BATTLE

A Post-Apocalyptic/Dystopian Adventure

The Traveler Series Book Five

Tom Abrahams

A PITON PRESS BOOK

BATTLE

The Traveler Series Book Five
© 2017 by Tom Abrahams
All Rights Reserved

Cover Design by Hristo Kovatliev
Edited by Felicia A. Sullivan
Proofread by Pauline Nolet
Proofread by Patricia Wilson
Interior design by Stef McDaid at WriteIntoPrint.com

tomabrahamsbooks.com

FREE PREFERRED READERS CLUB: Sign up
for information on discounts, events, and release dates:

eepurl.com/bWCRQ5

PITON PRESS

WORKS BY TOM ABRAHAMS

THE TRAVELER
POST APOCALYPTIC/DYSTOPIAN SERIES
HOME
CANYON
WALL
RISING
BATTLE

THE SPACEMAN CHRONICLES
POST-APOCALYPTIC THRILLERS
SPACEMAN
DESCENT
RETROGRADE

PERSEID COLLAPSE: PILGRIMAGE SERIES NOVELLAS
CROSSING
REFUGE
ADVENT

RED LINE: **AN EXTINCTION CYCLE NOVEL**

POLITICAL CONSPIRACIES
SEDITION
INTENTION

JACKSON QUICK ADVENTURES
ALLEGIANCE
ALLEGIANCE BURNED
HIDDEN ALLEGIANCE

For Courtney, Sam, & Luke

My heroes

*"If everyone fought for their own convictions,
there would be no war."*

—Leo Tolstoy

CHAPTER 1

"I'm getting too old for this," Marcus Battle muttered under his breath.

He wiggled his fingers above the grip of the Glock at his hip. His feet were shoulder width apart on the cracked, hole-riddled asphalt, and he straddled the faded single yellow line that ran through town. Despite the dry chill of a late West Texas winter, Marcus was in short sleeves. Sweat coated the back of his neck and under his arms.

His muscles tensed and his focus sharpened on the target standing thirty yards from him in the street. He drew slow, even breaths.

"You're the one they used to call Mad Max," sneered the target. "I heard tell of you all over the territory south of the wall."

Marcus positioned his shoulders over his toes. It was the best position from which to fire his weapon.

"They say you ended the Cartel single-handedly," said the target. "Turned your back on the Dwellers, got north of the wall, and came back to kill most of the Llano River Clan."

The target had the story mostly right. While there was a defiance in the man's voice, there was also fear. Marcus could hear it as the man recounted the dime-store tales of Marcus Battle's violent adventures. He was the most recent in a long succession of would-be sharks who'd circled Baird and dove into its waters in hopes of besting its legendary sheriff.

Marcus wasn't really the sheriff. There wasn't such a thing south of the wall in the territory once known as Texas. But he'd found people to lead in the town of Baird. They'd wanted his help and he'd given it freely.

For six months it had been easy. Until word got out. Things changed. Now, almost weekly, some young gun or guns came calling. They called out Marcus by name or reputation and demanded the chance to seek out glory.

This one was tall and thin. His arms were comically long and his sleeves stopped short of his wrists. His baggy pants ended at his calves. "I also heard you ain't got no family," said the target, smiling. "You're here 'cause your home is gone. They say you got nowhere to go and nobody to go to, so you're here. That's pathetic, if you ask me."

At first Marcus had tried to talk them out of their mission, to offer them refuge from the violence and unease that plagued the lawless, wild south. None of them accepted. One by one they'd failed in their quest and Marcus had buried them himself a mile outside town. Marcus's fingers had blistered then thickened with calluses from the frequency of the work.

The target adjusted his stance. His hand still hovered above the holster at his side. "I used to believe what they say!" he shouted. "I used to believe the stories. I thought you were a giant full of muscles!"

Another body to put in the ground, Marcus thought.

He rubbed the side of his thumb against his twitchy trigger finger.

"You don't look so tough," said the target. "You look old. I ain't impressed one b—"

The nine-millimeter round drilled through the center of the challenger's forehead and exploded out the back of his head. Marcus already had the Glock back in his holster and snapped shut by the time the silenced target went limp and collapsed to the ground face-first. His mouth was still open in the shape of a B when his brain stopped working and his heart stopped. He hadn't drawn his weapon.

"That was anticlimactic," said Lou. She was up against the brick façade of a building to Marcus's right. "You didn't let him complete his thought."

Marcus sighed and scratched his beard. It was time to shave again. "I'd heard enough," he said and closed the distance to Lou. "I half expected you to put a blade in him before I had a chance to fire."

Lou shrugged. She put a hand on one of the knives in her waistband. "I considered it," she said. "He *was* a talkative one."

Marcus stepped up the curb onto the wide cement sidewalk that separated the street from the long rows of buildings lining both sides of the main boulevard that ran through the center of Baird. From the look of the place, it could have been 1894 as easily as it was 2044.

Marcus moved next to Lou. "Just once," he said, "I'd like for these punks to take me up on my offer of sanctuary, forgiven transgressions, et cetera. They're too stubborn, too confident in their own abilities."

"Yeah," Lou said, folding her arms across her chest, "but they only have to be better than you once. You have to be better than them every time."

Marcus rubbed his aching neck, digging his thumb into a knot below the back of his head. Lou was right. It only took one hotshot with a quicker draw, or one who decided to snipe him without warning.

He nudged Lou with his shoulder. "Let's hope that's later rather than sooner," he said. "You gonna help me with the body?"

Lou looked at her empty wrist as if she wore a watch. She tapped it. "I guess so. I ain't got nowhere else to be."

They dragged the body to the side of the street and loaded it into a wheelbarrow he kept next to a building they used as a jail for trespassers and ne'er-do-wells who didn't rise to the level of an execution. Lou grabbed a shovel leaning against the building and tossed it atop the dead man's body.

Marcus gripped the handles of the wheelbarrow, tilted it forward on its warped wheel, and pushed it towards the burial plots. It was a long mile to the burial ground. His leg ached. He worked hard not to limp against the pain.

"Did you ever read *War and Peace*?" asked Lou as they reached the edge of town. She was playing with her knives, flipping one in each hand as she walked alongside Marcus.

"The book?" asked Marcus.

"No," said Lou, "the musical."

Marcus adjusted his grip on the wheelbarrow and furrowed his brow. "Musical?"

Lou shook her head. "Sheesh. Of course the book. You can't read a musical, Marcus. Sometimes you amaze me."

Marcus puffed his chest. "Thank you," he said. "My goal in life is to amaze Louise."

Lou scowled but ignored the sarcastic use of her full name. "My dad made me read it. He insisted it was a classic."

"You never told me your dad was sadistic," said Marcus. "That book is long."

"Longer than some, not as long as others," Lou said. "He said Tolstoy wrote a book without giving the story a hero. He was right. There really isn't one. The characters kind of move around and interact without motivation even. Sometimes they can't explain why they do what they do."

"Never read it," said Marcus.

Lou nodded. "Not surprised."

Marcus dropped the wheelbarrow and arched his back. He sucked in a deep breath of air and exhaled through puffed cheeks. He planted his hands on his hips, twisted from side to side as if doing simple calisthenics, and bent over to lift the wheelbarrow again. He motioned forward with his chin and led Lou closer to the burial ground.

"He profiled several well-to-do families and how they coped with a changing society," said Lou. She picked at her fingernails with a knife blade she'd drawn from her waistband. "A lot of the political stuff was over my head, but I got the gist."

Grunting, Marcus drove the dead weight up a rise in the thin dirt path he'd worn through the weeds and brush. "What's the gist of this conversation?" he asked. "What's your point?"

"Why is it," she asked without looking up from her fingers, "that no matter what kind of dirt you get trapped under your nails, it's always the same dark gray color when you pick it out? It's like the snot of the fingers."

Marcus ignored the question and repeated his own. "What's with the talk about Tolstoy?"

"I'm saying you don't always have to be the hero, Marcus. For that matter, you don't ever have to be the hero."

Marcus juggled the weight of the wheelbarrow, pushing harder against the rise. He was nearly at its end; then there would be a gentle slope leading all the way to the burial ground.

Lou flicked the dirt off the end of a nail. "You put too much pressure on yourself is all I'm saying. The world doesn't need heroes anymore, Marcus. It needs survivors."

Marcus stuck out his lower lip and blew the sweat on the tip of his nose. He reached the top of the rise and leaned back to control the dead weight moving downhill. His back protested, but he managed.

"You don't have to face off against every one of these punks who shows up trying to best you," said Lou. "You could refuse. You could retire. You could—"

"Put myself out to pasture?"

Lou bounded down the hill with long strides. She caught up to

Marcus and passed him, using her momentum to jog by the time she reached the bottom of the slope. She skidded to a stop and faced Marcus while he strained to control the load on the way down.

"You said it," she told him. "I wasn't suggesting we sell your parts for glue. I was only saying the burden isn't *all* on your shoulders. You have me. You have Rudy."

Marcus dropped the legs of the barrel into the weeds and rubbed his hands against his shirt. He walked to a nearby scrub oak and plucked a pickaxe from the dirt. He'd stored it there after his earlier kill two weeks ago. He crossed the short distance back to the wheelbarrow and Lou. She'd pulled out her second knife and was juggling both blades.

"They're getting more frequent," said Marcus. "It feels like I was just here."

Lou kept her eyes on the blades as she flipped them into the air from one hand to another. "You were," she said. "That's my point. One of these days…"

Marcus smirked and lowered the shovel to the ground. He scanned the plot for a good, clean spot to bury his latest suitor. He was running out of room. The field was covered with stone markers Marcus had laid at the head of every grave. Some of the rocks were large; others weren't much bigger than a skipping stone. Each represented a man killed in the year since he'd agreed to become the de facto sheriff of Baird and the surrounding farms.

He'd thwarted every threat so far, but as Marcus eyed the perfect spot to bury the latest of them and hoisted the shovel to start digging into the dry, cracked earth, he knew none of them had been serious. None of them had come with any support, let alone an army. They'd been stupid enough to come alone.

Marcus slung the pick into the dirt several times to loosen the dirt. He tossed it aside, drove the shovel into the ground, and heaved out a spadeful of dirt. He repeated the move mechanically, load after load, until he'd dug a hole deep enough to stand inside. He stopped to take a swig of water from Lou's canteen and thanked her.

She was right. One of these days, somebody smart enough would bring reinforcements. They'd bring an army. And somebody would be digging his grave.

CHAPTER 2

FEBRUARY 5, 2044, 4:34 PM
SCOURGE + 11 YEARS, 4 MONTHS
KERRVILLE, TEXAS

Each pushup hurt more than the last. Junior was up to one hundred and thirty when he stopped, his body posed in a straight plank above the ground beneath it. Sweat dripped from his face and neck. His arms shook with exhaustion, his chest burned, but he held his position.

He envisioned the face of the man who'd brought him so much pain, so much sorrow, so many sleepless nights. A well of anger-laced adrenaline coursed through his body and he grunted, managing another twenty pushups before collapsing into the dirt.

Junior lay there for several minutes. Then he rolled onto his back and mustered up the strength to sit up and push himself to his feet. He looked skyward. It was a bright day, warm for the hill country, and a steady breeze blew from the south. He reached one arm across his body and caught his elbow to pull it inward. He did the same with the other arm. The sore muscles in the backs of his arms stretched painfully and Junior clenched his jaw to mitigate the burn. He flapped his arms at his sides and rolled his neck from side to side.

He looked down at one shoulder then the other, paying attention to the irregular keloid sprays that marked the spots of his injuries some sixteen months earlier. He rubbed one of them with his thumb. It was a miracle he'd survived the twin injuries, dealt minutes apart. Without antibiotics, most people would have died. Somehow, he'd staved off infection and lived.

Again, the face of the man who'd hurt him appeared in his mind's eye. It was the face that provided a constant source of inspiration as Junior pushed through the long days and nights of work he'd endured to repair his body and make it stronger.

His boyish appearance and small stature belied his age. He was in his early twenties and was more than a year older than when he'd faced his enemy that one and only time.

His rehabilitation had taken too long, but he knew he was finally ready for his mission. It was time to find the man who'd changed his life.

Junior walked over to his horse, his legs tingling from his exercise, and pulled a shirt from one of two large saddlebags. He slipped it over his head, his muscles straining against the fabric. He rubbed his hands across his sweaty, shaved head and wiped them on the shirt.

He ran his hand across the long gun in the saddle scabbard, letting his fingers trail along the steel barrel. It might as well have been a sculpture as a weapon. Junior had run out of ammunition for the rifle and he hadn't been able to find any to replace it. Still, he kept the weapon that had belonged to his father. It was identical to the FDE brown AR-10 he'd long carried before losing it the day he was shot in both arms. Someday he'd come across the jacketed lead and feed it into the beast. Someday.

In the meantime, he had his twin single-action bone-handled Colt revolvers. They weren't ideal, but he had ammunition for them. That made them priceless.

He slid his hand underneath the dual-holstered belt he'd hung around the saddle horn and slapped it around his waist. It felt good there. Junior gripped the Colts, slid his fingers inside the trigger guards, dropped his hands down, and rolled the guns forward once before swinging them backwards into a spin. He spun them backwards several times, lifted his hands, and stopped the weapons into a flat aim directly in front of him.

He spun them down and back again in perfect sync and slid them back into their holsters. He repeated the well-practiced move twice more.

"You'd be dead three times over by the time you finished the move, Junior," said a man, chuckling as he approached from behind. His hands were stained dark with blood. "It's parlor tricks."

Junior slipped the guns into the holsters and looked over his shoulder at his compadre, Gil Grissom. He sneered at Gil and spat into the dirt in front of Grissom's leather shoes.

"Watch it," said Grissom. "This is my last pair."

"It calms me," said Junior.

"Spitting on my shoes?"

"No," said Junior, "spinning the guns. It's relaxing. Takes my mind off things."

Grissom dug the toe of his shoe and dragged it across the dirt. "Keep your relaxing off my shoes," he said. "I got a rabbit. It's over by the fire."

Junior ran a hand across his head and sniffed. He cleared his throat and hawked another wad of spit onto the ground at Grissom's feet. "Come on. We got work to do."

Grissom grumbled and followed Junior to the charred remains of the campfire they'd built the night before. They plopped down on the ground opposite each other.

Junior eyed the fully dressed rabbit on the ground next to the char. He glared at Grissom. "We gonna eat it or stare at it?"

Grissom huffed. He took the meat of the animal and skewered it on a wooden spit fashioned from a mesquite branch.

Youthfully awkward was a kind way to describe Gil Grissom. Unlike Junior, he looked every bit his youthful age. His eyebrows were thick, his nose too big for his face, his cheeks dotted with pink outcroppings of acne. Above his upper lip and at his chin were dark wisps of hair. His neck was long and thin, and his Adam's apple strained underneath the surface of his pale skin. His curly mop of hair sat unevenly atop his head like a bad wig.

"You don't have to be mean all the time," said Grissom. "I ain't never done nothing to you other than maybe ribbing you sometimes."

Junior shifted in the dirt, his abdominal muscles sore from the workout. "You're not funny. I'd laugh if you were funny."

Grissom twisted the meat to the middle of the spit and raised himself onto his knees to approach the fire pit. He dropped the spit into the twin wooden branches he'd put on either side of the fire. He took some thinly stripped bark and put it underneath the rabbit meat, and some dry leaves from a pile at his side, crumbled them in his hands, and sprinkled them atop the kindling pile. Using flint, he sparked the pile and blew the embers,, relighting the coals he'd used the night before. Minutes later, the rabbit was cooking.

"Be an hour," said Grissom, scooting away from the growing flames. "Maybe an hour and a half."

Junior nodded and pulled his knees up to his chest. He wrapped his arms around his legs and clasped his fingers in front of them. He stretched his back as he balanced his weight.

He looked past the flames, through the undulating heat above them and to the rolling hills to the west. The sun was perched atop them, framing them with a bright orange hue that stretched along the wave of uneven ground known as the Texas Hill Country.

"Where we headed?" asked Grissom. "We've been here for three days now. Probably time to move on."

"The horses needed the rest," said Junior. "We've been riding them hard since El Paso."

"We head out tomorrow, then?"

Junior nodded again, his eyes still fixated on the low-sitting sun. "Yeah. We'll ride for San Antonio, try to pick up some help there. Probably find some good men there."

Grissom rolled the spit by twisting it with his fingers. "Nobody in El Paso wanted any part of it," he said. "You think folks in San Antonio are going to be different?"

Without moving his head, Junior's eyes left the distant hills and settled on Grissom. He licked his lips but said nothing.

Grissom shifted uncomfortably and scratched at the acne on one cheek. "I'm just asking," he said. "I mean, we're asking a lot and not paying much. That's all I'm saying."

Junior shook his head. "We're offering people the chance to be legends. That should be enough."

CHAPTER 3

"Nebraska, huh?" said the short man pumping gas. "You headed north?"

"East," said Taskar, the driver of a funeral hearse long past its prime. He made his living transporting people and things back and forth across the wall.

The gas station attendant switched hands on the pump. "East? What's east, if you don't mind my asking?"

Taskar rubbed one hand across the worn leather on the steering wheel. He glanced at the controls on the driver's side door and considered rolling up his window.

"You got work back east?" the man pressed. "I hear there's more and more work out there. Especially in the big cities, I hear there's lots to be had."

Taskar thumped his index finger on the wheel. "The government still controls everything. They're the ones who have the jobs."

The man looked over his shoulder at the slow-moving numbers of the low-pressure pump. "I ain't the government and I got a job," he said, his drawl dragging out every syllable into two.

Taskar reached into the center console and pulled out a wad of cash. "Good for you. What do I owe you?"

"Ain't done yet," said the man. "Next filling station heading east isn't for another couple hundred miles. Might wanna let me finish."

Taskar slid the rubber band from around the roll of bills and started counting. Money wasn't worth what it had been before the Scourge, and it was only in the last couple of years the government had started circulating it again.

The pump clanked to a halt and the man drew the nozzle from the tank. He replaced it on the pump and stepped to the window. He whistled when he saw the cash.

"My," said the man, "that's a lot of dough. You must be doing government work. They're the only ones who pay—"

"How much?"

The man looked over his shoulder at the numbers on the pump. "Three hundred," he said, and held out his hand.

Taskar peeled off a trio of hundred-dollar bills and slapped it into the man's waiting palm. "Thanks." He kept the window down and slammed the hearse into drive.

He eased onto the highway and, with his knees controlling the wheel, wrapped the roll with the rubber band and put it back into the center console. He'd reached sixty miles per hour within a few seconds and was cruising on relatively new tires that hummed on the asphalt and concrete that made up the existing highways north of the wall.

He adjusted his weight in the cracked leather seat and put his arm on the open window, letting his hand drift in the chilly wind. It was too cold to have the window down, especially given the head congestion with which Taskar had been coping, but he wasn't about to waste gasoline on air-conditioning. Plus, the cold air kept him awake. His newest job required expediency. He couldn't afford a nap.

Taskar picked up a map from the passenger's seat and looked at the lines he'd drawn to his destination. He probably had another thirteen or fourteen hours and nine hundred miles ahead of him.

He glanced in the rearview mirror and saw, in the distance, the tall sign for the service station as it sank below the horizon. Taskar thought about how curt he'd been with the curious man pumping gas. He could have been nicer. He could have answered the man's questions, or at least pretended to answer them, but that wasn't Taskar's way.

He didn't like questions. His profession as a post-Scourge incognito courier demanded discretion. All he needed to know was where to go and when. He didn't want names; he didn't want sob stories or fantastic tales of the new gold rush. He wanted half up front and the rest of the payment at the destination.

This job was different.

Two weeks earlier he'd been driving north, having navigated past the wall for the umpteenth time in the last decade. He'd dropped off his fare near Oklahoma City and stopped at a hole-in-the-wall restaurant to get some coffee and a smoked meat sandwich.

He'd sat down at his regular spot in the back corner and opened the wax paper wrapping his sandwich when a woman sat down in the seat across from him. She'd planted her hands flat on the table and blew out a breath.

"Can I help you?" asked Taskar.

"You're the one who provides illicit transportation services?"

Taskar had wrapped his callused fingers around the soft white bread and shoved a corner of the sandwich into his mouth. He'd chewed the cold meat and with his mouth full replied, "Depends."

The woman had rubbed her hands on the table, as if she were wiping it clean with her fingers. "On what does it depend, Mr. Taskar?"

Taskar had swallowed his mouthful and took a swig of room temperature water. "Who are you?"

"I'm a client."

It wasn't unusual for people he didn't know to approach him for work. It wasn't weird that she seemed to relish the clandestine nature of their conversation. Still, he'd sensed something was different about the woman. Something was…off.

"Who recommended me?"

The woman had smiled. "People."

Taskar had studied her for a moment then took another bite. The meat was too dry and it had stuck to the roof of his mouth. Then it hit him. "You're government."

The woman's eye had twitched and she'd nodded almost imperceptibly. She'd slid her fingers inward, raising her palms from the table, and held them there as would a concert pianist about to begin a concerto. "I'm the person who wants to pay you a sizable amount of money to transport something from this side of the wall to the other," she'd said. "That's all that matters."

Taskar had set his sandwich down on the wax paper and swallowed another gulp of the water. "These last couple of years have gotten tougher," he'd said. "When it was as bad here as it was south of the wall, nobody but the Cartel cared who came or went. Most people thought they'd find a better life here, made the trek, then headed back south again."

"I recall," the woman had said.

"Now that the government has the power back on in the cities, has communication back in parts, and people are starting to make a go of things again, it isn't so easy to go back and forth."

"What are you saying?"

Taskar had run his tongue along the roof of his mouth and smacked his lips. He'd lowered his voice. "I'm saying there are a lot of risks involved. There are wheels to grease. Going south is a lot easier than coming north."

The woman had smirked. "That's not a problem," she'd assured him, "from a compensatory standpoint or from a logistical one. We'll take care of it. All of it. You just show up where I tell you to show up on the date I tell you to be there."

From under the table, she'd produced a roll of cash larger than any Taskar had ever seen in person. It had told him two things: this was a job worth taking, and it was a job he knew he shouldn't take.

The woman had placed the roll on the table, stood from her seat, and walked out without saying another word. Taskar had scanned the room and then quickly plucked the money roll from the table. Wrapped around it and tucked underneath a rubber band was a piece of paper with an address and a date.

That piece of paper was now stuck to his rearview mirror. The date was tomorrow, February 7, 2044. The address was 1600 Clifton Road, Atlanta, Georgia.

Atlanta. He hadn't been that far east since the Scourge. He'd driven to and from New Orleans, or what was left of it, Little Rock, and even Birmingham, Alabama. One trip took him west to Phoenix and another to Denver. He'd turned down a trip to Chicago. Not enough money in it, too much risk and not enough reward. He wondered what Atlanta was like.

He'd heard rumors the new government had a huge presence in Atlanta. The city had recovered more quickly than most, and survivors from other cities and towns had flocked there, accelerating its regrowth. A big reason for that was electricity. There were two hydroelectric dams, one north of the city and one south, that never stopped producing power after the Scourge.

Taskar slid down in his seat. The cruise control was broken and his ankle was already sore from the driving he'd done. It would be a long trek.

From the driver's side window, he saw clouds gathering in the distance. They were gray, almost black, and some were perched above curtains of rain. He tried to figure out which way the clouds were headed. As much as he knew the land needed rain, he didn't want to deal with it on his road trip. He hadn't replaced the windshield wipers in four years. He sucked in a deep breath. The cold air didn't yet smell like rain. That was good. His eyes drifted from the clouds, back to the road, and down to the money in the center console. He could only imagine what he might do with twice that much once the job was over.

He looked at himself in the rearview mirror. "You could give this up," he said aloud. "You could find a little place, settle down, get out of the game."

A smile crept across his face as he thought about the possibilities and envisioned a life unrecognizable from the one he lived now. He put one hand on the money, gripping it with his fingers.

He hoped this job was worth it. He really did. Even though in the back of his mind, he knew it wasn't.

CHAPTER 4

Lomas Ward stood in the plaza and shoved his hands into his pockets. He spun around on his worn leather heels and looked at the decrepit skyline of his city. He remembered a time when it gleamed with promise. But it was so long ago it was hard to impose his memory over the ever-present sepia that cast itself onto everything and everyone. That promise died with Lomas's parents and siblings in the days and months after the Scourge. That promise was before his life crumbled around him. It was before the offer.

At thirty-five, Lomas had lived half his life in this sick world, one where civilization peeled back to unearth the worst in people. He'd tried to make a go of it, to find work, raise a family, and provide a home filled with love and the promise of a better future. Some people with better connections than Lomas had managed much better. Many more had done much worse. Lomas had heard about life south of the wall, the stories of barbarism and lawlessness. He considered himself among the fortunate.

That was gone now. All he had was the offer.

19

They'd come to him at his lowest, in the hours after his wife had died from a gunshot wound. He was grieving her in the clinic's chapel on bended knee when a firm hand touched his shoulder. In his grief, he thought at first it was the hand of God. It wasn't.

As he stood here in the plaza, feeling the cool northerly breeze on his face, he wondered if maybe the hand did belong to an angel.

"We'll find your children a good home," they'd told him. "They'll never have to worry about food or violence again," they'd promised. "They'll go to a connected family."

Lomas had thought they were joking until the earnestness in the wrinkles above their eyes and around their mouths convinced him they were on the level.

"But you have to sign on the dotted line," they'd insisted. "You have to sign before somebody else beats you to it. This is a limited-time offer."

They'd given him twenty hours to think about it, one last night to spend with his sons.

He'd made the choice that produced a thick knot in his throat that was still there two days later as he stood in the plaza.

Lomas adjusted his collar on his neck, folding the stained fabric along the creases. He rubbed his bloodshot eyes with his knuckles and rubbed the thick, puffy circles that threatened to close them.

He stuffed his hands back into his pockets, tugging his pants beneath his hips, and turned back to the nondescript building behind him. It was the kind of place he'd probably passed a thousand times and never noticed. The multistory brick façade was windowless except for a rectangular transom above a wide metal door. Lomas approached the door and raised his hand. He hesitated, his balled fist hovering between his past and future. He bit his lower lip and, as instructed, knocked several times, waited, and knocked again.

A hollow voice blared through a stainless steel speaker box next to the door. *"Lomas Ward?"*

Lomas stared at the box, searching for a button to push. There wasn't one.

"*Lomas Ward?*" asked the voice again.

Lomas looked over his shoulder and back at the speaker. "Yes," he said tentatively, his eyes still searching for the microphone. "I'm Lomas. I'm here to see—"

A loud buzzer followed a metallic click at the door. "*Please pull on the door to enter.*"

Lomas gripped the door handle in front of him and tugged. The door opened outward, revealing a square waiting room bathed in white light. He crossed the threshold, and when the door clacked shut behind him, the buzzer stopped.

He looked overhead at fluorescent tubes of light. He hadn't seen bulbs like that in years. Most everything was low-power LEDs in the places that had power. These lights were much brighter than those to which he was accustomed, and he squinted, surveying the space around him. There was a single chair in one corner with a hand-printed sign above it that read SIT HERE.

"*Please sit in the chair provided,*" the voice said, as if on cue. "*Someone will be with you in a moment.*"

Lomas noticed a door that didn't have a handle or knob. "I'm here to see Dr. Morel. Charles Mor—"

"*Someone will be with you in a moment,*" said the hollow voice. "*Please be seated in the chair provided.*"

Lomas stepped over to the chair and sat down. It was hard and uncomfortable, and he shifted his weight to try to relax. It was futile. He planted his elbows on his knees and his head in his hands.

His boys' faces flashed in his mind. Their small features, their smiles, their hands in his, their arms wrapped around his neck. Lomas swallowed against the thick knot in his throat and pushed the images aside. He'd done what he had to do. He'd given them a future they deserved, a future he couldn't otherwise provide.

Lomas sat in the chair for close to thirty minutes. When the door opened, it wasn't Dr. Charles Morel, one of the men who'd convinced him to trade his future for that of his children. It was a tall, rail-thin woman with jet-black hair pulled tight against her oval head into a long ponytail. Her cartoonish arched eyebrows conveyed a permanent sense of disapproval and her tight-fitting clothes gave the clear idea that she was among the connected. The Scourge hadn't done to her what it had done to most everyone else.

The woman stood in the doorway, holding it ajar with a booted foot. She held a digital tablet in her hands. Lomas hadn't seen one in a dozen years. He sat back in the chair, gripping his knees with his fingers.

"Lomas Ward," the woman said in a husky voice that sounded devoid of femininity, "I'm Gwendolyn Sharp. Please come with me." The woman's facial expression didn't change as she spoke.

"I thought I was meeting Dr. Morel," he said, unmoved from his seat. "Dr. Morel told me—"

"I'm unaware of any arrangements you may have discussed with Dr. Morel," said Gwendolyn Sharp, her boots shoulder width apart. She leaned her shoulder into the door. "I am aware, however, that you are to come with me. Now."

She smiled in a way that told Lomas it wasn't a smile at all. Her nostrils were pinched together in such an unnatural way he couldn't imagine it was easy for her to breathe. Maybe that accounted for her acerbic demeanor. Lomas rubbed his knees with his palms and glanced at the large door through which he'd entered.

Sharp sighed. "Are you having second thoughts about your participation?"

Lomas swallowed hard and pressed his lips together. There wasn't a correct answer here despite the woman offering what was clearly a rhetorical question. "No," Lomas lied.

Sharp motioned with her head toward the space beyond the door. "Let's go, then. We've things to do."

Lomas pushed himself to his feet and moved past Sharp into a narrow hallway. It shared the same lighting as the waiting room. He walked with his eyes glued to the reflective glow emanating from the row of fixtures that ran along the center of the high ceiling. The hard linoleum floor clacked against Sharp's shoes and squeaked underneath Lomas's. It felt like a hospital, the antiseptic odor lingering in the air amplifying the sensation that he was about to strip and don a paper gown.

His eyes drifted to the doors that populated the freshly painted white concrete walls. They were white too, unmarked, and decorated with identical alphanumeric keypads. Lomas opened his mouth to ask Sharp what he'd find behind the doors, but decided against it.

When they reached the door at the end of the hallway, Sharp stood in front of the alphanumeric panel, shielded it with her body, and glanced over her shoulder at Lomas and punched five buttons. The door clicked and buzzed until Sharp rotated the handle and shouldered the door inward.

Lomas followed her past the doorway and into what looked like a doctor's examination room. At its center was a large bed covered in disposable paper. There was a pillow affixed to the head of the table, and hanging from the ceiling above it was a moveable light.

On one side of the room were a sink and a cabinet. On the other were open shelves containing stacks of towels and boxes of powdered rubber gloves. Next to the shelf was a wall-mounted otoscope with various attachments.

"Please seat yourself on the table," ordered Sharp. She tapped her computer tablet and dragged her finger across the screen.

Lomas stepped up onto a platform at the base of the examination table and swiveled around to sit on it. The paper crinkled under his weight and he tried adjusting it. Sharp nodded and left the room, closing the door behind her.

Lomas tried to remember what Dr. Morel had told him. He tried to recall the step-by-step explanation as to what he could expect once he agreed to work with the doctor and his team. His mind was swimming with so many details he couldn't remember which ones were real and which ones he'd imagined in his sleepless stupor. He didn't recall sitting in an exam room as being part of the deal.

Lomas lay back on the table, resting his head on the pillow. He looked up at the overhead light and tried to clear his thoughts. Instead, his vision grew fuzzy from exhaustion. His mind drifted, and he fell asleep.

When he awoke, Dr. Morel was standing next to the table, gently shaking Lomas by his shoulder. "Lomas," he said softly, "I need you to wake up. We have to get started."

Lomas blinked his eyes open and yawned. "I'm sorry," he said, the thick, sour taste of sleep in his mouth.

Dr. Morel smiled. His eyes narrowed with the grin, exposing his deep crow's-feet. "It's not a problem, Lomas. But if you could sit up, that would be very helpful."

Lomas used the edges of the table to pull himself upright. His feet dangled off the end of the table. There were two other people in the room. Sharp and a man who'd been with Dr. Morel when Lomas had agreed to trade his sons' lives for his freedom. That man, whose name Lomas didn't know, was holding a syringe in one hand and a length of rubber tubing in the other. Lomas swallowed hard. An uncomfortable heat swelled in his cheeks and on the back of his neck.

"Could I have your arm, please?" Dr. Morel asked.

Lomas stared at the syringe. "What exactly is happening here? What are you doing to me?"

Dr. Morel cleared his throat. "Well," he said in a tone laced with waning patience, "what's happening is exactly what I told you would happen, and what we're doing is what we told you we would do."

Lomas shook his head, a wave of nausea welling in his gut. "You never said anything about needles."

Dr. Morel rolled his eyes. "I guess that's technically accurate, Lomas," he said, "but I did tell you that you would be involved in a tactical effort aimed at lessening the burden on our natural resources.

I did tell you there could be taxing elements that would test your endurance."

Lomas shuddered, his hands trembling. "You told me I would be a secret hero, like an undercover agent. You told me I would make life better for my kids and their kids. You never talked about needles. I would remember if you talked about needles."

Sharp stepped forward toward Dr. Morel. "Do we need the restraints?" she whispered into his ear loudly enough for Lomas to hear her.

Dr. Morel shook his head and looked Lomas in the eyes. His smile was gone. "That won't be necessary," he said. "Will it, Lomas?"

Lomas's muscles tensed. His eyes darted from Morel to Sharp to the needle to the door and back to Morel. The man with the needle moved a step, blocking the door.

"Your boys are in good hands," said Morel. "They are in good spirits and had a wonderful lunch. I think it was beef stew. When was the last time they had a hot meal, Lomas?"

Lomas's shoulders slumped. He lowered his head, swallowed past the lump, bit the inside of his cheek to keep himself from crying, and offered his arm to Dr. Morel.

Morel reached onto the shelf and pulled out a pair of gloves. He blew into the openings and slid them onto his hands. He stepped across the room and opened the cabinet next to him, withdrew a bottle of isopropyl alcohol, popped its flip top, and doused a circular cotton pad. "I need to clean the injection site," he said to Lomas and wiped the cotton pad on a spot just below the crook of his elbow. "There. That's good."

The silent man standing at the door moved across the room to Dr. Morel. He offered the rubber tubing and the syringe. The doctor thanked the man, took the tubing, and wrapped it above Lomas's elbow.

"Make a fist, please. Hold it."

Lomas did as he was told. He balled his hand into a fist and squeezed. Morel then took the syringe and pushed the plunger enough for a drop of clear liquid to drip from the tip. Then he tapped a vein in Lomas's arm and placed the needle against the skin.

"Why do you need my blood?" asked Lomas, his voice shaking. "What are you going to do with it?"

Morel chuckled, slid the needle into Lomas's vein, and pushed the plunger. "Oh," he said, "we're not *taking* anything from you. We're *giving* you something."

CHAPTER 5

Rudy Gallardo stood on the front porch of his home, his shoulder against one of the tapered Craftsman-style posts that accented the wraparound decking that surrounded three sides of the farmhouse, his mutt named Fifty panting at his side. His arms were folded across his chest expectantly, his legs crossed at the ankles. He looked bored, or irritated, or a little bit of both.

Marcus waved at Rudy and smiled weakly. "Hey," he said, trudging up the long dirt path that led to the house. "Sorry I'm late. I lost track of time."

Fifty licked his chops and wagged his tail. He bounded down the wooden porch steps with his oversized meaty paws and clomped his way to Marcus.

"Don't apologize to me," he said. "It's Norma who cooked the food."

Every Saturday for the past year, Rudy had hosted a big meal at his house. Marcus was always late. Without exception. He ran his hand along Fifty's head and led the dog up the steps to the porch, his boots announcing his arrival on the old treated pine. He offered his hand to Rudy.

"How are you?" Marcus asked. "Good day?"

Rudy slapped Marcus on the back and pulled open the storm door, its hinges creaking. Marcus moved past him into the house with Fifty herding him along the hallway toward the large eat-in kitchen. He glanced back over his shoulder at Rudy and motioned to the door.

"You should get that fixed," he said, as he'd told Rudy every Saturday night for the past year.

"Fresh out of WD-40," said Rudy. "Plus it's a nice alarm if people try to sneak into the house." It was the same answer as the fifty before it. He called down the hall to the kitchen to announce Marcus's arrival.

Norma stood at the butcher-block island, her hands on her hips. "Let me guess. You lost track of time."

Marcus snorted. "You know me so well," he said, crossing the room to hug his host. She planted a platonic air kiss on his cheek and shooed him to the table. Lou was sitting there petting Fifty. The dog focused his attention on her whenever she was around.

Marcus sidled up next to Lou and sat beside her on the bench that ran the length of one side of the long rectangular table. On the other side sat two of the women who'd been held captive with Norma in San Angelo. They were always quiet. Neither ever said much other than whispering to each other or asking for a helping of food. They lived with the Gallardos and, in exchange for a roof over their heads and at least two meals a day, helped work the farm.

At one end of the table, Rudy found his seat. Norma sat at the other end. She surveyed the table, her guests, her husband, and pointed at Lou. "Your turn to say grace."

Lou lowered her chin. "I said it last week."

Marcus shook his head. "Nope, I did."

Lou frowned and clasped her hands together in prayer. "Fine. I'll do it, but I'm not good at it."

"Of course you are," said Norma. "Don't be ridiculous."

Lou took a deep breath and exhaled. She lowered her head and rested her forehead on her thumbs as she prayed. "For as high as the heavens are above the earth, so great is His love for those who fear Him. As far as the east is from the west, so far has He removed our transgressions from us. Thank you for our lives and for this food. Amen."

Marcus glanced at Lou. "Psalms?"

Lou shrugged. "I don't know. I've heard you say it in your sleep. When you're napping at work."

"In my sleep?"

Lou nodded and reached for the bowl of carrots. She plucked a handful, dropped them onto her plate and passed the bowl to Marcus. "Yep, all the time. You mumble, you groan, you speak Bible."

Marcus used a large spoon to shovel some carrots onto his plate and passed it to Rudy. "Huh. I had no idea."

Lou slid a carrot into her mouth and snapped off a piece with her teeth. "Not true." She chuckled. "I've told you that you talk in your sleep. I've asked you about some of the names you blurt out."

Marcus shook his head. "No, that's not what I mean. I had no idea I was quoting scripture."

Lou's eyebrows arched with surprise. "Scripture? That's a new word. Never heard you use that."

Norma picked up a bowl of broccoli, which she'd picked from the garden earlier that day. "There's nothing wrong with that," she said to Lou, her tone judgmental. "A little prayer never does anyone harm."

"That's not my point," said Lou, taking the broccoli bowl from Norma. "I'm just saying it surprised me, that's all. I didn't know he was religious."

Lou picked out a couple of florets with her hand and dropped them amongst the carrots, passing the bowl to Marcus. She picked a carrot up from her plate, broke it in half, and offered it to Fifty. The dog sniffed it but declined. Lou shrugged and popped the piece in her mouth.

"I don't talk about it," said Marcus. "That kind of thing is between a man and his God. Can we change the subject?"

"Excellent dinner," Rudy said to his wife. "You've outdone yourself, as you always do."

The table concurred with full mouths. The Saturday suppers were always good. Whatever was in season in the garden out back was on the table. It was fresh, sometimes cooked over burning mesquite, and always filling.

"I hope rattlesnake is okay," said Norma. She had a plate of thinly stripped meat in her hands. "It's the best I could do tonight. Haven't seen too many varmints out there. Rabbits, possums, armadillos, they're all tougher to come by these days."

"Anything you made for us is fine," said Lou. "The drought is doing a number on everyone. We get a day of rain and then another month passes."

"What's it been now?" asked Rudy, waving his fork as he spoke. "Three years? Four?"

Norma shook her head. "All I know is that if it weren't for what's left of the well, we'd have had to give up on this place a long time ago."

Marcus stabbed at a piece of the snake on his plate. He twirled the utensil around in his hand, swirling the stringy meat on the plate, only vaguely aware of what he was doing. His mind was elsewhere.

"Something wrong, Marcus?" Norma asked.

Marcus blankly stirred the fork around the plate, spinning it as if the meat were spaghetti noodles. His eyes were open. He wasn't blinking.

"This about the prayer thing?" asked Lou. "You pouting?"

The two women across the table snickered and whispered to each other. Neither of them had put food on their plates yet.

Marcus blinked. He looked at Lou and shook his head. "No," he said. "I'm thinking."

"About?" Rudy prompted.

Marcus laid the fork on the plate and pinched the bridge of his nose. He grimaced and eyed each person at the table. "I'm gonna quit."

The room fell silent. Rudy's face crinkled with concern. Norma's jaw dropped. The two women across the table looked at each other with wide eyes. Lou scooted away from Marcus. She held her fork in her hand, her fingers blanching white as she tightened her grip.

"You took what I said out of context," said Lou. "Or you twisted it somehow. You can't quit. This town needs you. *We* need you."

Rudy's forehead creased more deeply. "What do you mean?" he asked, looking between Lou and Marcus. "I don't understand what's happening here."

"I didn't take anything out of context," said Marcus. "I didn't twist what you said, Lou. This is not about heroism. It's about sanity and survival."

Lou chuckled sarcastically. "Sanity? You gave that up long before we met. You've as much as admitted it. You used to name your guns and talk to ghosts."

"That's not fair," said Marcus. "I—"

"What is going *on* here?" Rudy said again, his voice straining with confusion.

"You quitting isn't fair," said Lou. "You giving up isn't fair."

Rudy stood from his seat, pushing his chair away from the table with the backs of his legs. He slammed a fist down on the table. His face was red, his eyes narrowed with anger. "Answer my questions," he demanded. "This is *my* house. You're at *my* table. Answer me, or I swear to—"

"Rudy," Norma said firmly, "calm down."

Marcus raised his hands in surrender. "It's okay," he said. "It's fine. Rudy, I'll answer you. I didn't mean to cause an uproar."

Rudy plopped down in his chair, his balled fists planted on the table. He nodded at Marcus. "Go ahead."

"After the kid I killed a couple of days ago, I got to thinking," Marcus said. "Lou mentioned something about not always needing to be the hero. She didn't mean any harm by suggesting it, but she had a point."

Lou threw up her hands. "I *knew* you took it out of context."

Marcus shook his head. "No. I thought about my life. I was a warrior. I saw people killed. I killed people. Then I tried to escape it. The violence, I mean. I wanted a quiet, safe existence with my family. Life had other plans."

"So?" said Lou. "What does that have to do with quitting now?"

"Sure," said Marcus, "the Scourge brought with it more violence. I engaged, I killed, saw people killed. I retreated again. But that violence found me. Like Al Pacino said in *The Godfather*, 'Just when I thought I was out, they pull me back.'"

"Mario Puzo wrote *The Godfather*," said Lou. "I read it. There wasn't anybody named Al Pacino."

Marcus rolled his eyes. "Regardless. Violence keeps finding me. I'm sick of it. I'm getting old. I'm tired. I need out."

"Why now?" asked Rudy. "Why tell us here at dinner?"

"The whole prayer thing," said Marcus.

"I *knew* it," said Lou.

"No," Marcus said, "not you picking on me. I don't give a flip about you making fun of me. That's par for the course. It just got me thinking about Sylvia and all the praying I did. I don't know that she'd like the man I am nowadays. Lola knew who I'd become. Sylvia and Wesson didn't. I've come to a place where I want to be the man they'd be proud to have around."

"So you'll be a monk?" asked Lou. "You'll live some solitary existence? Hello? You just said you've tried it and it didn't work. You know insanity is doing the same thing over and over again and expecting a different result, right?"

"I'm not going anywhere," Marcus said. "I'm staying here in Baird. But I don't want to be the point person for death-dealing anymore. I want to slide into an uneasy peace."

Marcus gauged the room. The whisper-twins had started eating, clearly having lost interest in the conversation. Lou was sitting board straight with her hands in her lap. She wasn't looking at Marcus, though she clearly had him in her peripheral vision. Norma hadn't moved. Rudy's face had relaxed, but his glare maintained the same red-eyed intensity as when he'd stood and blurted out his frustration.

"So you're not leaving," said Rudy, "which is good. But what exactly is it you're doing? What do you mean by an uneasy peace?"

Marcus sighed. "I mean I don't want to be sheriff anymore. Somebody else needs to take the reins, somebody who's as skilled as I am and has a connection to this place and its people."

Marcus looked around the room as he spoke, but his stare landed on Rudy. He didn't have to say what he was thinking. Everybody knew.

"No," said Norma. "Not going to happen, Marcus. I'm not letting Rudy take that risk. It's too much."

Marcus picked up his fork, slid the room-temperature meat into his mouth, and chewed. It actually tasted like chicken, at least what he recalled chicken tasted like. It had been years since he'd had any.

"You want me to be sheriff?" asked Rudy. "*Me*? Why me?"

"It doesn't matter," said Norma. "You're not putting a target on your back for every ne'er-do-well who rides into Baird."

Marcus swallowed and stabbed at another bite on the plate. "I'm not asking him to put a target on his back. The target is me, not the job."

Norma shook her head. "That makes no sense, Marcus Battle," she chided in a voice louder than Marcus had ever heard her employ. "If you're the target, then how is you giving up the job going to make a difference? All you'd be doing is putting my husband in the crosshairs along with you. Is that what you want? You want someone else to take some of the heat?"

"Now hold on, Norma," Marcus said. "I'm not saying—"

"What *are* you saying?" Norma pressed, tears welling in her eyes.

Rudy puffed his chest and raised his chin. "He's saying I should take the lead," said Rudy. "He's saying I could make a difference for our friends and neighbors."

Norma cocked her head to one side, her hair falling across her face. "Are you serious?" she hissed. "You'd consider this?"

Rudy shrugged. "I don't know. I'm not saying yes *or* no."

Norma ran her hands through her hair. Her eyes were slits, her mouth set firmly. In a measured, but clearly volcanic tone, she said, "After what we've been through, you'd think about it? You'd think about having whatever hell-sent group of bandits, or posse, or whatever be the end of you?"

"We don't know that would happen again," said Rudy. "The Cartel is gone. The Dwellers dissolved into oblivion; the Llano River Clan scattered. For more than a year, no organized gang has attacked us. It's been one-offs, loners, and vigilantes. That's it."

"That's it," Norma scoffed. "You're an idiot, Rudy Gallardo. I love you, but you're naive if you think no gang is coming for this place someday. Someone will fill the vacuum. It *will* happen. I don't want you in their sights when it does."

Rudy sucked in a deep breath of air. He sank back in his chair, apparently considering his wife's concerns. He scratched his neck and then rubbed his hand along the back of his neck.

"I could *so* use my knives to cut the tension in this room." Lou snickered. "This is the best Saturday dinner in a long—"

"Not funny," said Marcus.

"Not funny at all," said Norma. She pushed herself back from the table. With tears streaming down her cheeks, she stormed from the kitchen. Her footsteps echoed through the hallway. The screen door slammed open against the exterior of the house and then banged shut.

"Rudy, I'm sorry," said Marcus. "I didn't mean for it to go that way. I don't want you and Norma fighting on account of my issues."

"If they were at odds because of your issues," Lou chirped, "they'd have gotten divorced or shot each other by now."

Marcus glowered. "You're not funny at all."

"I'm hilarious," Lou countered.

"It's fine," said Rudy, ignoring Lou. "I get where you're coming from. I do. I should have had her back, at least here at the table. We could have talked about it later, just the two of us."

"Still," Marcus said, "I ruined dinner. I'm going to go apologize."

"No," Rudy said, "that will only make things worse. I'll deal with it later. You can help with the cleanup though. I'd appreciate that."

"No problem."

"I do appreciate it though," said Rudy.

Marcus took another bite of snake. "What?"

"Your having confidence in me."

Lou giggled and shook her head. She took a swig of water from her glass and smacked her lips when she slapped it back on the table.

"Passive-aggressive?" asked Marcus.

"No," said Lou. "It's that you're the funny one now."

"I'm going to talk to my wife," said Rudy. He feigned a smile and excused himself, disappearing through the open arch that led into the hallway.

Marcus looked at the two women across from him. He blinked with effect. They took the hint and cleared their plates, then left the kitchen to do whatever it was the two of them did.

Marcus put his hand on Lou's shoulder. She shrugged him off. "What's going on?" he asked.

Lou squeezed her eyes shut and dropped her shoulders. When she opened them again, they were glossy with tears. She swallowed hard. When she spoke, her voice cracked. "You didn't ask *me*," she said, pain etched in her voice.

"I didn't ask you what?" Marcus asked, dumfounded. "If I should quit?"

"No, *Dorothy*." She shook her head and pointed at herself with a balled fist. "You didn't ask *me* to be the sheriff."

Marcus sat there for a moment considering her outrage. Lou? He scratched his head. "I didn't even think about it."

Lou rolled her eyes and threw back her head in a way that only teenagers can effectively do. She clamped a hand over the Astros baseball cap on the top of her head to keep it from flying off. "I didn't even think about it," she repeated in a baritone voice, mocking Marcus. "I didn't even think. Why would I think? I'm Marcus Battle. I act all introspective; I quote old movies. I name my guns, I don't read books, I think Al Pacino was in *The Godfather*. Maybe he was in *War and Peace* too."

"C'mon," he said, "give me a break. I didn't think about it because never, in a million years, would I think you'd want that responsibility."

"Why?" she asked. "Because you think I couldn't handle it?"

"No," said Marcus, frustration welling in his voice, "because I don't want you living the same kind of nasty existence I have."

"My existence has been pretty nasty, Marcus. You and I both know that. I'm perfectly capable of living with my demons. More than you, apparently."

Marcus never wanted to be the sheriff, or whatever he was, in and around Baird. He took the job because Rudy had asked it of him, and because the townsfolk were desperate for someone who could fend off the scavengers who'd come to peck at and steal what they'd worked too hard to have. There were other reasons too.

He couldn't go back to his own ranch. He'd seen to that himself, having burned it after Lola, Sawyer, and Penny had died there. There was no point in staying in that haunted place anymore.

He'd grown fond of Lou. She was a good kid who needed an adult in her life to equip her with some sort of parental guidance. He was more a friend than father, but that was a sliding scale depending on the circumstance. She'd decided to stay in Baird and live in an outbuilding on Rudy's property. It gave her a roof over her head and provided easy joint custody of Fifty with the Gallardos.

He didn't want to be alone again. He was acutely self-aware of what it had done to his psyche in the five years after the Scourge. Another long bout of solitude would surely have driven him over the edge.

A couple of the townsfolk were former low-level Cartel suppliers who knew of Marcus as Mad Max. They recalled his larger-than-life persona and his reputation as an unstoppable solo force and lone vigilante, and had put Marcus on a pedestal. They played to his ego.

Rather than become a never-ending drifter in a western wasteland, Marcus took those plusses and subtracted the only minus, which was being the top law enforcer in a lawless land. The math was simple; he took the job. The town gave him a place southeast of town. It was next to what was once known as T P Lake. It was more of a pond now, but it did provide Marcus and his horse with a water source. There were a cluster of shotgun houses and travel trailers on the edges of the pond. Though Marcus lived by himself, he wasn't alone.

Sitting here listening to Lou, he wondered if he was wrong to take the job in the first place. If it was always going to end badly, which it was bound to according to the post-Scourge order of things, he might have been better off wandering, slipping into oblivion.

"I'm sorry," he said. "I should have asked if it was something that might interest you. I should have. I didn't. Given Norma's reaction to Rudy taking the job, I'm sure it's yours if you want it."

Lou pushed herself from the table and picked up her plate. "Thanks, Marcus. I appreciate the apology. But wow. As good as you are with a gun, you are equally as feeble with people."

She dropped her plate into the sink, took a sponge from a bucket of water on the counter, and squeezed it over her plate. Then she rubbed the sponge on a brick of homemade lye and oil soap and scrubbed her plate. She washed the others in the sink too. When she was nearly finished, Marcus stood and carried his own plate to the sink.

He reached out to put an arm on Lou's shoulder, but she wiped her wet hands on his shirt. "You need to think about what you said here tonight. Probably need to consider why you said it too. Get over yourself, Marcus," she said. "We've all lost. We've all killed. We've all had trouble sleeping because of the things we've done to stay alive. You don't hold a patent on pain."

Marcus took a step back and stuffed his hands into his pockets. He nodded without saying anything.

Lou patted him on the chest and walked out of the kitchen. She whistled for the dog and he gave chase, his long nails clacking on the wooden floor.

"I'm going back to my place," she said without facing him. "I have some knitting to do. Maybe I'll play with makeup."

CHAPTER 6

FEBRUARY 6, 2044, 9:40 PM
SCOURGE + 11 YEARS, 4 MONTHS
SAN ANTONIO, TEXAS

The San Antonio River Walk was a meandering cesspool of trash and muck. The water that ran through what had once been the city's tourism jewel was poisoned by the carelessness of the Cartel, the Dwellers, and anyone else who tried to wield power in the Mission City.

Junior slid a sweat-soiled bandana over his nose and mouth as he and Grissom rode along the water toward the city's most famous mission. The dank odor of the bandana was far easier to breathe than the fetid air that hung low over and around the River Walk. The two traveled east on Crockett Street and crossed Losoya Street. They were close to their destination after an arduous ride that had taken longer than either of them had expected.

"It's up here," said Junior.

"You think we'll find what we're looking for here?" asked Grissom.

Junior adjusted the bandana on the bridge of his nose and shifted his weight in the saddle. He winced as his chafed skin rubbed against his jeans. He didn't answer Grissom. He'd already told his compadre countless times over the past day and a half that this would be the place they'd find who and what they needed. Good people didn't go to the Alamo.

The sun had set three hours earlier and the moon was a week away from being at its fullest light. They clomped along in the relative dark, guided by a decades-old laminated map Junior kept inside a box that had belonged to his father.

Their horses had walked a half block when Junior spotted their destination. Its exterior was lit with oil-burning wicks that flickered wildly and gave the limestone façade the glow of a medieval castle.

"The Alamo," said Junior. "This is it."

He eased his horse to an unoccupied hitching post in front of the wide plaza that led to the mission's entrance. There were a dozen other horses standing watch already.

Men stumbled around the plaza. One stood against the trunk of a large two-hundred-year-old pecan tree. His arm was outstretched, giving balance against the tree while the man relieved himself onto the dirt at its roots.

From inside the building there was laughter and music. Junior hitched up his pants and touched the grips on both Colt revolvers at his hips. He looked over his shoulder at Grissom, who was slower to ready himself.

Junior spat onto the stone plaza. "You coming?" he asked Grissom. "Or you staying here?"

Grissom finished tying off his horse and hurried to Junior's side. Junior moved purposefully to the Alamo's entrance.

They reached the entrance to the mission on its southern side, where the prison once sat. Junior moseyed through the sally port and into the large open space on the west side of the small complex. He ignored the dozens of eyes that followed his advance as he and Grissom weaved their way through the maze of tables occupied by men and women, as they made their way to the large bar at the far end of the space. At the bar, Junior planted his elbows on the polished oak and surveyed the room.

To one side, and running the length of the rectangular space, were a series of rooms. During the famous thirteen-day siege two hundred and eight years earlier, almost to the day, those rooms had served as officers' quarters. Now they were the post-Scourge version of VIP rooms, where men paid extra to spend private time with the women employed at the bar.

A meat hook of a hand gripped his shoulder from behind the bar. An equally animalistic voice pulled him around to face the broad-shouldered, thick-necked barkeep. "If you stand here," he said gruffly, "you gotta buy something. No freeloading."

Junior pulled a hundred-dollar bill from his pocket and slapped it on the bar. "Whatever you got for me and my friend."

"That'll get you two shots of mash," said the bear of a bartender.

Junior scowled. "Two shots? I could get a whole tank of gasoline for three hundred."

The bartender shrugged, his neck disappearing into his shoulders. "Go drink a tank of gasoline, then."

"What'll fifty get me?" asked Junior.

"One shot, genius."

Junior motioned toward Grissom "One shot, then," he said. "For my friend."

Grissom bellied up to the bar. "Gee," he said with a gap-toothed smile. "Thanks, Junior."

Junior waved him off. "I've got a job," he said to the bartender. "I need some men for it. I heard this was a good place to find men."

The bartender stepped back from Junior, his eyes darting around the room. He grunted something Junior couldn't decipher and walked away, disappearing through an opening at one end of the bar that led into another room.

Junior stood there for a moment. Then he tightened his hands into fists and pounded them onto the bar. He cursed and spun around to face the party behind him.

Grissom downed his shot and coughed. He wiped his mouth with the back of his hand and mimicked Junior's position at the bar. "What just happened?"

"We got the brush-off," said Junior. "Now I've got to work the room on my own."

Opposite the VIP rooms sat a woman playing guitar. She alternately sang and hummed as she played, her long fingers dancing across the strings and plucking at them with ridiculous skill. The melody distracted Junior from the task at hand, but he refocused and moved from the bar to search for the right people.

"I'll be back," he told Grissom as he drifted into the crowd. "Stay here."

At the center of the room, a few couples swayed to the rhythm. He ignored them and worked past them toward a group of tables at which several armed men sat with their drinks. He approached several of them and was ignored or told to go away. Nobody was interested in what he had to offer.

He started to wave at Grissom, ready to give up on the place and move on when a table he hadn't tried caught his attention. It wasn't the table, but one man in particular, who had a certain look about him. There was an unmistakable aura around that man. A glow almost, that emanated from him. He was a leader of men, a person who could get things done. Junior was sure of it.

The man sat between two others. While they talked across him, laughing and arguing and drinking, he sat quietly. His stubbled head and thick, wiry beard were a sharp contrast to the mess of slovenly survivors around him.

Junior walked straight up to him. He looked at the floor, scanning their feet, and then looked at each one of them in the eyes and settled on his target. The others who'd been carrying on stopped and stared. One of them slammed his palm onto the table.

"Do we know you?" he asked.

Junior shook his head. "Not yet."

"What do you want?"

Junior looked at the man's hands and then at the bearded man in the middle. "I've got a job. I need men. The pay is horrible, but the reward is great."

"Not interested," said the man.

Junior's eyes stayed focused on his target. "I didn't ask you. I asked him." He nodded at the bald man with the wiry, unkempt beard.

As the others laughed, oohed and ahhed, the rude man cursed at Junior and threatened to come around the table. The bearded man stopped him. The table grew quiet. Guitar music strummed and glasses clinked in the background, as if providing a soundtrack.

"What's the job?" asked the bearded man.

"Revenge."

The bearded man rubbed his head with his palm. "That's vague," he said with a thick Southern drawl. "Revenge comes in a lot of different colors."

"This is the blackest kind of revenge," said Junior. "I want to kill the man who killed my father."

The rude man sneered and looked around the table for validation. "Kill him yourself. What kind of person asks someone else to do his killing for him?"

The others grumbled their agreement. The bearded man did not. He tilted his head to one side and narrowed his eyes. He stared at Junior and tilted his head in the other direction. He was expressionless even when he finally spoke.

"Just one man?" he asked.

Junior nodded. "Not any man," he explained. "He's charmed or cursed, I don't know which. But a single man can't kill him."

The others at the table laughed.

The rude man, who clearly hadn't taken the hint from the bearded man, playfully punched him in the shoulder as he mocked Junior. "What is he, a ghost?" He laughed, then feigned Junior's tone. "*A single man can't kill him?"*

The bearded man wiped the grin from his cohort's face. "You're not funny," he said. "You're drunk. You're belligerent when you're drunk, and that means you're not funny."

The bearded man then offered his hand to Junior. "I'd like to apologize for my friend's rude behavior. We're not animals here."

Junior shook the man's hand. "I'm not interested in what he has to say anyhow," he said. "I'm talking to you. I'm called Junior."

"I'm Bumppo," said the bearded man. "Have a seat."

Junior looked across the room to Grissom, who was still at the bar with an empty glass, nodded reassuringly at him, and took the lone remaining chair at the table.

Bumppo poured a shot of mash into an empty glass and slid it across the table to Junior. "It's on me."

Junior shook his head. "I can't," he said. "That's fifty dollars."

Bumppo laughed and the rest of the table, save the drunk bully, laughed with him. "Fifty dollars?" he asked. "Who told you that? I paid a hundred for the bottle."

Junior gritted his teeth but didn't admit to being taken by the barkeep. He took the shot and downed it. The sting of it burned his tongue and throat on the way down, but he relished it. He hadn't had a drink in weeks.

Bumppo raised his glass toward Junior and then slung it down his throat. "It's lousy," he said, wincing, "but it's what we have."

"Thank you," said Junior.

"Tell me more about this immortal man you can't handle on your own," said Bumppo. "The prospect intrigues me."

"You've done this sort of work before?" asked Junior.

From beneath Bumppo's beard, a sly smile spread across his face. His eyes shrank to slits. "Yeah," he said, drawing chuckles from the others at the table, "we've worked the entire color wheel, if you know what I mean. What's the pay?"

"Ten thousand."

"That ain't a lot," said Bumppo. "We'd usually take three times that for a job as precarious as the one you appear to be offering."

"It's all I've got."

"Where is it?" asked Bumppo. "And who is it?"

"He's in a town called Baird," said Junior. "His name is—"

The smile disappeared from Bumppo's face. "Marcus Battle."

Junior swallowed hard. "How did you—"

Bumppo's eyes were wide. He rubbed his head with both hands. "Everybody knows who Marcus Battle is. Plenty of people have tried to off that man. Back when we were in the Cartel, we heard stories about him. He could kill twenty men with a switchblade and a lit match."

The obnoxious man pointed his finger at Junior. "He wouldn't even need the match, I bet. He's one bad hombre."

Junior wasn't surprised by their reaction. He'd have been more shocked had they never heard of Battle. "He's getting old," he said. "He's not what he used to be."

"That's like saying the sun doesn't burn as hot as it used to," said Bumppo. "It'll still fry you if you get too close."

"If we kill him, we'll be legends. We become the men who killed Mad Max."

Bumppo poured himself another shot and downed it. His fingers were wrapped around the glass, which he tapped gently on the table.

Junior sighed. He pushed back from the table. "So you're not interested," he said. "I get it. I'll find someone else."

"I didn't say that," Bumppo countered. He eyed the bar. "Give us a minute though."

Junior smiled with one corner of his mouth and nodded confidently. "All right. Come see me when you're ready."

He stood and meandered through the crowd back to Grissom. The musician still strummed her guitar, but it was more aggressive. Her fingers moved quickly and she sang with an anger Junior hadn't previously noticed. Resisting the urge to look over his shoulder at her or toward Bumppo's table, he eased up to the bar. He reached across the polished wood and snatched the uncorked bottle of mash. He wrapped his fingers around the long neck and emptied a healthy pour into Grissom's glass.

"You have the money for that?" asked Grissom.

"We're not paying for it," said Junior. "Drink it."

Grissom swallowed the mash and whistled. "Whew," he said. "Okay. What's up with you? Are those men gonna help us?"

"They're gonna help," said Junior. "They just haven't figured it out yet."

Grissom inched closer and lowered his voice. "How do you know? What did they say? Did you tell them who we're after? Did you say how much the job pays?"

Junior swayed with the rhythm of the music that filled the room. "That guitarist is good," he said. "She plays with emotion. I like that."

"Junior," Grissom pressed, "what is—"

Junior put his finger to his lips. "Shhh. Listen."

He caught each pluck of the strings, the resonance of them as they vibrated against the musician's finger. One note melted into the next. Her voice blended perfectly as she sang the song.

"They'll do the job because they need the money," he said to Grissom after a moment. "They haven't cleaned themselves in weeks. The leader's head is unshaven. Their hands are filthy. Their boots and shoes are worn through. And they're desperate."

"Desperate?"

"Only the desperate come to the Alamo," said Junior. "It's why we're here, right? We're desperate to find men to help us. We've exhausted every other reasonable possibility, so we're left with the ones nobody else would have."

"You told them the job only pays twenty?"

"I told them it pays ten."

Grissom's eyes popped and he bit his lower lip, trying to contain his glee. "You're a smart man. Your father would be proud."

The music stopped. "He would be," Junior said with a nod. He sucked in a deep breath of the stale air and the bartender emerged from the darkened doorway through which he'd disappeared minutes ago.

"I need another glass," said Junior. "We're going to finish the bottle here."

The bartender dropped his meat-hook hands onto the polished wood. "That's gonna cost you. Looking at the bottle, you already owe me for another glass."

Junior shook his head. "You already charged us for the bottle," he said firmly, "so I don't owe you anything."

The bartender growled and slid his hefty frame across the bar, his finger an inch from Junior's face. "You're gonna pay me for—"

Without warning, Junior grabbed the man's finger with his hand and bent it backwards, snapping it with one quick move. The man eked out a high-pitched squeal and tried to free his broken finger from Junior's grip but couldn't.

Junior used the finger to yank the man toward him with one hand while he slid his other around the bartender's neck and pushed downward rapidly, slamming the man's forehead onto the wood. Junior gripped a handful of the bartender's hair and held him down, leaning close to the man's ear. "No. I'm. Not."

He let go of the barkeep and the man stumbled backward, holding his injured hand at the wrist. His eyes jittered with fear and he banged into the shelf that held several bottles of mash. One of them teetered and fell to the floor with a smash. The bartender stood there, dazed, mumbling to himself. He'd gone from what he thought was the upper hand to a simpering victim in a matter of seconds.

Junior pulled a Colt from its holster and set it on the bar, his fingers draped across the grip. "I'm going to need that second glass."

The bartender eyed the gun, obliged, and used his good hand to gently deliver it at arm's length. He shakily rested the bottle on the wood and stepped back to cradle his wounded hand.

"Ain't you afraid he's gonna come back and shoot you?" asked Grissom.

Junior raised his glass and motioned for Grissom to raise his. "That's his shooting hand that's all mangled," he said and slammed the mash against the back of his throat. "He's not coming back to do squat."

"I think we're in," Bumppo said from behind the pair. "It's gonna have to be fifteen grand though. Can't do it for less than that."

Junior scratched his temple and shrugged. "No can do."

Grissom stepped back with surprise, cocking his head like a clucking bird, and eyed Junior warily. He didn't say anything. Junior ignored him.

Bumppo grumbled under his breath and moved to the bar, squeezing his frame between Grissom and Junior. He leaned on his forearms and clasped his hands. He looked to Junior like a Catholic resting on the pew in front of him, about to pray.

"You came to me," he said with a sardonic chuckle. "I'm guessing you can't find anyone else to help you or you wouldn't be here getting into finger fights with the bartender."

Junior's lips were pressed tight and curled into his mouth between his teeth. He looked straight ahead at the wall of grain alcohol varietals held captive in bottles on wooden shelving. He could taste the remains of the mash in his throat. He wasn't budging. Ten thousand dollars was all he was paying and that was all Bumppo was going to get.

"Marcus Battle ain't one to mess with," said the bald, bearded, would-be assassin. "You need us more than we need you. It's gotta be fifteen."

Junior inhaled quickly through his nostrils, pulling a gob of snot-laced spit into his mouth. He drew it forward with his tongue and spat the nasty wad of it at the liquor wall behind the bar, where it splattered and snaked down the limestone.

"I'm guessing you need the money more than I do," said Junior. "Anybody willing to do it for less than twenty will do it for ten."

Bumppo squeezed his laced fingers together until they were white. "I'll do ten if you give us the money up front."

A smile crept along the edges of Junior's mouth. He'd won. "Five up front. Five when Battle is dead."

Bumppo glanced over his shoulder at the men he'd left at his table. He exhaled with histrionic resignation. "Okay," he said. "That's a thousand per man now and another thousand when the job is finished."

Junior reached into his pocket and pulled out a roll of cash. He casually handed it to Bumppo without looking at him. "It's all there," he said. "Five grand in hundred-dollar bills."

Bumppo snatched the roll of money and shook it at Junior. "Best money you ever spent," he said. "Consider Marcus Battle dead. We leave for Baird in the morning."

"Two hundred fifty miles to Baird," said Junior. "That's a three-day ride, easy. We'll stop in San Angelo along the way. So let's make it early in the morning. We'll meet you out front in the plaza at sunup."

"Done," said Bumppo.

Junior shook the man's hand, sealing the deal. He hoped he'd found the right kind of desperate man.

CHAPTER 7

Taskar knuckled the sleep from his eyes and yawned, thumping a rhythm on the steering wheel with his thumbs. Coupled with the warbling hum of the tires against the interstate asphalt, and the rattle of his water bottle against the edge of the cup holder, the thumping complemented a nice melody. It was almost musical.

"Welcome To Georgia," a bent blue sign announced in bold white lettering. "We're Glad Georgia's On Your Mind." At the bottom of the sign was the name of the governor at the time of the Scourge a decade earlier.

"Christopher Bridges," Taskar said to himself. "Gonna guess he's no longer in office."

He reached to the center console, found the water bottle, and flipped its top to take a drink. Finally, after a long night of driving, he was in his destination state. A green mileage sign told him Atlanta was only fifty-three miles away.

Taskar took his foot off the accelerator for a second and rolled his ankle around in a circle. The ache had stretched from the top of his foot, up his leg, and to his knee.

The hearse lurched and slowed until he reapplied pressure to the gas pedal. The vehicle sputtered for a moment and then jerked into gear. The speedometer read forty-five miles per hour.

"Not far now," he muttered. "Not far at all."

Taskar closed the cap on the water bottle and set it back into the cup holder. He twisted it until it made the familiar rattle and then thumped the wheel with his thumbs. Humming along with the tires, he improvised a tune with the cup, his thumb furnishing the instrumentals.

Taskar would like to have been a musician. That was the plan, in fact, until the Scourge changed everything.

He'd been working at the Korisko Larkin Staskiewicz Funeral Home in Omaha as a funeral bugler and stand-in pallbearer. It had been a good after-school job for a sixteen-year-old.

His mother, a florist who'd done a lot of work for the home, had gotten him the job. She'd been proud of her Boy Scout and his musical abilities.

"He plays alto sax, the piano, and the guitar," she'd told the funeral director. "He's such a good boy."

"Can he play the bugle?" the man had asked. "We don't want to resort to a digital recording of 'Taps'. It's an insult to our veterans, I think. We much prefer a live performance."

She blinked but nodded. "Of course," she'd told them, and Taskar had been hired at twenty dollars per service, even though he couldn't play the valveless brass instrument.

Instead of panicking, Taskar had bought himself a secondhand instrument at a pawnshop and taught himself to play it. After a few months, he'd been promoted and got an extra five dollars for helping carry caskets if needed.

One afternoon, after the burial of an Air Force veteran, the funeral director had turned to Taskar as the boy was slipping his bugle back into its case. He'd wiped his sweaty brow and whistled.

"You sure are a good musician," he'd said. "I mean, for never having played the bugle, you certainly have a talent."

Taskar had snapped the lid shut and blushed. "How did you know that?" he asked. "Did my mom tell you?"

The director had picked up a folding chair and loaded it onto a cart. "No," he'd said with a smile. "I knew when I hired you."

"How?"

"Your mother mentioned that you played a woodwind and two stringed instruments. She never mentioned a brass," the director had said. "Still, I figured, here's a mother who loves her son and believes in him. So, I believed in you."

Taskar was a talented musician. He played by ear and could compose melodies on the fly. He was an improviser who understood the language of music. He'd wanted to attend the Berklee College of Music in Boston and hoped to one day play professionally as a session musician or in a band.

That had ended with the Scourge. His mother had been among the first in Omaha to contract the illness. She'd given it to his twin sisters, and then his father had succumbed. Taskar had been alone. He'd sought help and refuge at the funeral home. For weeks he'd managed there. Then, predictably, everyone affiliated with it had also contracted the ampicillin- and tetracycline-resistant viral pneumonia. The director had collapsed in Taskar's arms as the boy tried to cool his fever in the shower. Within hours Taskar had been orphaned again.

Unsure of what to do, he had taken a bag full of food from the cupboard and bottled water from the break room refrigerator, plucked the keys to the hearse from a pegboard by the back door, and climbed into the driver's seat. He'd no clue where to go or what he was doing.

A block from the funeral home, at the corner of F Street and South Fiftieth, he'd slowed to a stop. He'd gripped the wheel, considering his options. North or south? Or east until he could merge onto Interstate 80?

Despite the relative lack of vehicles still on the roads, he'd heard horror stories of impassable pileups on highways through the Midwest and heartland and decided south was the best choice. When he'd swung the wheel and tentatively pressed the accelerator, a woman had appeared at his window. She'd been wild-eyed, her red cheeks glistening with tears, and her hair had sprayed across her head as if she'd played with a light socket.

Her rapping knuckles and unintelligible pleas had startled Taskar, but he'd stopped the hearse and cracked the window. The woman had plied her fingers through the narrow opening and stuck her face to it like someone gasping for air before drowning. Her fingernails had been chipped and the red polish was missing in spots.

"Pleeaase!" she'd wailed. "Help me. I need to go to Kansas City. My parents are in Kansas City."

Taskar had taken his hands from the wheel and held them up in surrender, trying to calm the woman.

"Pleeaase!" she'd repeated amidst raspy gasps for air. "I can pay you. I can give you money."

"Are your parents alive?" he'd asked.

The woman had bitten her lip, her chin quivering, and she'd nodded loosely. "Yes, but my mother's sick. I have to get there."

Taskar had studied the woman. She'd seemed sincere. Like so many people at that time, she'd been at her wit's end, and her mania was to be expected. He hadn't considered whether she was a thief playing him or something more sinister. Still naive in those early days after the Scourge, he'd given in to the guilt.

He'd motioned to the front passenger's seat. "Okay, hop in."

The woman had pulled her fingers from the crack and danced up and down with excitement. She'd thanked him repeatedly as she'd skirted her way around the front of the hearse.

She'd flung open the passenger's side door and rolled into her seat. She'd been barefoot. It was only once she was sitting next to him, struggling with the seatbelt, that Taskar had noticed the woman was in her pajamas.

He pressed the accelerator and started the two-hundred-mile journey south as the woman, still on the edge of hyperventilating, had reached into her pajama top and pulled out a stack of folded bills.

"I've got one thousand dollars," she'd said. "I can pay for whatever gas you need plus five hundred. That okay?"

Taskar had checked the fuel gauge and nodded. "I should have enough gas to get you to Kansas City, even if I stay off the highways. Plus, I don't know how many places are going to have fuel anyhow."

The woman had thanked him again, and five hours later, he'd dropped her off at her parents' home. He hadn't stuck around to find out if the woman's mother was still alive. If she was, it likely wouldn't be for long.

Armed with the five hundred dollars in cash, he'd managed to find a gas station that would sell him half a tank for a hundred dollars. He'd taken the deal, and while the station owner pumped the gas, a young couple had approached Taskar and asked if they could hitch a ride.

He'd asked them where they'd wanted to go and if they could pay him. They'd said Wichita and offered a case of bottled water, ten cans of Chef Boyardee Beefaroni, and a weather radio.

He'd taken it. His unplanned career as a post-apocalyptic chauffeur had begun. He traveled back and forth across the wall countless times. He'd been from the Rockies to the Appalachians. He'd never been to Atlanta. Until now.

The sun was still rising in the sky straight ahead of him as he drove east. He flipped down the visor and fumbled for a bent pair of Ray-Bans he kept in the driver's side door pocket.

Beneath the glare was a city built upon its own ashes. One hundred and eighty years earlier, Atlanta had burned.

November 15, 1864, General William Sherman and his Union troops set fire to the city, one that Sherman believed had done more to help the Confederacy than any other save Richmond. Thirty percent of Atlanta was burned to the ground. Famously, one Georgian was quoted as having said, "Hell has laid her egg and here it hatched."

Under the glow of the morning sun, it appeared to Taskar as if it were on fire again and he wondered what hell he might be entering. He gripped the wheel with one hand, adjusted his Ray-Bans with the other, and pressed harder on the accelerator. The faster he understood what he'd gotten himself into, the better.

CHAPTER 8

Lomas Ward awoke with a headache in a bright white room he didn't recognize. He was cold and drenched in sweat. His shirt was stuck to his lower back and underneath his arms. He blinked to try to focus on the ceiling above him but struggled. Each thump of his quickened pulse aggravated the throb that ran across his forehead from one temple to the other.

He tried sitting up, but couldn't. There was something holding him in place, flat against a cot or table. Sweat dripped into his eyes and he squeezed them shut.

A familiar voice caused him to open them again. *"Lomas,"* said Dr. Morel, *"can you hear me?"*

Lomas searched the room despite the muscular ache in his eyes, but didn't see the doctor. His chest tightened and he coughed. When the doctor spoke again, he could tell the voice was piped in through a speaker.

"Lomas," said Dr. Morel, *"how are you feeling?"*

Lomas lay back against the thin, damp pillow underneath his head. He stared at the ceiling. His head pulsed with a sharp, debilitating pain. He swallowed against the sandpaper in his throat and coughed again. An explosion of stinging pain jabbed against his chest. A loud buzz and metallic click drew his attention. A figure in a large blue biohazard suit appeared from beyond a newly opened door and clunked its way into the room. The door buzzed again and the door shut. The figure connected a tube on the suit to a coiled hose along the wall, then moved toward Lomas.

"I'm not certain this is a best protocol," said Dr. Morel over the speaker. *"We could wait to assess the progress until—"*

"I'm fine," said Gwendolyn Sharp. "I've done this before without consequence."

The figure stopped at Lomas's bedside. Even through the haze of his discomfort, he recognized her face behind the mask.

"We're designated BSL 3," said Dr. Morel, referring to the room's designation as a biosafety level three laboratory.

Sharp awkwardly faced a white spherical camera perched in the corner of the room behind Lomas's head. "So?" she said. "I'm not breathing his air. There are no sharp objects except for me. It's fine."

Morel sighed through the intercom. Sharp smirked and bent over to look at Lomas. She spoke about him as if he wasn't there. "Please record my observations," she said. "The time is 10:06 a.m. Eastern Standard Time, 7 February 2044. This is Dr. Gwendolyn Sharp, Senior Research Virologist, CDC, Atlanta, Georgia."

"What are you doing?" asked Lomas in a wispy voice he didn't recognize as his own.

She ignored him. "Patient CV-01 is exhibiting symptoms consistent with a viral form of the *Yersinia pestsis* bacteria to which he was previously immune. Note an obvious inflammation around the eyes and nostrils."

Lomas struggled against the binds that held him flat against the table. He strained until he used up what little strength he had remaining. His body shuddered.

Sharp slid close to Lomas until her mask was inches from his face.

"The patient is perspiring. There is nasal mucus draining from the nostrils and rheum collecting in the corners of his eyes."

Lomas swallowed past the razor-blade pain in his throat. "What did you do to me?"

Sharp stood up straight and shifted toward the camera. "The patient is requesting information about his condition. Your thoughts, Dr. Morel?"

"Tell him," said Morel. *"There's nothing he can do about it now."*

Sharp looked back down at Lomas. Her blurry image shimmered in the cloud of his aching eyes and pounding head. He could smell the plastic of her suit, could almost taste its organic compounds on his tongue, the odor was so strong. Still, he couldn't even be sure this was real. Maybe it was a dream.

"Is this happening?" he asked, expecting to wake up.

Sharp responded flatly, without emotion. "Yes, this is happening. You're infected with a modified virus. It will kill you. Are you experiencing any abdominal pain?"

Lomas searched Sharp's face for any hint that she might be joking. He found none. He started to speak but coughed. He clamped his jaw against the swelling pain in his chest.

"Tussis is present," said Dr. Sharp. "We are at nineteen hours incubation. The onset of these symptoms is accelerated beyond our expectations."

"Is that a problem? We need enough time for phase two."

"We should be fine," said Sharp. "We've yet to identify any bloody sputum, and the secondary viral infection has a longer incubation period. We have at least three days, by my estimation, until they are fully present, and another two or three before we reach morbidity."

Sharp's blue, angular image danced in front of Lomas's eyes. He tried blinking past the blurred shimmy of the virologist in her Tychem suit. He wanted to reach up and grab her by the mask and tear at it with his hands until her face was exposed. Then he would cough on her, spit on her, give her whatever it was they'd injected into his body. He sucked in a shallow, raspy breath. Moving his lips and emitting a sound was taxing.

"Morbidity?" he asked.

"Yes," said Sharp. "I told you, what you have will kill you. Within a week you'll have served your purpose and we'll know whether or not what we've given you is as effective as we anticipate it to be."

Lomas tightened his fists into balls. His chin quivered, his chest heaved, and his pulse quickened, worsening the throb of the headache. He tried suppressing the wave of tears he knew was coming, but couldn't. He lay there, strapped to an exam bed, sobbing. His chest and hips pressed against the straps that held his body in place.

"Are you experiencing any abdominal pain?" asked Dr. Sharp.

Lomas didn't respond. He relaxed his fists and laid his sweating palms flat on the table. His body shuddered again against the perceived chill in the room.

Sharp stood motionless for a moment, pivoted away from Lomas, and moved back toward the door. There were a series of hums and clicks; the door opened and closed. She was gone.

Lomas inhaled a shallow breath through his nose. He could taste the thick phlegm building at the back of his throat. He tried cataloging his ailments: headache, coughing, sore throat, fever, tightness in his chest, muscular weakness, burning in his eyes. Soon, he knew he would add stomach pain to the list. He silently prayed for a quick end to the suffering. He didn't think he could handle another three or four or more days of this, especially if it was going to get worse.

He told himself to stop thinking about it. He willed himself to envision his boys in their new home.

They were smiling. Their eyes were free from the worry he so often saw reflected in them when he tucked them in at night. They were rubbing their bellies from the home-cooked meal made-to-order. Chances were, they'd asked for grilled cheese sandwiches. They loved cheese, but it was a delicacy in the Ward household.

They were clean and smelled like Irish Spring soap. Their hair was washed and brushed. They wore proper-fitting clothes that were absent the stains, tears, and holes common in the wardrobe he'd been able to supply them.

And most of all, he hoped, they didn't miss him, that they'd already adapted to their new environs and forgotten all about their dad. He couldn't bear the thought of his boys missing him, of wondering where he'd gone, if he'd abandoned them or given up on them. He'd much rather believe they'd wiped him from their young memories.

The idea that they hadn't was as painful as the chest-drilling coughs that came with more frequency. Lomas told himself he'd done a good thing by his boys. He knew that if he kept repeating it to himself, he might eventually believe it.

* * *

Gwendolyn Sharp dabbed a cloth towel on her forehead, absorbing the thin sheen of sweat that had formed on her forehead during the trip into the lab. Once she was finished, she tossed the cloth into an aluminum container marked INCINERATOR.

She finished disrobing and tossed the rest of her clothing and undergarments into the same container. Then she stepped into a floor-to-ceiling rectangular box that resembled a twentieth-century phone booth, shut the door behind her, and raised her hands above her head. She stood with her feet a bit more than shoulder width apart.

"Ready," she said. A blast of cold water sprayed her body from all directions. It was an identical spray to the one she'd undergone minutes earlier while still wearing the single-use biohazard suit.

The water stopped and a voice warned her to close her eyes and mouth. She did as instructed and a wash of antibacterial foam coated her body. The voice counted down from ten; then a secondary spray of icy water cleansed the soap from her skin and hair.

Goose bumps populated her skin as she wrung the excess water from her hair and walked from the shower room, through a code-panel equipped door, and into an adjacent space with towels, a stainless steel bench, and a locker.

She shivered and dried off her slender, toned body. She was a runner who managed ten miles a day on a treadmill in her room at the facility. It was her time to exercise, think, de-stress, and plot.

Once in her clothes, she slinked into the hallway, around a corner, and into an office space replete with a wall of surveillance monitors and high-powered computers connected to the facility's basement mainframe.

She ground her teeth in a Pavlovian response to the ever-present low-pitched hum in the room that was at once unnerving and soothing to Sharp. She was acutely aware of it every time she stepped into the office. It subconsciously reminded her of the overwhelming project with which her team had been tasked. As she got to work, the hum melted into the white noise of the room and it was comforting. She drifted over to the far corner of the room and Dr. Morel.

He was pounding away at the keyboard at his terminal. The clacking of his keys smacked of desperation. He didn't notice her as she approached.

She put her hand on his shoulder and he jumped at the surprise of her touch. "What did you think?" she asked.

Morel kept pecking at the keys. "About what? The patient's symptoms, his lack of understanding, his frustration?"

"We should start referring to them as subjects as opposed to patients," Sharp said. "Calling them patients makes it sound as though we're trying to save them."

Morel stopped typing. Without looking at Sharp, he sighed. "We are trying to save people. That's the whole point of this, isn't it?"

"Is it?" she asked coyly. "I think *subjects* is more proper regardless of the endgame. How are the others?"

Morel rolled his chair backward past his colleague and spun to face a wall of monitors. Sharp faced the wall with him. She folded her arms across her chest and scanned the large color displays.

Morel pointed to a screen in the top row. "CV-02 isn't showing symptoms yet," he said. "She's less restless now though, getting weaker. Temperature is still normal."

Sharp focused on the woman in the picture. She was older in appearance, her white hair wiry and unkempt. Her eyes were half open. She was flat on her back and not struggling or moving. Sharp stepped closer to the monitor.

"Can I see the vitals on CV-02?" she asked.

Morel rolled back to his desk. He picked up a tablet-sized handheld remote and tapped the screen several times until a multicolored graphic overlay appeared on the monitor with the image of the woman strapped to the exam table.

"Her pulse is very low," said Sharp. "And her oxygen intake is suboptimal. Did we do a VO2 max test when she arrived so we have a baseline oxygen utilization measurement?"

"No," Morel replied. "She wasn't able to generate any intensity in her workout. We couldn't even complete a standard stress test."

Sharp sighed. "Not sure she's a great patien—subject."

"As long as she's infected and contagious, it doesn't matter. She's not going to be running any marathons."

Sharp spun from the display and scowled at her colleague. "She needs to survive the infection long enough to be effective. So it does matter, Dr. Morel. It matters a great deal. There is a tremendous amount at stake here. Or aren't you aware of that?"

Morel shrank in his chair. He frowned and looked blankly at the tablet in his hands. "I'm aware," he mumbled.

"Show me CV-18 and CV-19," she said. "What's their status?"

He tapped his tablet and switched two displays. "They're infected.

They have elevated body temperatures and the most recent CBC indicates spikes in their white blood cell counts."

"They're sick?"

Morel hesitated. He looked at the screens, the bodies of the two lying motionless on their respective tables. Both were drenched with sweat. Fluids drained from a bag attached to an IV pole and into their veins.

Sharp snapped her fingers. "Morel?" she said. "They're sick?"

He blinked and nodded. "Yes. They're sick."

Sharp pointed at the image of a woman lying quietly on her table. "What about this one?"

Morel squinted to focus on the display. "CV-07. That subject is not showing any signs of infection."

"When was the subject exposed?"

Morel tapped the tablet first, then expanded the detail on the screen with his index finger and thumb. "Four days ago. We subsequently introduced a second dose. Virtually no effect."

"Virtually means some," said Sharp. She had her hands on her hips as she stared at the woman who appeared peaceful and asleep.

"Her white blood cell count is elevated."

"Elaborate."

Morel swiped the tablet. "Both the T and B lymphocytes are active. There's a spike in B cell antibodies. We're also seeing neutrophils present where we should see bacteria."

"What makes her so special?"

"She's not necessarily special," answered Morel. "CV-09 is also relatively asymptomatic."

"Are they the only ones?"

"So far," said Morel, "but that gives us an eighty percent infection rate. That's higher than the sixty-six percent mortality rate of the Scourge by itself."

"We've increased its efficiency by fourteen percent?"

"With this incredibly small sample, yes. It could fluctuate

drastically once we see it in the real world."

"What about the others?" Sharp asked. She motioned toward a screen in the middle of the wall. "CV-04? How about him?"

CV-04 was a waif. If he weren't shirtless, it might have been difficult determining his sex. His chest and abdomen were heaving. His eyes were squeezed tight with pain. He was drenched in sweat and other fluids. There was dried blood on his philtrum, the narrow indention that ran vertically from his nose to his upper lip, and what appeared to be vomit on his chin and neck. His mouth was moving, as if he were mumbling or talking. His eyes drifted wildly around the room. His wrists and ankles strained against the binds that held him down.

"Vitals are indicative of infection," answered Morel. "It appears the subject is exhibiting symptoms of both viral elements."

Sharp's eyes were fixed on the pain-racked man. He was clearly everything they'd hoped to achieve. "Have you interviewed him?"

"No. Another one of our researchers did the interview just as the abdominal discomfort was becoming an issue. That was yesterday."

A smile crept across her face as the man coughed up a spray of blood. "He's the first to fully contract YPH5N1?"

"Yes."

"Turn on the audio."

Morel tapped the tablet to amplify the ambient noise in CV-04's room. The man was, in fact, talking between coughing fits. He was cursing the scientists who brought him there, the diseases themselves, and the unrelenting pain.

He looked directly at the camera through which Sharp could see him. "I didn't ask for this," he growled. "I didn't want this. This isn't human. This is evil. I didn't sign up for this."

Sharp took a step closer to the screen. "Fascinating," she said softly, to herself.

"What?" asked Morel.

She shrugged. "That he thinks we care."

Morel didn't respond but did mute the volume. He stepped back to his desk and sat in his chair, setting the remote beside the keyboard.

"So," Sharp said, "the others are in the initial stages, correct?"

Morel nodded. "Yes," he said. "Of the ten we have. None of the other seven have exhibited any symptoms yet, though I'm certain they will within the next twenty-four hours."

"Deployment then?" she asked. "What's the schedule?"

"As planned," said Morel. "CV-01 and CV-02 go first to test our hypothesis. None of the others are slated for deployment. As you requested, they are test patients only."

"Subjects."

"Test *subjects*," Morel corrected. "We'll use them to gauge the progress of the disease in the two deployed subjects. Then we'll dissect the corpses to learn more about what we've created."

"Then?"

"Then—" Morel sighed "—as you requested, we'll recruit another ten subjects. That's when the full-scale deployment occurs. That's when we are operational."

"Good. Has your team selected a test deployment site?"

"We have."

He faced his computer, tapped on the keyboard, and then touched the display to pull up a large interactive map. Running across the center of the map was a thick, dark line marked WALL.

"This is the wall," he said. "And—"

"Seriously, Morel?" Sharp asked rhetorically. "I know where the wall is. I know what it is. I know why it's there. I don't need a primer."

"That's not—"

"Just give me the information I need."

Morel pointed to a spot on the screen. The map zoomed, narrowing the area displayed on the monitor. "Abilene."

"Why Abilene?"

"Based on what we know of the population size, its mobility, and the climate, we believe it's an ideal test location for YPH5N1."

"Very well," she said. "If your team's research finds it appropriate, then Abilene it is. Make it happen. Have you secured the transportation I arranged?"

"Yes," said Morel. "It should be here any minute now."

CHAPTER 9

Marcus rolled away from the open window and the sunlight that shone through it. He took a deep breath and exhaled loudly, touching his neck with his fingers. He opened his eyes. He had no idea what time it was, but from the sunlight that cast across his room, he figured it had to be close to midday. He'd only awakened because of the nightmare that had punctured his final moments of uneasy sleep.

His sweaty body was tangled in the lone sheet he used for warmth, and he blindly reached for a bottle of water next to him on the floor. He knocked over an empty jar of moonshine one of his neighbors had given him as a Christmas gift.

He pushed aside the empty mason jar and found the water. Gripping it tightly, he slid it across the scraped wood planks and rolled onto his back. He slid himself against the wall and drew a long pull of the water.

His head ached and his mouth was dry. The water helped both as he glugged it until the bottle was empty.

Marcus could still taste the sweet moonshine on the roof of his mouth and tongue. It had been a while since he'd had anything to numb his pain, to take the edge off the sharp corners of life.

A pair of his neighbors, Blake Peele and Aaron Cay, had stopped by to spend some time with him. He'd tried to shoo them away, but they'd persisted, so he'd invited them into his sparsely decorated house and they'd sat around drinking, talking about nothing.

"You're pretty much the coolest dude I've ever met," Blake had admitted. "You look like a regular guy; then you go all crazy on people."

Marcus had downed a shot and smacked his lips. "I don't go crazy," he said, pouring another round.

"Yeah, you do. I've seen you end a man's life faster than a flash of lightning," Aaron had said, snapping his fingers for emphasis.

Blake had laughed, nodding enthusiastically.

"It's not like I set out to kill people," Marcus had said. "It just happens. Death seems to find me."

"I wish I could be like you," Blake had said, wiping his chin with the back of his hand. "You know, like some sort of ruthless killing machine."

Marcus had eyed both with a frown, their naive excitement grating on him. He'd bitten down on the inside of his cheek to keep himself from spouting off something nasty. The boys didn't know better.

He slugged another shot and made them an offer. "You wanna know what it's like to be me?" he'd asked rhetorically. "I'll make you a deal. The next time we got a big threat coming to town, you can be my deputies."

The men had shaken his hand in gratitude. They'd toasted their forthcoming jobs as *the* Marcus Battle's deputies.

"If I call on you," Marcus had cautioned, "it's a big deal. It means you'll be doing some killing. It also means you could be the ones getting killed."

Blake and Aaron had laughed off the suggestion. They'd had another round of drinks and had left Marcus with dreams of glory in their heads.

For Marcus, it was increasingly difficult to sleep. He couldn't be sure if it was the onset of arthritis in his knees and shoulders or the ghosts of those he'd sent to their graves that kept him restless. It was probably both, though the previous night had most definitely been the latter.

He tilted his head back and shook the remaining droplets of water from the bottle and licked them onto the roof of his mouth. His room was getting warm from the sunlight and he shook free of the sheet, which was damp from his night sweats.

Marcus slept on the floor as a sort of self-imposed penance. When Sylvia died in the early days of the Scourge, he'd tried sleeping in their bed alone. It was uncomfortable. So he'd moved to the floor beside the bed. He'd slept there until the house burned down. When he'd returned to the ranch, he'd slept on the barn floor for several months until Lola coaxed him into the canvas cot to sleep next to her.

Now, more than a year removed from her bloody death, he was again most comfortable on a hard floor. Though comfort was a relative term, given his insomnia.

His moonshine-amplified nightmare from the night before was fresh in his mind as he sat against the cool plaster wall behind him. The man was coming for him. He could taste the gun smoke that trailed from his weapon and up into his nostrils after he slugged the man with a pair of bullets.

In the real world, that man was buried in the graveyard outside town. The weeds and grass had grown over the grave and the mound of dirt that marked the freshness of the burial had long since eroded.

In the dream, though, the man kept coming. It didn't matter how many bullets drilled through his body. They were inconsequential, and the target moved unfazed. He was growling and taunting Marcus, assuring him there was nothing that would stop his advance.

"You're a dead man, Marcus Battle," said the seemingly immortal threat, laughing as he spoke. "You don't have enough ammo to end me. Go ahead. Empty the magazine."

Countless nights, Marcus found himself at odds with someone he'd killed. In the dreams, though, they'd come back from the dead and were unstoppable. The literal ghosts of his past were haunting him. The bad guys, the thugs, the would-be notoriety-seekers were tough enough to cope with. Their deaths clung to Marcus's memories like the tiny burrs that stuck to his jeans when he wandered into untamed fields, looking for birds or small game. But they paled to the nightmares fueled by the ghosts of the ones he'd loved. When they came calling, when their relentless pursuit haunted him in his dreams, he couldn't shake the unease of their memory for days afterward. Nightmares involving Sylvia were the worst.

She came at him with questions he couldn't answer, with reminders of his obsessions and failures. She was his guilty conscience manifested in an angry, unforgiving reminder of how he'd inflicted the most pain on the ones for whom he'd have gratefully died in their places.

"Alpha male," her withering, sick frame would taunt. "Always know best, do you? Take us from our friends and family. Isolate us in the name of preparation. What a joke."

Of course, Sylvia would never have spoken to her husband that way. And the gentle apparition to whom he'd spent the better part of five years post-Scourge talking to and whose counsel he sought was nothing like that seething slither that manifested herself in his dreams.

She was too much. She reminded him of his shortcomings, of his single-mindedness, his inability to take the advice of others.

Marcus stood and stretched his lower back and aching shoulders. He knew these demons were the real reason he needed to retreat from the world of activism. Lou had merely reminded him of that need, she hadn't been the cause.

He crossed the room to the bathroom and rested his weight on the inoperable porcelain sink, looking at his face in the mirror. He ran a finger across the long, deep crease that ran across his forehead.

It was deeper, more pronounced, than he remembered. It had new friends above and below it. His crow's-feet fanned farther away from the corners of his eyes, and increasingly, the stubble on his face was white. There were large freckles on his cheeks and across his forehead that hadn't been there months ago. He smiled and eyed his teeth.

They weren't sparkling white, but for a decade without a visit to the dentist, they looked okay. Nothing was sparkling white anymore, except maybe for the thin hair at his temples.

Marcus looked into his own eyes, recalling the nightmare. He touched his neck, where the ghost had grabbed him with long, bony fingers that gripped with an otherworldly intensity.

If he was going to save any semblance of the man he'd once been, let alone a shred of humanity, he needed to stop killing. He also understood that might be like telling a scorpion it couldn't use its stinger or a snake its bite. Some things were made for a single purpose.

A loud, hurried knock at his front door pulled Marcus from his reflection. He stepped back into the bedroom and snatched his Glock from the dresser, the lone piece of traditional furniture in the room. He checked the magazine and slapped it back into the grip, crossing the floor in his bare feet and moving into the front room.

The visitor pounded on the door again. Marcus slid to the side of the door, pressing his back against the plaster wall. But there was low mumbling beyond the door, an exchange of some kind. There was more than one visitor.

More knocking, and then whoever it was tried the handle, wiggling it. Marcus slid his finger onto the trigger, his finger resting on the thin safety that split the center of the trigger. He slid from the wall and raised the weapon, aiming it at what he figured would be center mass for whoever it was came calling. His pulse raced but his breathing was steady. He could empty the magazine into the pine door and take out both visitors within seconds.

He steadied himself and focused beyond the door, imagining his targets readying their own weapons. He exhaled and…

"Are you in there, Dorothy?" asked Lou, her voice muffled through the pine. "C'mon, dude. Answer the door."

Marcus pulled his finger from the trigger. He lowered the weapon and swung the door inward. Lou and Rudy stood next to one another. A smirk crept across Lou's face and she pushed herself past Marcus into the house, thumping him on the arm as she passed. In the grass close to the lake, about thirty yards from the house, Fifty was licking himself.

"You look awful," she said. "Rough night?"

Marcus nodded toward the front room, motioning Rudy into his house. Once they were both inside, he pushed the door shut and glared at Lou. She was standing in the middle of the room, hands on her hips.

"You have any idea how close you came to getting killed?" he asked. "You come banging on my door without warning me who you are?"

"You were going to shoot us? Seriously? You *are* paranoid."

"It's not paranoia when people really do want to kill you."

"We need you downtown," said Rudy.

Marcus pulled a thin flannel shirt from the square table that separated the living area from a cramped galley kitchen. He sniffed it and, with all but the top button fastened, slid it over his head and across his arms.

"What for?" he asked.

"We've got a visitor who claims he's got some important information," said Lou. "Says he needs to talk to you."

Wearing his jeans from the day before, Marcus plopped into the lone chair at the table and slid on a dirt-stained boot sock. He scratched at the salt-and-pepper scruff on his neck and sighed. The jeans were tighter than he liked. But in the post-apocalypse, one wore what one could find. He adjusted them self-consciously and eyed Lou.

"Why me?" he asked. "Can't you handle it? I mean, you want to be sheriff and all."

Rudy shot Lou a look with a knitted brow. "What?"

Lou's cheeks reddened. "That's not what I said, Marcus."

"What did you say, then?" asked Rudy. "I didn't say I wasn't doing it. Norma and I need to have a heart-to-heart, that's all."

Marcus winked at Lou and shrugged. "I'm not lying, am I?"

"No," said Lou. "I mean, yes. I mean—"

"Spit it out," said Marcus, pulling on a boot. "Tell the man what you said."

Lou touched the brim of her Astros cap with both hands and tugged at it. Her knuckles were white as she pulled the cap down and then slid it back up on her head. "I said I was hurt that Marcus didn't think to ask me if I'd be interested in the job," she said through clenched teeth. "I didn't try to steal it from you or say you wouldn't be good at it."

Rudy chewed on the inside of his cheek and nodded. "I guess I see that. Why didn't you ask her, Marcus?"

Marcus pushed his heel into the second boot and stood up. "Don't you have someone you need me to meet?"

"You're a jerk," Lou said under her breath. "A full-fledged, misogynistic jerk."

"Misogynistic?" Marcus asked. "Good word. Remind me to look it up when we get back from town. By the way, I thought I *wasn't* Dorothy."

"Changed my mind," said Lou. "Dorothy was an immature, whiny narcissist. That fits you."

Marcus walked gingerly back to the bedroom for a minute and, when he returned, was wearing his gun belt. "Let's go," he said, opening the front door. "Somebody wants to see me."

* * *

The Baird jail at the center of town wasn't much. The former Callahan County jail, it was a faded red brick two-story building that looked more like an early twentieth-century mansion than a house of incarceration.

Marcus used the second floor to store weapons, explosives, and detonators, what little they had. There was also a room that housed the old radio communications hardware. There were a couple of old computers, some even older typewriters, and a half-dozen solar-powered two-way radios that got occasional but infrequent use. Only a couple of them still worked and they were unreliable.

The first floor was a single cell and an office. What had once been multiple cells was reconstructed as one larger secure space. Most of the iron that made up the bars and doors for the other cells before the Scourge had been sawed off and recycled in one way or another. Marcus used the old reception area as his office in the center of town. It served its purpose, containing threats and would-be threats. But given what looters had done to it over the years, it looked like something Otis Campbell might wander into every Saturday morning after a drunken Friday night in Mayberry.

The man who'd come to town asking for Marcus Battle, as so many ill-intended men had before him, was thought a threat. Rudy had treated him politely, but relieved him of his rifle, which hung on a rack on a wall opposite the cell, and asked him to wait patiently inside the locked cage.

Reluctantly, the man had obliged. He was pressed against the bars when Marcus, Rudy, and Lou waltzed into the room. Marcus figured the man was in his mid-thirties. He was tall, standing at least six feet four. His thick brown hair covered his ears and the nape of his neck. His deep-set eyes were round, as was his face. His mouth was wide and sat halfway between the tip of his nose and his clean-shaven dimpled chin. His clothes fit him reasonably well, which was saying something.

"You're looking for me?" asked Marcus.

The man nodded. "Can I get some water? I ain't had nothin' to drink since last night, I don't think. I'm parched."

"Sure," said Marcus, "we can get you some water. But let's start with why you're here. You looking for a fight? I'm not much for men who come here looking for a fight. Men like that aren't much for leaving here alive."

The man tightened his grip on the bars. He shook his head. "I don't want a fight, Mr. Battle. Not at all. But I know someone who does and I come here to warn you."

Marcus stepped back from the man. "Why?"

"Why what?" asked the man. "Why don't I want to fight?"

"No," said Marcus. "Why do you want to warn me? I don't know you."

The man shrugged. "I guess I thought it wouldn't be a fair fight if I didn't warn you. I don't want to see you get killed. You being a legend and all."

"What's your name?" Marcus asked.

The man looked at his feet and rewrapped his fingers around the bars. "Does it matter?"

Marcus took a couple of steps and stopped at the bars, only inches from the caged man. He spoke softly as a parent would to a child. "It kinda does, friend. How am I supposed to believe what you're telling me if you won't be straight up about who you are?"

The man kicked one of the bars with the toe of his boot. "Dallas," he said. "Dallas Stoudenmire."

"Okay then, Dallas," said Marcus, "tell me where you're from and what exactly you know."

"El Paso. I was a sheep rancher before the Scourge. Sold wool and meat from a shop on my land. Managed to keep the flock for a few years after the Scourge, but the Cartel ended that. I still manage to farm the land. Gourds mostly, some beans and okra. It does okay without much rain."

"So you keep to yourself?"

The man let go of the bars and moved away from Battle. He sat on the wood bench at the opposite end of the cell, his back against the cement block wall, and folded his hands in his lap. His shoulders hunched forward and he looked down at his boots.

"I did," he said softly. "Llano River Clan made it tough for a while. I killed plenty of them when they got too close. I'm a good shot. But it didn't matter. They took…" The man pulled his hand up to his face and ran his fingers through his hair.

Lou's hands were stuffed into her jeans pockets, a finger sticking through the holes in the bottom of them. "Took what?"

She, Rudy, and Marcus already knew the answer. They knew firsthand what the LRC had done, what they'd taken from Marcus and tried to take from Rudy.

The man looked up at them, bleary-eyed. "My girl," he said. "We'd been together since high school. We were each other's best friend, you know. Then one day she's gone. Only girl I ever loved."

"I'm sorry to hear that," said Marcus.

The man wiped his hands across his face and puffed air from his cheeks. "That's why I'm here, I guess. I don't want to see nobody else get ambushed if I know it's coming. Even if it's somebody I ain't never met."

"What exactly do you know?" asked Rudy.

"I know there's a gang headed here to kill Marcus Battle," said Dallas. "They tried to get me to join 'em five days ago. I told 'em I wasn't interested."

"Who are they?" asked Lou. "They have a name?"

"Junior," said Dallas.

"The Junior gang?" asked Rudy.

"No," said Dallas. "The leader. His name was Junior. He showed up at the market where we trade goods. You know, to help each other out. I give a guy some okra and he gives me homemade soap. That sort of thing."

"Got it," said Marcus.

"He shows up and holds court, so to speak. Tells everybody at the market he was out to avenge the death of his father. Said Marcus Battle killed him and had it coming. Was willing to pay for men to join his cause."

Marcus scratched his neck. "How many men?"

"Just Junior and one other. A man named Grissom," said Dallas. "Nobody took him up on the offer. Nobody wanted a piece of you."

Lou laughed condescendingly and walked toward the cell. "Wait," she said, waving her hands and shaking her head. "You rode your pony all the way here to tell us two men have a grudge against Marcus? We can handle two men without warning. What's your game, Dallas?"

Dallas cocked his head to the side. "No game," he said defensively. "I'm telling you they're gonna come with a bunch of men. They're gonna have a posse. I got no doubt about that."

Lou pressed her hands against the cell bars and peered through the gap. "How so?"

"After they left El Paso, they were headed to the Alamo."

"How do you know that?" asked Marcus.

Dallas shrugged. "They said if we changed our minds, we could meet them there."

"What's important about the Alamo?" asked Rudy.

Lou looked at him askance. "Don't you remember the Alamo?"

"Funny," Rudy said flatly. "Seriously though, what's with the Alamo?"

"It's a bad place for bad men," said Marcus. "Left over from the Cartel days. Moonshine, drugs, women, and guns for hire."

Rudy shook his head. "I had no idea."

"Chances are Junior found what he wanted there," Marcus said. "No telling how many men are headed this way. And we know San

Angelo still has leftovers from the LRC. He could pick up a few more if he hits that town on his way north."

"What do you think?" asked Rudy.

Marcus held up a finger and slid past Rudy to the wall holding the gun rack. Next to the rack was a hook holding a key ring. Marcus plucked the ring from the hook and moved past Rudy to the cell door. He slid the key into the lock and looked over his shoulder at Rudy as he spoke. "I think we let Dallas out of his cell," he said, turning the key. "And we get ready for a fight."

He pulled open the heavy door and planted a boot at its corner to stop it from swinging shut. Lou moved back, giving Marcus a skeptical side-eye.

Dallas stood from the bench and hesitantly inched to the opening. "You're letting me go?"

"I didn't say that," said Marcus. "You're staying with us. You're going to help us fight."

Dallas froze. "Wait, what?"

Lou's jaw dropped. "Yeah. What?"

Marcus moseyed back to the wall and rehung the keys. He reached over to the rifle on the rack and pulled it down with one hand.

"Dallas said he killed plenty of LRC back in El Paso," said Marcus. "He said he was a good shot. Don't you think we're going to need as many good shots as we can get if there's a posse coming this way?"

Dallas waved his hands in front of his body in protest. "I didn't say I was interested in fighting. Just 'cause I wanted to warn you don't mean I want to be involved."

"You already involved yourself." Marcus checked the bolt action on the rifle, aiming the weapon at the floor. "You said you don't want to see me die. So stick around and make sure that doesn't happen."

"Are you sure this is a good idea?" asked Rudy. "We don't know if this man is who he says he is. This could be part of Junior's plan."

"If there *is* a Junior," added Lou. "Dallas here, if that's even his real name, could be a scammer of some kind."

Marcus held the weapon with both hands and then extended it toward Dallas. He smiled at the man. "Take your weapon. You're staying here. At least for a day or two while you rest up. Then I guess you're going to want to stay and help us fight. You can bunk with me."

Dallas moved forward with skepticism but took the rifle and held it at his waist. "Thank you."

Lou huffed. "Marcus—"

"Lou," he said, "this man here is who he says he is. His pain was real. It was on his face. His breath smells like fresh spinach, which grows in El Paso this time of year. His horse out there is exhausted from a long ride. The saddle it wears has an El Paso Saddlery stamp on the side. And I believe his name is Dallas Stoudenmire."

"How do you know?"

"I just do," said Marcus. "No man names himself Stoudenmire by choice. Battle might be stupid for a last name, but Stoudenmire is downright ridiculous."

CHAPTER 10

FEBRUARY 7, 2044, 2:14 PM
SCOURGE + 11 YEARS, 4 MONTHS
KERRVILLE, TEXAS

Junior chewed on thick weed, rolling it around on his tongue and twisting it with his fingers. He was thirsty but didn't want his posse to see him drinking too much water. *Real* men could go without. He needed to project strength to the loose band of hired mercenaries he was leading into battle against the man who'd altered the course of his life.

He held the reins loosely in one hand and swayed effortlessly in the saddle as they rode north on what used to be Texas State Highway 10. The air was dry and he sucked on the weed.

"We're about a third of the way to San Angelo," said Grissom, riding beside him. "We could be there by this time tomorrow."

Junior inhaled deeply through his nostrils.

"I think we need more men," said Grissom. "These guys are good, but do you think seven is enough?"

Junior held the weed in his teeth as he answered, "That's why we're stopping in San Angelo. Battle did some damage there. We'll no doubt find some people looking to make good. Might not even have to pay them."

Grissom tightened his grip on his horse's reins and used the horn to adjust himself in the saddle. He looked over his shoulder at the five men trailing them, leaned toward his boss, and whispered, "You never told me exactly what he did."

"Who?"

"Battle," said Grissom. "I know he killed your pop and he hurt you. But what did he do?"

Junior rolled the weed around on his tongue. Grissom was right. He'd never fully explained what happened. He'd never detailed the September day that Marcus Battle had put a pair of bullets in him or the day, a month later, Battle had murdered his father. He'd only spoken of it vaguely.

"It was late September," he began, "around nine o'clock in the morning. There were six of us. We rode up on this ranch we'd spotted the day before. It was near Rising Star, a little nothing town near Abilene. We'd passed by it I don't know how many times without noticing it. But we did that time, so we hit it."

"Battle's place?"

"Yeah. It was Battle's. There was this woman standing in the grass. She was a pretty one. Older, mind you, but still pretty. One of the fellas calls out to her, asks her if she might be able to spare some food. Before she can answer, this kid fires off a rifle shot from inside a treehouse."

"Did he hit anyone?"

Junior shook his head. "Nah. I think it was a warning shot. But the woman, his momma I think, screams; then she starts running. They knew from the outset we weren't there for food or nothing."

"So she ran."

Junior nodded. "Two of the fellas, Rolf and Shimey, chased after her and followed her into a building. The others went into another building, a barn. I took aim at the kid in the treehouse."

"You shot him?"

Junior mimed aiming a rifle and pulling the trigger. "Dead," he said with a smirk. "Kid fell from the treehouse. Hit the ground hard."

"Where was Battle?"

"Thing is," said Junior, "I don't know where he came from. One second he wasn't anywhere and the next he was in my face. He got the drop on me with a Glock. I acted all scared and nervous like I was a lookout."

"He shot you?"

"Twice," said Junior. "Once in each shoulder. Coulda killed me. Those shots burned like the devil. I thought I was gonna die from the blood loss."

"Then what?"

"I shooed my horse back to the highway and I hid in the grass in case he came back looking for me out of spite," said Junior. "I gotta tell you, Grissom, I've seen a lot of crazy things in my life, but I ain't never seen the straight-up death stare that man Battle carries on his face. It's like he's not even human. He's all rage and anger. But it's controlled all smart-like and such."

"Did he come back?"

"No," said Junior. "He took care of Rolf and Shimey. Shot 'em dead in the grass. Then he went into the barn. That's where the others were. He didn't come back out."

"What do you mean?"

"They thought he was dead," said Junior. "They put I don't know how many bullets in him. But he wouldn't die. He even talked to my dad as he lay there bleeding out."

"What did he say?"

"Said he was gonna kill him."

"I'm sorry," said Grissom.

Junior pulled the weed from his mouth, twirling it between his thumb and forefinger. "For what?"

"Him killing your dad."

Junior slid the weed back between his teeth. "Yeah," he said. "That's the thing. He *didn't* kill my dad. He was just responsible."

"What do you mean?"

"His dog killed my dad," said Junior. He chuckled and then looked Grissom in the eyes. "Can you believe that? A mangy mutt killed Hank Barbas on the edge of the Concho River. Chewed him to pieces."

Grissom swallowed hard but didn't respond. He shifted his boots in the stirrups.

"My dad saved my life, you know," said Junior. "He picked me up out of that grass, all bleeding and such. He carried me on his horse and got me help. Saved my life. That's what a father does for a son."

Grissom forced an uncomfortable smile. "He was a good dad," he offered.

"Damn straight," said Junior. "And a good son gets even. We'll find what we need in San Angelo. People there remember what Marcus Battle did."

CHAPTER 11

Taskar rested on the hood of the hearse. The engine was running. He held the wad of cash in his hands and stared at the green-hued glass building in front him.

This was the place. He'd checked the address again and again, hoping he was wrong. He wasn't.

1600 Clifton Road.

The Centers for Disease Control and Prevention.

"This is a bad idea," he mumbled. "Money or no money." He'd been standing there for close to an hour, unable or unwilling to take the final steps of the journey. He'd finally made the decision to return the cash and leave when the woman who'd hired him emerged from the entrance of the building and marched purposefully toward him. She was wearing a white lab coat and light green doctor's scrubs. When she approached Taskar, she greeted him with a tepid familiarity, offering enough warmth to indicate she remembered who he was and nothing more. Her name tag read DR. G. SHARP.

"You're late," she said.

"I'm not la—"

"You were to be here at four o'clock sharp," she said. "It's close to four twenty."

"I've been here. I ju—"

"We have a schedule to keep. If you can't be punctual and adhere to a very strict protocol, then we may need to have a discussion."

Taskar extended the wad of cash in her direction. "That's the thing," he said. "I don't want the job. This is not for me. I don't do diseases. Not control, not prevention."

Sharp bristled. Her eyes twitched, and she dropped her hands into her white lab coat pockets. Her mouth curled into a disapproving frown. "You don't have a choice," she said flatly, not looking at the cash.

Taskar withdrew the money and chuckled. "Sure I do."

"No, you don't."

Taskar tried to gauge the woman's lack of expression. She was serious. But what could she do about it? He adjusted his hold on the ball of cash and tossed it underhanded at the woman. It hit her in the midsection and dropped to the ground. She was unmoved. Taskar shook his head and gripped the handle to the driver's door.

"I'd stop if I were you," Sharp warned. "There are armed men positioned on the roof of the building. They will fire if I give the signal."

Taskar froze with his hand on the handle. "Are you serious?" he asked over his shoulder.

"Take a look, Timothy," she said, using his given name. Nobody had called him that since he was a child. "Look up. You'll see two of them. There are three more you won't see."

Taskar swallowed hard and slid his fingers from the door handle. He turned around, his feet dragging in the gravel, and looked toward the green-hued glass. He scanned the rooftop and found two armed men perched at the edge and aiming their rifles straight at him.

A hint of a triumphant smile flashed across Sharp's otherwise stone-chiseled face. "Now look at your chest," she said, her eyes locked on his.

Taskar lowered his chin to his chest. There were four dancing red dots targeting him. "What is this?"

"We have a deal," said Sharp. "It's nonnegotiable at this point. Follow me."

Sharp spun on her heel, hands still buried in her lab coat pockets, and led the reluctant Taskar toward the front entrance of the building. He picked up the money from the ground, stuffed it into his pocket, and trudged across the plaza. Sharp held the door open for him and he stepped into the building.

A rush of cool air blasted him from the top of the door frame, sending a chill down the back of his neck. Then again, it might not have been the air that caused the involuntary shiver.

Rather than a lobby or a main reception area, Taskar was standing amid what appeared to be a cross between a field hospital and the sort of decontamination units he'd seen in horror movies more than a decade ago.

There were several large white plastic tents that stretched toward the ceiling of the three-story atrium. They were labeled with various acronyms Taskar couldn't decipher. Between and amongst the tents were computer terminals and examination tables. There were also black granite lab tables that reminded him of high school chemistry class. People in a variety of colored full-body protective suits moved from spot to spot. Some of them, however, were standing guard. They were armed and stood at the ready as if any improper flinch could unleash a hail of semiautomatic gunfire. Sharp motioned to one of them and the guard hurried to her side.

"This is Blankenship," she said to Taskar. "He'll be accompanying us." She reached out and touched Taskar on the shoulder. "Timothy, walk with me, please."

He pointed at the people in the suits. "Shouldn't I be wearing one of those?"

Sharp shook her head. "Not yet." She motioned toward a wall of elevators at the far end of the atrium, walked with purpose to them, and flashed a badge at a magnetic panel above the floor indicators. The panel's light switched from red to green and Sharp pressed the DOWN button.

"Where are we going?" asked Taskar.

"You'll see when we get there. Have patience, Timothy."

The elevator buzzed and the twin stainless steel doors slid apart. They stepped into the car and the door slid shut behind them. Sharp again pressed her badge to a panel and, when prompted, touched her index finger to a fingerprint-recognition pad. When the corresponding lights blinked green, she pushed the button at the bottom of the numeric bank.

The elevator shuddered and whooshed downward. Taskar felt the momentary loss of gravity in his feet and his stomach lurched. Blankenship stood in the corner of the elevator car. Condensation from his breath bloomed on the plastic face guard of his hood. Taskar noticed an illuminated square box at his chest, a red numeric display at its center.

"That's an oxygenator," said Sharp. "Our mobile biohazard suits have self-contained oxygen supplies. Its new technology developed here in this building."

Taskar nodded. He could feel Blankenship staring at him.

"It's a lot to take in, Timothy," said Sharp. "Most of it, however, has nothing to do with you and what we're asking of you. Stay focused."

"How do you know my first name?" he asked. "Nobody knows it. Well, nobody who's still alive."

"Why wouldn't I know your name?" Sharp asked. "I know everything else about you."

The elevator slowed and an artificial voice announced their arrival at their destination floor. It was something called the "observatory lab."

The doors whooshed apart and Sharp led Taskar out of the car and into a hallway that forked into three directions.

"We've done our due diligence on all of our transporters," she said, "just as we did on each of our subjects. It's important that we understand the psychology of those with whom we are entrusting our future. We cannot afford to take chances where they're unnecessary to take."

Taskar hustled to keep up with Sharp's brisk pace along the narrow, brightly lit hallway. He tried matching the rhythm of her heels clicking on the hard cement flooring. He hadn't seen a woman wear high heels in years. He'd almost forgotten they existed.

"Who are you exactly?" he asked. "I know you're the CDC. But seriously, *who* are you?"

Dr. Sharp slowed and allowed Taskar to slide next to her as she walked. She tilted her head. "Interesting question. And it's without an easy answer."

"Try me," said Taskar.

She stopped walking. "Yes, we are the CDC," she said, "and we spent much of the first post-Scourge years trying to isolate the virus in a way that we could inoculate for it, prevent it from ever coming back, identifying why the survivors were immune to its ridiculously high morbidity."

"Spent?"

She raised her chin and pulled her shoulders back. "Perceptive, Timothy. We stopped working backwards several years ago. Our mission changed. Now we are much more...forward looking. Many of us are not CDC-centric anymore. There is a heavy military presence here, as you may have noticed."

"Impossible to miss."

"Yes," said Sharp. "Regrettable, but necessary, given the work we're performing here. It's highly sensitive and is at the direction of those in the highest levels of government."

"What exactly is the work you're performing here?" asked Taskar.

"Especially if it's not making sure the Scourge doesn't happen again."

Sharp raised her eyebrows but said nothing. She motioned toward the end of the hall with her head and began walking. Taskar again kept pace with the click of her heels until they'd passed an intersecting hallway and reached a coded door. Sharp opened it through a multistep process that included the key card, a manually entered code, and a biometric scanner.

The door clicked open and she pulled it toward her, stepping out of the way for Taskar to cross the threshold first. "Go ahead," she encouraged. Taskar entered the room to the sound of a vibrating hum. He could feel it in his chest as he walked into the space filled with computers and a wall of monitors along one side. At the back of the room Dr. Morel sat in a rolling chair, pecking at his keyboard with his index fingers and thumbs, and apparently hadn't heard the door open.

Dr. Sharp took Taskar by the arm and led him from the entry to the opposite end of the room. She moved quickly and seemed irritated, more so than usual. She let go of his arm when they'd reached Dr. Morel. He spun in his chair and rolled backward when Sharp called his name.

He smiled and stood. "Ah," he said warmly, "you're here, Timothy. Good to see you. We wondered if you were going to make it. You ran a bit late."

Taskar swallowed and started to explain. "I wasn't late, I—"

"It's a moot point," Sharp cut in. "He's here and ready to go. Shall we show him the cargo and explain the protocol?"

The smile shrank from Morel's face and he nodded. He glanced past Taskar to the bank of monitors on the far wall and pointed at them. "This is it over here," he said, sliding past his visitors to move closer to the wall. Blankenship kept his distance, legs shoulder width apart, his rifle across his chest. "Each of these displays presents an opportunity," he said less as if lecturing to a class of college students than pitching a room of venture capitalists. "They are all unique and all of them will play a very critical role in shaping the future of our society." Morel stepped to the monitors. He spoke passionately about a post-Scourge renaissance fueled by their research and its implementation.

Taskar, however, wasn't listening. His eyes were fixed on the horrors he saw on the screens. It was a freak show of agony, and a thin stream of bile crept up his throat.

On one screen, a man with a label marked CV-04 was covered in blood. From his nose to his abdomen, there were varying shades of red. It was obvious to Taskar that much of the blood had dried and the fresher, brighter red was new. The man was so thin he appeared skeletal. His veins webbed underneath the surface, his ribs and joints straining against his translucent skin. He was strapped to the stainless steel table at his chest, wrists, and ankles. It was inhuman.

Another monitor displayed CV-01, a man groaning in pain. He was drenched in sweat. There was a pool of it on the floor to the side of the table. He wasn't bleeding, but his pants were soiled and thick yellow snot trailed from his nose. His eyes were squeezed closed, his muscles were taut, and his skin was raw and bleeding at the binds. He'd clearly been fighting his restraints.

But it was CV-02 that Taskar knew would haunt him. The camera was zoomed in on the woman's gray face. Her white hair covered one open eye, but the other stared back into the lens and through Taskar. Her eyebrows were arched and deep creases ran along the sides of her nose. Her mouth was open as if she were accepting a pill to place on the tongue that hung from her mouth. The picture combined to paint the woman's final painful moments. It was almost as if she'd died mid-wail.

He pointed at the monitor, his finger shaking. "That one's not breathing," he said. "I think that woman is dead."

Morel stopped his dissertation about the common good and survival of the fittest. He snapped his attention to the monitor behind his head. "What?" he asked worriedly. "Oh no. Oh no."

Sharp huffed. "Are you serious? Has it flatlined?"

Morel shuffled back to his desk and picked up an electronic tablet. "I was monitoring her," he said, tapping the tablet's screen. "She was recovering. Her vitals had improved, albeit nominally, but they were retracing toward better numbers."

Sharp stepped to within a foot of the monitor for CV-04 and growled to Morel, "Retracing? Losing the subject isn't a *nominal* improvement. This is not good, Dr. Morel. Not good at all."

Morel stabbed at the tablet with his finger. He bit his lower lip as his eyes scanned the information on the screen in front of him. He stopped, his finger still touching the tablet, and looked up at Sharp. "This could be good," he said. "It's not necessarily a bad thing."

"What is going on here?" asked Taskar. "What is it you're doing to these people?"

"Subjects," corrected Sharp. "They are subjects. Not patients, not people, subjects."

"Remember, Dr. Sharp," said Morel, "we learn from each of these…subjects. The autopsy will provide valuable information. We chose each of these peop—subjects for their individual characteristics. This one was older, had preexisting anomalies, and was introduced to a variant, concentrated strain of the YPH5N1. It's maybe a little too aggressive."

"Strain?" asked Taskar. "Strain of what?"

Sharp sighed. "Perhaps," she said to Morel. "But as I told you, we have a timetable for delivery. We need as many beta introductions as we can achieve in the real world. This lab is one thing. South of the wall is something altogether different."

Taskar unconsciously backed away from the wall of monitors, from the mad scientists to whom he'd unknowingly sworn a blood oath.

Sharp shifted her attention from Morel to Taskar. Her brow furrowed. "What's your problem?"

Taskar bumped into a desk, groping at it behind his back to gain his balance. He shook his head in disbelief and pointed at the monitors and his voice croaked when he spoke. "You're sending *them* with *me?*" he asked, not wanting to know the answer. His eyes skipped from one of the scientists to the other and back again. He could tell they were surprised that he was only now understanding his mission. A wave of heat rolled across his body. His stomach gurgled, and his throat was suddenly dry.

Sharp clicked her heels toward Taskar and spoke softly, the edge having disappeared from her tone. "Have you ever heard the story of Fort Pitt, Timothy?"

He shook his head. He hadn't.

"It was 1763," she said. "The British were at war with the Native Americans. There was an uprising among the natives in what became Pennsylvania and they were winning. They'd burned the houses of those who lived near the fort, so all of the British settlers were forced to live inside the fort."

Taskar shifted his weight uncomfortably. He wiped the sheen of sweat from his temples and ran his finger inside his shirt collar.

"As you can imagine," Sharp continued, "this is the eighteenth century and more than a full decade ahead of the American Revolution. Conditions were difficult at best. Add all of those people to the confined fort and the situation was likely untenable. The British military was concerned about the rapid spread of disease, especially because there was already an outbreak of smallpox."

Sharp dipped her hands back into her deep lab coat pockets. She began pacing in front of Taskar as she gave her history lesson.

"There was a man who lived there by the name of William Trent. He wrote in a journal that when two of the Indian chiefs came to broker some sort of surrender with the British, the Brits offered the chiefs some blankets as a token of their respect. Those blankets were infested with smallpox. Not long after there was a smallpox epidemic among the Native Americans that greatly reduced their numbers and lessened the threat."

Taskar shook his head. "What are you saying?"

Sharp crossed the distance between herself and Taskar. She stopped in front of him, inches from his face. "I'm saying you're a chief and I'm handing you a blanket."

"I'm not going," said Taskar. "I'm not infecting people south of the wall. For what? Why would I *do* that? You can't make me."

Sharp looked over Taskar's shoulder and motioned toward Blankenship with her chin. Her tone shifted. "You're right," she said with the hint of a knowing smile. "I can't make you. But what I can do is have Blankenship kill you. Right here, right now."

Taskar felt Blankenship's presence behind him, heard the soft whir of the oxygenator supplying clean air to the postmodern mercenary.

Sharp shrugged nonchalantly. "We could put a bullet in the back of your head and go get one of our other handsomely paid transporters to take your subject to the destination. Do you like that option?"

Trembling, Taskar shook his head. He glanced at Morel, who averted his eyes. It was as if the scientist could empathize with Taskar's plight.

"Option two would be forcibly injecting you with our beautiful concoction, YPH5N1," she added. "We could find out if you're one of the lucky twenty percent who we think are immune. Nobody's survived it yet, but our research suggests a little more than two in ten won't contract the illness. We could use you as one of our distribution platforms too. Are you amenable to that?"

Taskar's eyes drifted to Morel. He was busy tapping the tablet and seemed to be ignoring Sharp's sadistic version of *Let's Make A Deal*.

Her smile evaporated. "Then I suggest you do what you're told," she snapped. "Blankenship will accompany you on your journey. If you fail to deliver the subject to the agreed location, Blankenship has his orders."

Taskar didn't like any of the options. All of them, he imagined, ended up with his death. Either he ate it now, ate it when not finishing the journey, or ate it when his cargo ultimately infected him through close contact.

If he chose option one, they'd get someone else to do his job and he'd have gained nothing. Options two and three at least gave him time to figure out a way to avoid spreading the infection to the masses south of the wall. Among his choices, he really had none.

"Fine," he said. "I'll do it."

"Smart man," said Sharp. "Let's get you ready to go."

CHAPTER 12

The morning brought with it a gentle breeze, high, wispy clouds, and a yellow sun that cast a warm glow across the lake bordering Marcus's home. There was no hint of rain, nor any sign of the danger to come.

Marcus had stayed up late learning more about Dallas Stoudenmire, the carrier pigeon of a man who'd warned them about the approaching posse that sought his head. He'd questioned him about who the threat might be.

"Junior?" Marcus had asked as he boiled water on a single-burner stove. "That's all you got? No first name, no last name?"

Stoudenmire couldn't offer any hints. He'd even described the man and the one named Grissom who rode with him. Nothing rang a bell with Marcus.

"You've killed that many men?" Dallas had asked. "I mean, enough that you got no idea who it could be wants you dead?"

Marcus had nodded and lowered the heat of the stove. He didn't want the rolling boil to bubble over the pot's edges.

"How many?"

Marcus had hesitated. He'd watched the water bubble and pop, recounting the faces of the dozens of men he'd killed or been responsible for killing. "Too many."

They'd eaten breakfast silently after that. There wasn't much to say.

* * *

Hours later, Marcus stood behind Dallas, his hand on the grip of his holstered Glock. Dallas had his rifle pulled tight against his shoulder. He took aim at a tin can target fifty yards downrange. They'd been there for an hour while Marcus gauged Dallas's eye.

Lou stood off to one side, up against the thin trunk of an anemic oak, juggling her knives and whistling the Guns 'n Roses classic "Patience." Rudy was sitting on a rotting stump, elbows on his knees and Fifty at his feet. The dog's head rested on his front paws.

Dallas lowered the weapon and looked over at Lou. "Do you have to whistle?" he asked. "I'm trying to concentrate."

Lou pulled a knife out of the air, twirled it with her fingers, and slid it into a scabbard at her hip. She spun the other blade on her finger like it was a basketball.

"You think it's gonna be quiet when the storm comes?" she asked. "When the posse rides into town on big horses with their guns blazing?"

"She's got a point," said Rudy.

Lou puckered her lips to start whistling again, but Marcus shot her a look that politely asked her to stop. She rolled her eyes. "Anybody could hit the bull's-eye with dead silence."

Dallas ignored her, rested his finger on the rifle's trigger, and applied pressure. The rifle kicked against his shoulder, but he kept the muzzle flat. The bullet zipped the fifty yards and pinged straight through the center of the can. It was his tenth consecutive hit.

"Guess I'm as good as anybody," drawled Dallas.

"Don't mind her," said Marcus. "She's an acquired taste."

Rudy chuckled. "I'm still trying to acquire it."

The men laughed.

Lou smirked and faked an overly dramatic chuckle. "What's the point of this?" she asked. "That Arlington here can shoot as well as the rest of us?"

"It's Dallas," said the newcomer.

"Sorry," said Lou. "Frisco."

He huffed and corrected her again. "Dallas."

She smiled and shrugged. "McKinney?"

Dallas handed the weapon to Marcus and marched toward Lou. He stopped when Fifty raised his head and bared his teeth, snarling a warning to keep his distance. He raised his hands and took a half step back. His eyes stayed on the dog as he addressed Lou. "What's your problem?" he asked. "I came here to help you guys. You act like I'm the enemy."

"Are you asking the dog or me?" said Lou. "The dog thinks you *are* the enemy."

"I'm asking you."

"People have to earn my respect," she said. "It doesn't work the other way around."

Dallas looked away from Fifty and the dog grumbled. He yawned, licked his chops, and lowered his head.

"Okay," Dallas said, "but that doesn't explain the nastiness."

"Sure it does," said Marcus. "Lou's got her reasons not to trust folks. Like most of us, she's been through a lot and doesn't take easy to strangers."

"All true," echoed Rudy.

"Heck," said Marcus. "Consider yourself lucky that all she's doing is hazing you with the names of Dallas suburbs. She tried to kill me."

Dallas glanced at Lou and back at Marcus.

Marcus nodded. "Seriously."

"If I wanted to kill you," said Lou, "you'd be dead."

"Okay, enough of the backtalk," Marcus said. "We need to do a little planning. Not too many townsfolk are going to want to get involved in this. They're as sick as I am of the would-be Battle killers who come to town."

"Did you just refer to yourself in the third person?" asked Lou.

Marcus held his finger up to his lips to silence her. "We might be able to get a couple of guys to help out. My neighbors, Aaron and Blake, will want in. But mostly, it's going to be the four of us."

"Aaron and Blake?" asked Lou. "The handymen? The Aaron and Blake who fix gaskets and door hinges?"

"Yes," said Marcus. "They'll be good. They can handle themselves, I think."

Lou sighed. Dallas looked at her, then Marcus, and back at Lou.

"So six against dozens?" asked Dallas. "That's suicide."

"And this is why I don't respect you," said Lou.

"We've had worse odds," said Rudy. "This is our turf. We know it. We'll be ready for them."

"Wouldn't it be helpful if we knew exactly how many people we were facing?" asked Dallas. "Then we'd know how to set up our defenses."

"Why does that matter?" asked Lou. "A gunfight is a gunfight."

"Says the woman who brings a knife," Dallas shot back.

Marcus half expected Lou to quick draw a blade and fling it blade first into Dallas's gut.

She smirked. "Maybe I'll respect you yet."

"He has a point," said Marcus. "Not about the knife, but about knowing what we're up against. We need a little recon."

"How do you suppose we do that?" asked Rudy.

"Not we," said Marcus. "Me. I do this alone. I'm heading to the jail. Gotta set up some welcome gifts for our visitors. Then I'll head out. The three of you round up whoever you think will join us. Get the town prepped. Tell everyone to stay at home and lock the doors."

He expected protests but didn't get any. He walked over to Dallas and handed the kid his rifle. "I expect they're no more than two days out. Maybe closer. They'll be coming north. If I leave now, I'll catch 'em no matter the exact direction."

"Are you seriously leaving Wylie here with us?" asked Lou.

"Yes," said Marcus. "He's a good shot and, from what I can tell, a good man. Remember, Lou, sometimes you get more with sugar than with vinegar."

Lou huffed. "Fine. I'll be nice."

"Even if she isn't," said Rudy, "we'll be ready when you get back."

CHAPTER 13

FEBRUARY 8, 2044, 9:31 PM
SCOURGE + 11 YEARS, 4 MONTHS
COLEMAN, TEXAS

Junior Barbas slid from his saddle and planted his feet in the dirt. He wrapped his reins around a mesquite and stretched the stiffness from his lower back and shoulders, drew a deep breath of the cool south-central Texas air, and looked up to the dark sky above. Stars flickered and danced. The moon was somewhere between half and full. Dark clouds drifted across its white light. There was something deceptively peaceful about his surroundings.

The rest of his men stopped their horses, gathering in the clearing a few yards from the highway, where there was a watering hole for the animals to rehydrate.

Grissom crossed the dirt and stood next to his friend. "I think all twenty are still with us," he said. "None of 'em dropped off along the way."

Junior grabbed his elbow with his opposite hand and pulled it toward his chest. He grunted, stretching his aching muscles.

"They're asking if they should go ahead and set up camp."

Junior repeated the exercise with his other elbow. "Sure," he said.

"Tell 'em to get a good night's sleep. Tomorrow's gonna be a big day."

After Grissom walked away, Junior pulled a glass bottle from a saddlebag. He uncapped it and walked toward the pond. Halfway there, Bumppo joined him.

"We do the job tomorrow," he said. "Leave early, finish early, get paid early."

Junior kept walking, forcing Bumppo to keep pace. "Yeah," he said, "tomorrow."

They reached the water's edge. The sound of frogs croaking stopped when Junior dipped his bottle into the pond. The murky drink gurgled its way into the narrow opening.

"Do you know the lay of the land?" asked Bumppo. "I mean to say, you been to Baird?"

Junior shook his head. With the bottle full, he drew it from the pond and wiped the neck dry with his thumb. He was crouched on his feet like a baseball catcher. Bumppo was on one knee next to him.

"Do you think we need to do a little recon?" Bumppo asked. "Find out what it is we're up against? With a man like Battle on the other side, might not be a bad idea."

Junior snorted, spit into the pond, and wiped his face with the back of his hand. "Yeah. Not a bad idea."

"I could send one of my guys if you want," said Bumppo. "He'll ride fast, sneak up on the town like a ghost, get a lay of the land, and head back."

Junior dug his elbows into his knees and pressed himself to his feet. Without answering Bumppo, he slugged back to his horse, dragging his feet along the surface of the dry, cracked earth. From the feel of the ground under his feet, he could tell he was walking on what used to be the bottom of the pond behind him. He looked back up at the stars, specks of light from the center of places untouched by the Scourge, unaffected by this drought. Clouds sailed across the sky. They needed rain.

He finally answered Bumppo as he reached his horse. "Okay. You send one of yours and I'll send Grissom. Two's better than one."

"All right," Bumppo replied. "They can head out now if you want. More time they have to make the round trip, the more time we have to formulate a plan."

Junior yanked a camping pot from his saddlebag and tapped it like a tambourine. "Formulate," he said, facing his hired gun. "Form-yoooo-late." He chuckled. "That's a mighty fine word, formulate. You got a lot of fancy words, Bumppo? You got a lot of smart things up your sleeve? Lots of ideas? Lots of plans?"

"What? I don't—"

Junior's tone melted into seething distrust and he slithered closer to Bumppo. "You ride all quiet like for the last day, talking all hushed to your men and the fellas we picked up from San Angelo. You don't bother talking to me."

"Serious—"

Junior jabbed the pot at Bumppo's chest, knocking him off balance. "Then you come over here telling me we need recon. You offer to send one of your men, talk about formulating things."

"I wasn't—"

"You listen to me," said Junior. The muscles in his arms flexed. His lips curled as he bared his teeth. "You're working for me. I paid you. You understand? I make the decisions. Not you."

Bumppo stepped back and raised his hands in surrender, trying to deescalate the sudden tension. The madman was pointing with the pot toward a tall, broad-shouldered man called Whisper. "Get your man, the one over there. That one. He goes with Grissom. Got it?"

"Got it."

Bumppo backed away, his eyes on Junior, and walked the short distance to Whisper. The man's vocal cords were damaged and he could barely speak. He was unpacking his saddlebag for the night. A cigarette hung from his lips, the orange glow of the tobacco intensifying as he sucked on the hand-rolled smoke.

"Hey," said Bumppo, "might want to put that stuff back. I got a job for you."

Whisper scratched at the long scar across his neck that interrupted the thick knots of curls that made up his black beard and pinched the cigarette, pulling it from his mouth to blow a ring of smoke into Bumppo's face.

"We need recon on this town we hit tomorrow," Bumppo said. "You and Junior's guy, Grissom, are going to ride up to Baird. Check out the main street, see what it looks like, maybe find some spots we can exploit. Then ride back and tell us what's what."

"Why I gotta ride with some other dude I don't know?" asked Whisper. The rasp in his voice was like gravel on glass. He took another drag, his cheeks pulling inward to inhale.

"'Cause I'm asking," Bumppo replied simply.

Whisper stuffed his canteen and ragged blanket back into his bag. He climbed back onto his horse and flicked away the ashes from the end of the butt. "Who's the dude?"

Bumppo winced at the shard in his man's voice. He nodded toward Grissom, who was getting a talk from Junior. Grissom nodded like his head was on a loose spring and glanced over at Whisper. When they were finished talking, Junior marched toward them, his hands balled into fists at his sides.

"You best get going," he said. "Time's running out."

* * *

Marcus hadn't ridden much in the last year. On occasion, he'd take his Appaloosa on lazy rides into the high grass meadows that surrounded Baird on all sides. Time had reclaimed what used to be farms and working ranches. Now they were overgrown open spaces with dying vegetation that ached for water. Marcus thought the horse liked their walks. She'd whinny and prance and always seemed a little sad at the notion of heading home when Marcus led her back along the path they'd taken out of town.

She was underfed and barely hydrated, but Marcus tended to her as best he could. He'd feed her before he fed himself at night, though he knew he should take her on walks and gallops more often than he did.

She'd long since lost her shoes and he wasn't a skilled farrier, so she went without them, but she didn't appear to mind. It didn't affect her gait or her attitude.

She was eager to run south when Marcus had climbed aboard the comfortable, worn leather saddle that clung to her back. He had to hold her back and calm her excitement. She reminded him of Fifty when Lou offered to take him for a walk or play fetch.

The air was crisp. A southerly breeze blew at his face as they moved with purpose parallel to the highway. Marcus was a good fifty yards from the paved road. He didn't want more than the rustle of the dying vegetation against his horse or the clop of the shoeless hooves on the dry earth to call attention to their trek.

The moon shone with enough light to see varying shades of blue-gray in the distance, although Marcus couldn't discern much more than rough outlines of old highway markers or distant ramshackle buildings long-since abandoned or burned.

He'd been riding for a couple of hours, his eyes weary from straining to make out anything of value, when he saw it. A faint orange glow. It was such a tiny prick of light he almost thought his eyes were tricking him at first. But it grew and then virtually disappeared. Seconds later the familiar odor of stale tobacco smoke sailing on the breeze wafted past him.

Marcus stopped his horse and quietly slid to the ground. He slid his rifle from the saddle scabbard and checked the Springfield's bolt to make sure he'd reloaded the five-round magazine. He knew the mag in the grip of the Glock was full. He remembered thumbing in the rounds that morning.

Leaving the horse to chew at the breezy wisps of grass and weeds in the field, Marcus lowered himself to a low crouch and worked his way toward the oncoming traveler. He didn't know yet how many men might be approaching or if they were even a threat. He did know that anyone heading north to Baird was usually a threat. That was how it was, plain and simple.

He was five yards from the road, lying flat against the cracked earth, hearing the clop of worn horseshoes on the pavement, listening for clues as to who was approaching.

The first voice was nervous. The second was rough and laced with rasp. Marcus could only hear the words that traveled between breezy swirls of air blowing north.

"...many raids...killed...years..." said the first.

"...plenty...thirty...since the Scourge..." rasped the second.

"...plan..."

"...improvise..."

"...Junior...vengeful..."

"...paycheck..."

"...report back..."

There was no doubt, Marcus knew. These men were coming for him. They were scouting, looking for whatever they could find to make their attack more effective. That, in and of itself, was more than most had done.

Typically, the menace rode into town alone or in pairs. Sometimes a trio might ride into Baird, thinking they had the upper hand. They never did. Three shots and a pair of blades later, they were in a wheelbarrow on their way to the graveyard for misfit gunslingers.

Not these fellas. They were coming to win. He couldn't kill them, though. He needed intelligence. That was the whole point of this trip. He fought the instinct to drop them dead in the road.

Marcus waited for them to pass, watching eight hooves move past him, before he rolled out onto the road, leaving the rifle in the grass next to the road. He stood up and called out to the men, who were ten yards north of him. He raised his hands above his head and cleared his throat to speak with the voice of a man who needed water in the worst way.

"Hey, brothers," he called out, waving his hands. "Hey, fellas!"

Both men drew their weapons and twisted their bodies to face the surprise. One of them leveled a pistol at Marcus's head. The other stopped and maneuvered his horse perpendicular to the road.

"Who are you?" asked the one ready to fire, his voice trembling. "Where'd you come from?"

"I'm so glad I heard you," said Marcus. "I been out here for days. Ain't got no water. Could you spare a drop, or maybe help me into town?"

The anxious one's eyes darted from one side of the road to the other. He shifted in his saddle. "Who else is with you?"

Marcus took a couple of steps forward. "Nobody. I'm by myself."

"Stop moving," the man ordered. "Stay there."

Marcus stopped his advance. He raised his hands higher above his head. His shoulders were starting to burn. His neck ached with a familiar stiffness. He ignored both and focused on the armed man with the shaky hands.

The other rider eased his horse toward Marcus and urged the animal even with his nervous compadre. He took a long drag from his cigarette. The orange glow at its tip bloomed as the man sucked in his cheeks. His pistol was in his hand at his side. He slumped in his saddle with the disinterest of a man who'd rather be somewhere else.

"I just need a sip of water," said Marcus. "Maybe a ride? Wherever you're headed would be fine."

Nervous Nelly wagged the gun and shook his head. "What are you doing out here? How'd you get here?"

"I been wandering for a day or two," said Marcus. "Got lost. Ran out of supplies."

The cool customer with the cigarette pulled the butt from his mouth and flicked it to the road as he exhaled smoke through his nose. He scratched his neck. "What's your name?"

Marcus didn't hesitate. "Rufus Buck."

"That gun loaded, Rufus?" asked the raspy-voiced man. His eyes were on Marcus's hip.

Marcus followed the man's eyes to his Glock. He nodded. "It is," he said. "You can't be too careful. Where you headed?"

"My name's Whisper," said the smoker with a sly smile. "This here's Grissom."

Grissom squeezed his eyes and shook his head. "What are you doing?" he asked. "We don't know this man. For all we know, he's come to spy on us."

Whisper eased out of his saddle and unhooked a canteen from a bag. He walked toward Marcus. "He had the drop on us," he said, passing Grissom. "If he was gonna kill us, he would've shot us both in the back."

Marcus reached for the water and then raised it in a toast. "I ain't interested in anyone dying, let alone me."

He uncapped the metal canister and took a dramatically thirsty gulp. He sucked down a breath like a child drinking juice too fast, and swallowed another healthy pull. He handed back the canteen and wiped his mouth with the back of his forearm.

"Much obliged," he said.

"Rufus, huh?" asked Whisper, his eyes narrowing with suspicion. "That's an unusual name."

Marcus nodded. "Sure. I get plenty of flack for it."

Whisper's eyes traveled up and down Marcus's person. They lingered on his elbows, the bend of his arm, and his hands. "You shoot a lot?"

Marcus shrugged. "Some."

"We don't have time for this," Grissom said, his voice dripping with irritation. "He's got his drink. He's fine. We need to get to Baird."

As soon as he said it, Grissom pursed his lips. His eyes widened with the knowledge he'd leaked a secret.

Whisper's expression flattened with exasperation. He sighed and shook his head. "Guess you know where we're headed, Rufus."

Marcus feigned surprise. "Baird?" he asked. "We close to Baird? So we're not far from Abilene?"

"Yeah," said Whisper. "Not far."

Grissom waved the gun at Marcus. "Put your hands back above your head, Rufus. Keep 'em there."

Marcus did as he was told. "What's in Baird?"

"Nothing," Grissom said sharply. "Nothing's in Baird."

"Just a waypoint," said Whisper, the cadence of his raspy voice shifting to something less certain. "We're headed…farther north. Maybe…toward the wall."

"Can I tag along?" Marcus asked. "I'm good with a gun. I could help. I've been to Baird and—"

"We've got plenty of guns," said Grissom. "We—"

Whisper shook his head. "Keep your mouth shut, Grissom," he said and then stepped toward Marcus. "You've been to Baird? How long ago?"

Marcus took a couple of steps back. He shrugged with his weakening shoulders. "I don't know," he said. "A couple weeks ago, maybe. I thought I'd traveled farther than I have. Could be I been going in circles all this time."

"They got law there?"

Marcus eyed the gun in Whisper's hand, whose finger was rubbing the outside of the trigger guard.

"Yeah," said Marcus. "As much as anybody's got law. There's a man named Battle. He takes your guns when you get there. That's why I was offering to help out. If you wanted to keep your guns, I could—"

"You could what?" squeaked Grissom. "I don't like you, Rufus. I don't know you. I don't believe you."

Whisper backed away from Marcus. He raised a finger, asking him to wait, and he approached Grissom's horse. While Grissom kept his angry gaze aimed at Marcus, Whisper spoke softly to him. Occasionally he'd point at Marcus or glance at him momentarily as he made his case, whatever it was.

Grissom spoke under his breath, but his tense shoulders and wrinkled brow told Marcus he didn't like what Whisper had to say. Marcus rolled his neck from side to side. He flexed his fingers in and out. His triceps and biceps were thick with exhaustion, but he kept them as high as he could.

Finally, Whisper walked toward Marcus. "Look, Rufus," he said, "we can take you as far as Baird and you can show us what—"

Whisper stopped talking and moving. His eyes shifted beyond Marcus, over his shoulder. Marcus followed his gaze and glanced behind him.

His horse was there, chewing grass and standing in the middle of the road. Marcus cursed himself and the horse and turned back to Whisper.

"What is that, Rufus?" asked Whisper.

"I told you," said Grissom. "I knew—"

Without thinking about the impossibility of it, Marcus acted. In a series of quick, seamless movements, he lowered his arms, drew his Glock, zipped two shots at Whisper, dropped to one knee, and rolled into the grass.

Whisper dropped where he stood, collapsing to his knees and falling forward. His face smacked the pavement and his handgun rattled harmlessly from his hand, skittering across the road into the grass. He never managed a shot.

The shots startled all three horses. Marcus's backed away and trotted back into the grass. Whisper's snorted and galloped north. Grissom's horse reared with fright, throwing the unsuspecting rider from the saddle. He hit the ground awkwardly on his shoulder and lost his handgun.

He was groaning and writhing in pain on the cool pavement, crying out about the pain in his shoulder and the lack of feeling in his arm as Marcus approached. He stepped around the blood that spilled from Whisper's cracked nose and the wounds to his chest. Marcus noticed the slight reflection of the moon in the pooling black sheen that leeched across the fading lane marker.

He adjusted his grip on the Glock and marched to Grissom's side. He stood dispassionately over the sniveling man begging for his life as he held his disjointed shoulder at its socket. He raised the weapon and aimed it at Grissom's head.

"Shut up," he said. "Stop crying."

"Don't," said Grissom. "Don't kill me. Please."

Marcus held a finger to his lips. "Shhhh."

Grissom whimpered but stopped talking. Sweat bloomed in thick beads on his forehead and his upper lip. He was pale with shock. His pupils soaked in the moonlight and his body shuddered.

"How many men are you taking to Baird?"

Grissom's face twisted with confusion, as if he didn't understand the question. "What?"

"How. Many. Men?"

"I don't—"

Marcus tightened his hold on the Glock and squatted. He pressed the business end of the pistol to Grissom's drenched forehead. "I know you're headed to Baird to kill Marcus Battle. How many men are you bringing with you?"

Grissom swallowed hard. "T-t-twenty," he stuttered. "I mean nineteen. Is Whisper dead?"

"Yes."

"Nineteen."

"Who is Junior?"

Again, Grissom's wide-eyed response smacked of a man who couldn't comprehend what was being asked of him. The surprise gave way to recognition and his chest heaved. He opened his mouth to speak, closed it again, then announced the obvious. "You're Marcus Battle," he said. "Oh God. You're him."

Marcus tapped the barrel on Grissom's forehead and pressed it inward, applying pressure. "Who is Junior? Why does he want me dead?"

"Y-y-you killed his father."

"Who?"

"Hank Barbas."

Marcus withdrew the Glock and stood. He backed away a step from the groveling casualty on the road.

Hank Barbas? The red-bearded devil? The man who helped kill his family? *That* Hank Barbas?

Of all the men he'd offed, all the sons, husbands, and fathers whose lives he'd cut short with a bullet or bomb, it was Hank Barbas's son who'd mounted a coordinated attack against him?

"I didn't kill Hank Barbas," he muttered absently. "A dog killed him." Marcus squatted again and looked Grissom in the eyes. "Open your eyes and look at me."

Grissom, whose eyes were flooded with tears and sweat, nodded and visibly worked to keep his eyes open.

Marcus enunciated each word for crystal clarity. He wanted the injured man to understand every word through the fog of his pain.

"You go back to wherever you came from," he instructed. "You tell Junior that it doesn't matter whether he has nineteen men or nineteen hundred. If he comes to Baird, it's where he dies. It's where I let the same dog that killed his father chew on his carcass until all I have left to bury are the bones that dog doesn't want."

Grissom, still holding his shoulder in place, nodded his understanding.

Marcus stood and walked away. He whistled to his horse and the animal trotted to his side. He climbed aboard and walked to Grissom's side. From high in his saddle, Marcus looked down. "Best get going," he said, "before I change my mind and deliver the message myself."

Grissom struggled to his feet, his arm hanging limply at his side.

Marcus drove his heels into the horse's sides and she moved toward Baird. The wind had switched direction and was coming from the north now. It was cold, but Marcus couldn't feel it. He didn't feel anything.

CHAPTER 14

Taskar glanced in the rearview mirror. The man lying in the back amongst the quintet of large CDC-provisioned gasoline cans was coughing more vigorously than he had in hours. It was a wet, rattling cough that hurt Taskar's ears, even through the filter of industrial plastic.

He could almost see the deadly microbes and the spray of mucus exploding from the man's lungs and through his open mouth. He imagined the particulate dancing through the air like invisible pieces of a blown dandelion, floating with purpose in a widening arc to the front seat, where it curled around his head and neck, seeking out the current of air that would suck it into his nostrils and deep within his own lungs, where it could take hold. The virus would attach itself and start overtaking his cells one by one. They would mutate and expand and sicken him. Then he'd be coughing and wheezing, his own breath pricked with the crackle of infection.

It didn't matter that they'd outfitted him with his own hazmat suit or that he was breathing a self-contained supply of clean air. Somehow, he figured the YPH5N1, a lethal combination of the

Scourge and the swine flu, would kill him.

He shifted his shoulders toward the hazmat-suited twin sitting next to him. Blankenship hadn't slept a wink since they'd left Atlanta the previous night. He'd sat stoically, his large eyes focused on the road straight ahead like a robot on pause awaiting further instructions. He hadn't spoken, hummed, or even moved his hands from the rifle he held at his lap atop the seatbelt pulled high across his hips.

The man in the back hadn't played the statue game. He'd been talkative, in fact. He'd told them his name was Lomas and that he'd volunteered for the program to give his children a better life than the one he could offer. He'd told them he regretted his decision. He'd made a bad choice.

The only time he wasn't talking was when he was groaning in pain or coughing up the thick, virulent fluid that pooled in his lungs like the backwash in the bottom of a first grader's carton of milk.

Blankenship had asked him to be quiet. He ordered it. He'd threatened it.

Taskar reminded him there wasn't much anyone could do to frighten a man who was already inoperably sick. Blankenship had disagreed. He'd seen plenty of things that could frighten anyone, even a man who could feel death's grip. He done some of those things, he assured Taskar. But he didn't follow through. He sat facing forward, watching the world whoosh past them as they moved closer to the proposed ground zero.

Taskar adjusted the rearview mirror with his gloved hand. There was something foreign about his own car without the tactile sensation of touching the familiar molded plastic of that mirror or the worn leather of the wheel. Even the seat grooves molded to his body and shape weren't quite right. He sucked in a deep breath of the artificial air, inhaling the new-rubber scent of the hazmat suit. There was the faint odor of gasoline that he could taste in the back of his throat.

"I don't know how you got me through the wall," said Lomas, his voice carrying through the cabin. It was muffled but audible. "I can't believe them folks let you bring me south."

"He doesn't understand how it works," said Blankenship. His voice was without emotion.

Is he a robot?

"What do you mean?" asked Taskar. "How what works?"

The soldier peered at Taskar through the clear encased visor of his helmet. "The wall," he said. "How the wall works."

"You mean the guards are on the northern side?" he asked. "That since the Dwellers took over, nobody cares if you move south?"

Blankenship twisted forward, his suit crinkling. "Yes, that's correct."

Taskar looked at Lomas through the mirror. The man was strapped to a gurney, his head toward the back of the hearse, his eyes facing forward. He was confined at his wrists and ankles. There was also a wide restraint that ran across his chest. Taskar thought that particularly cruel given the heaving cough that strained the leather strap every time Lomas expelled the fluid from his irritated lungs.

"You hear what I'm saying?" he wheezed, his chin pulled to his chest so he could look at Taskar in the mirror. "Nobody's going to be safe. Not when the others follow us here. Everybody's going to get sick. Everybody is going to die. It's the Scourge all over again."

Taskar let those words play in his head. He listened to the hum and warble of the tires on the highway and the thump of his pulse in his head. He tried to focus on the road ahead. He pretended he was a robot and sat as still as he could as he steered the hearse west.

But the mirror kept pulling his attention toward the back of the hearse and Lomas's sermon. He was telling of things that had happened and warning of the things that would come. The sick man's voice rose and fell like a preacher full of spirit. Each word powered the next.

"It'll be like the locusts," he prophesied between worsening, barking coughs. "Sick people will descend carrying this incurable disease. It'll come in waves. That's what they said. One wave and then another. A tsunami of death. That's what they want. And I know why they want it."

"What is he talking about?" asked Taskar.

"He's babbling," said Blankenship. "He's delirious."

"They don't think I know," said Lomas. "They don't think anyone knows. But I heard them. I know. I knnnoowwww."

Lomas coughed. A short hack followed by a quick succession of staccato barks. Then he gasped for air, struggling as if surfacing from too long underwater. He arched his back and shook his head wildly. His eyes squeezed shut and tears streaked from their corners. One cough begat another and another. Now they were jagged, angry hawks audibly tearing at Lomas's chest and throat.

He was no longer mumbling non sequiturs or knowledge of secret conspiracies. He was fully engulfed in the throes of his rapidly progressing genetically modified disease.

Taskar gripped the wheel and shifted his upper body toward Blankenship. "Should we stop? Should we help him?"

"And do what?"

"I don't know. Loosen the binds. Pound on his back. Let him raise his hands above his head?"

"That's not happening."

The cough morphed into something less human. It was part growl, part moan, part retch. Taskar heard the rattle of the gurney's thin metal frame against the side of the hearse's interior. It was as though the wheeled bed was coming apart. The whole of the vehicle began to shimmy with Lomas's violent spasms.

Taskar tried to think of things worse than the sounds filling his car. Nails on a chalkboard? A drill grinding into a tooth? A metal blade scraping against glass? None of them made Timothy Taskar want to scream like Lomas's agonizing fight against the infection devouring his body.

Against his better judgment, he sheepishly checked the rearview through squinted eyes. His mouth gaped open, his body shuddering inside his protective suit.

The image reflected in the rectangular mirror was a study in blood. Lomas was covered in it. His face, his chest. The roof lining dripped. Taskar slammed on the brakes. The seatbelt snapped tight against his chest. In the passenger seat, Blankenship slid forward and braced himself against the dash with an extended arm. He faced Taskar with his upper body.

"What are you doing?" he asked. "Nobody told you to stop."

Taskar glanced one more time in the mirror; then he eyed Blankenship and his rifle. He knew instantly what to do. He flipped the hearse into park in the middle of what used to be called I-20, and unbuckled his constrictive seatbelt.

"He's dying," said Taskar. "We can't let him die, can we?"

Blankenship awkwardly moved himself such that he could see the rear of the hearse. His eyes expanded, scanning the blood-soaked tableau, and his mouth pursed with disgust. He met Taskar around the back of the vehicle.

Taskar fumbled with the handle through his trembling gloves, but he managed to swing open the tailgate, illuminating the vehicle in a bath of pale yellow light from the overhead bulbs. Lomas arched his back and neck, looking out toward the suited men. He coughed and choked on the bloody sputum. A fountain of it sprayed upward and outward, much of it landing back on Lomas, the rest of it sprinkling Taskar's suit and visor. The dying man was gargling, his hands flexing and contracting at his sides. His toes arched as if they were cramped into painful knots.

Blankenship stepped back. He cursed repeatedly, uttering words Taskar hadn't heard in years. He didn't even know the meaning of some of them. Apparently, the soldier wasn't a robot.

"Holy mother—" his final volley was muted by another cacophony of pain. "How much blood can he have left?"

Taskar swallowed against the dry lump in his throat. Sweat dripped into one eye and he tried blinking back the salty sting of it. He was breathing heavily and puffs of hot condensation clouded his visor. His legs, stiff from the drive, were weak. His knees shook and his ankles struggled to hold his weight as he slid into the hearse to work on releasing the hooks that held the gurney in place.

Even through the filter of his suit, the muffled groaning and bubbly cough spewing from Lomas was distracting. Taskar tried manipulating the hooks by touch.

Blankenship stood over Taskar's shoulder, one hand on his rifle's grip and the other on the underside of its barrel. "What are we doing?" he asked. "What's the goal here?"

Taskar didn't have an answer. The humidity in his helmet was thick and hot. The suit suddenly felt as if it were shrinking around him, like somebody had attached it to a vacuum hose and was sucking out the air. His pulse thumped against his chest, at his neck, and in his ears. He considered taking off the gloves, but thought better of it and managed to free the first two hooks. The other two were too far to reach. He stretched as far as he could, but his arms weren't close to long enough. He pivoted one hundred and eighty degrees and measured Blankenship with his eyes. The soldier was broad and muscular, but no taller. He wouldn't do.

Taskar's breath fogged his visor in the predawn. He planted his palms flat on the carpeted floor of the hearse. There was enough room to squeeze his suited body between the wheeled legs of the shaking gurney and the five gas cans pushed against the interior wall.

Blankenship's stance stiffened. He pulled back his shoulders and spread his stance. "Wait, what are you doing? You haven't answered my question."

Taskar blinked against another tendril of sweat and blew it from the corner of his twisted mouth. He pressed his gloved palms into the carpet and heaved himself headfirst into the vehicle. The oxygenator on the front of his suit pressed inward, pushing against his ribs, so he adjusted his body and angled himself at forty-five degrees. He slid forward and rolled his shoulder out from underneath his body, freeing it enough to reach the farther of the two hooks. He labored at it, his eyes wandering from the task to the trail of blood leaching along the gurney's upper rail. It traveled the length of the metal rail, twisting and throbbing like rain falling on a windshield, until it reached a bend in the frame and dripped to the floor in what Taskar imagined was a rhythmic beat.

He closed his eyes, the sting of sweat forcing them back open. He stretched them wide, pulling his skin taut against his cheeks, and took another shallow breath. The hook unlatched and he shortened his reach to the one inches from his face. He made quicker work of the connection than he had the other three and quickly slid himself from the cabin.

He pushed himself to his feet and shifted his weight to find the soldier. Blankenship was at the back corner of the hearse, his eyes planted firmly on Taskar's chest. Taskar followed the gaze and looked down at himself.

His chest was smeared with streaks of dark blood. He looked at his gloved hands. The palms were decorated with the same gruesome paint. He wiped them on his sides. It didn't matter.

"I need some help," he said. "I'm going to unlock these back wheels and you're going to help me pull the gurney from the hearse."

"Why?"

Taskar clicked the first lock, freeing the wheel. "We have to do something. If nothing else, we can't let him die before we get to Abilene."

Blankenship shrugged. "I guess."

Taskar unlocked the second wheel and stood behind Lomas. Blankenship moved around him on the other side.

"You're going to have to put down that rifle for a second," said Taskar. "I can't do this alone and you can't manage with one hand."

Blankenship wrapped his hands more tightly around the grip. "I can't do that."

Taskar huffed and glared at Blankenship through the dark spatter on his visor. "What am I going to do? Where am I going to go?"

Blankenship held the rifle out to the side and hesitated. He eyed the dying man in front of him and Taskar to his side. He laid the rifle up against the tailgate, setting its butt into a wide, weed-laced crack in the road.

"Okay," said Taskar. "These legs expand once we pull him out. So be ready for that when I press a latch underneath the bed."

Blankenship nodded his understanding from behind his visor. He gripped the front edge of the gurney with both gloved hands and awaited Taskar's command. Taskar counted down.

"Three...two...one..."

Both men pulled the gurney outward, its wheels rolling easily along the thin carpet inside the back of the hearse. It was halfway out of the vehicle. Lomas wasn't retching anymore. He wasn't coughing or spitting out the thick infectious fluid that filled his lungs. He was twitching. His mouth was open, his tongue hanging from the side like a tired, overheated puppy. His breaths were weak, shallow, and rapid.

Instead of hitting the latch to extend the legs, Taskar released his grip on the gurney and let it drop. It tilted awkwardly, Lomas's weight shifting against the restraints, and Blankenship stumbled backward away from the light. His eyes ballooned with confusion and Taskar grabbed the rifle. Blankenship let go of the gurney to regain his balance and the wheeled bed clattered diagonally from the back of the hearse to the ground.

Without hesitating, Taskar slipped his gloved finger onto the rifle's trigger, flipped off the safety with his thumb, aimed it at Blankenship, and applied pressure to the trigger twice in quick succession. A pair of rounds exploded from the rifle and burrowed into Blankenship's chest, ripping two perfect holes into the front of his hazmat suit above the oxygenator. A third shot drilled the air-supplying box with a thick thud that fried the display.

Blankenship grabbed at his chest in the dim cast from the hearse's interior lights, rolling on the ground like a turtle stuck on its back. His face guard fogged with his final breaths. His body spasmed and he went limp.

Taskar walked to the guard and stood over him. He pulled the rifle tight to his shoulder, aimed for the opaque face mask and pulled on the trigger a fourth time. The force of the shot jerked the dead man's body. Standing a few feet from the gurney, which had managed to stay awkwardly upright on the road, Taskar held the rifle with one hand, its barrel pointed at the ground.

"I'm sorry about this," he said to Lomas through his mask, keenly aware the dying man strapped to a mattress soaked in blood, sweat, and urine couldn't hear him. "But I can't let you suffer anymore, and I can't let you reach Abilene."

Taskar glanced over at Blankenship's shadowy corpse as he readied his aim for Lomas. Through his mask he eyed his target and rested his finger on the trigger. He took two steps closer to Lomas and adjusted the rifle against the fabric at his shoulder, nestling the butt into a comfortable position. He wanted to make sure a single shot did the trick. He drew the rifle down, putting the sights at the infected man's temple. As he began to apply pressure, Lomas's eyes opened, teared, and fluttered. He mouthed, "Thank you." By the time he finished forming the words, a true shot to his forehead ended his misery.

Taskar dropped to his knees and let go of the weapon. He planted his gloved hands on the road and sucked in a deep, ragged breath. As he exhaled, a knot in his throat swelled and an overwhelming sadness shook his body. He sobbed, one shallow breath chasing the next as he tried to suppress the emotional ambush.

When he finally calmed himself and sniffed back the snot that dripped from his nose, he pushed himself to his feet. He couldn't leave the body here as roadkill, an offering to the swooping carrion feeders sure to come. As he wandered the gory scene, mindlessly searching for his next move, he was preoccupied with the vision of a bird ripping into the dead man's flesh, devouring it, falling from the sky, and becoming the meal of an unwitting, famished family. The disease would spread and he'd still be responsible for it.

Weak-kneed, he managed to drag the lopsided gurney to the side of the road, dropping it on its side in a dry culvert meant for water runoff. He trudged back to Blankenship and dragged his body across the road, raking the suit against the rough asphalt as he moved in short bursts.

"I couldn't leave you alive," he muttered to the dead man. "You'd make sure we reached Abilene. Dead patient or not, you would've insisted, or you'd have killed me. I know that. This was self-defense."

He kicked Blankenship's body the final couple of feet until it flopped into the grassless, weed-free ditch next to the gurney and stood at the edge of the road, bent over at his waist. His head ached at his temples; his body quivered with exhaustion. His vision blurred. He was dehydrated.

Fighting the urge to collapse, he found his way back to the hearse and heaved out one of the gas cans. He carried it with both hands, the thick plastic banging against his knees, and dropped it at the highway shoulder next to the ditch. He fumbled with the spout until he managed to unlock the various safety mechanisms and tipped the can toward the edge of the road.

The can glugged, and post-Scourge, Texas-refined gasoline, as valuable as gold or a loaded AR-15, spilled into the culvert. When he thought he'd poured enough, he tilted back the can, picked it up, and heaved a splash on top of the bodies. He closed the spout and lugged the half-empty can back to the hearse.

From the glove box on the passenger's side, he withdrew a box of waterproof matches and gripped it tightly with his gloved hand. He used his other to brace himself against the open door frame. The suit felt tight again, tighter than it should. His nose itched, his neck and shoulders ached. A subtle vibrating current, somewhat less than a tremble, coursed through his extremities. The darkness, verging on daybreak, was closing in on him.

He sucked in the plastic-tasting air, his tongue coated in a thick, dry spit-paste, and put one booted foot in front of the other on his way back to the ditch. His shaking hands managed to slide open the slick plastic container and withdraw a long matchstick.

Taskar adjusted his grip on the box and struck the stick across its side, igniting the match head. It sparked and sizzled and he held it there for a moment, watching it burn shades of blue and orange. Wisps of smoke wafted from the burning wood and dissipated into tendrils that spiraled into the air above him. He walked a half-dozen steps toward the fuel-laden ditch and flicked it toward the target.

It found its fuel and the flames grew tall, cracking and popping as they spread across the ditch, lapping up the gasoline and engulfing the clothing, the suit, and the soiled mattress. The pyre was hot and strobed against the purple-hued black of the early morning west Texas sky.

Taskar had seen so much horror in the years since he'd been orphaned and sheltered in the funeral home. He'd experienced the oppression of the Cartel, the slippery, ineffective governance of the Dwellers, and the anarchy that held sway over the territory south of the wall now.

As a man with the rare duty of travelling both sides of the wall, of ferrying the good and the bad back and forth, he'd inhaled the intoxicating aroma of hope. He'd seen those living north of the wall rise from the ashes, become self-reliant, form a new government, and do their best to recreate some semblance of civilization. It was night and day, or so he thought.

Yet as he listened to his own breath inside the hot plastic cocoon surrounding his head and got lost in the angry flames that began to spread beyond the dead before dying in the dirt, he understood that both sides of the wall were the same. Both were replete with people looking out for themselves, self-serving survivalists whose primal instincts had overtaken more than two million years of cultural evolution.

At least in Texas it was in your face. It was kill or be killed and you knew it from the moment you crossed the wall. Up there, in the north, they masqueraded their intentions with a veil of civility.

Taskar backed away from the fire, appreciating the relative cool that came with distance, and with his hands on the hearse, worked his way around the back to close the tailgate. He eased his way back into the driver's seat and started the engine.

He drove southwest, not sure exactly where he was going. Maybe Abilene, where he could warn the people of what was coming one way or another. Maybe somewhere closer if he couldn't make it that far. He glanced to the passenger's side rearview mirror at the thickening smoke billow above the orange flames.

CHAPTER 15

FEBRUARY 9, 2044, 7:39 AM
SCOURGE + 11 YEARS, 4 MONTHS
ATLANTA, GEORGIA

"Do we know why she died?" asked Dr. Sharp of the broad-faced man standing in front of her. She was standing in the hallway outside a room called "No Man's Land" in which a team of suited pathologists worked while tethered to filtered air tubes.

No Man's Land was rated BSL 3 on a scale of one to four. Access was restricted. The room was separated from the rest of the facility by sealed double doors and a series of anterior rooms. The air handling was separate, filtered, and non-recirculated, unlike most BSL 3 labs. There were four bodies now, the most recent having been plopped onto a stainless steel table only minutes earlier. The broad-faced man, whose name was Bolnoy, snorted.

"She was infected," he said with an accent that gave away his Russian origins. "But you knew this, no?"

Bolnoy was a supervising pathologist who'd been observing and recording the findings of his team inside No Man's Land. They'd hypothesized that, like Ebola, the patient's death wasn't enough to end the threat of infection. This new mongrel virus, with bacterial components, was as lethal after killing its host as it was while that host fought to live.

Sharp poked at Bolnoy's chest with a finger and locked his eyes with hers. "I'm not in the mood," she sneered. "Don't play with me."

Bolnoy snorted again as if to suggest to his superior he wasn't intimidated. He likely wasn't. He'd seen the Scourge kill thousands in his native St. Petersburg and paid a hefty sum of money to secretly climb aboard a cruise ship docked in the Gulf of Finland at the eastern edge of his city. He'd stowed away on the ship until it reached its destination in Dover, England. By then, half the crew and most of the passengers were dead or dying from the disease.

It took him six months, and a lot of false starts, to find passage to the United States. He'd lucked into the job with the CDC through a friend of a friend. They needed people who could cut open bodies and knew anatomy.

He'd graduated with a medical degree from St. Petersburg Pavlov Medical State University. He'd joked all they'd need to do was show him a dead body and he'd start drooling. Nobody had laughed. But they'd hired him. He'd proven valuable and skilled, as well as irreverent and moody.

Now, as he stood in front of Sharp, he was an obstacle to the truth. She poked him again.

"Give me answers, Bolnoy," she demanded. "We can't send corpses out into the wild, even if they do retain their infectious properties."

"Dr. Sharp, you know this virus is viable for several days after the host dies," said Bolnoy, drawing out his words for effect. "I'm not telling you something you don't know. And it's entirely possible it lasts longer than that."

"I'm aware," said Dr. Sharp. "The influenza genome RNA segment gives the Scourge an added kick postmortem, which increases the infection rate by a factor of—"

"You don't know the answer to that," said Bolnoy. "What you're saying is theoretical. It's hypothesis."

Sharp bristled. "Which is exactly why we are testing the subjects in the wild. It's also why I need to know what about these dead subjects killed them faster than the others. It will inform our rollout and distribution to maximize the testing and the ultimate deployment."

Bolnoy looked through the double-layered glass that offered him a view of the autopsies in progress. He'd been in the room for the first of the procedures, a woman known as CV-02. It was grotesque. And there was something he knew Sharp wasn't telling him. There was something else in the deadly cocktail that caused the hemoptysis, the coughing up of blood. Maybe it was the unprecedented combination of a pneumonic plague and a deadly flu. Maybe there was some bacterial components of the polymerase causing a necrotizing pneumonia, otherwise called lung gangrene.

"I can speak to CV-02. The woman," said Bolnoy.

"The *subject*," corrected Sharp. "What about it?"

"CV-02's lungs were distended. We observed segmental atelectasis with a blackened pleura."

Bolnoy reached into his lab pocket and pulled from it a tin. He thumbed it open and removed a mint leaf. He crushed it between his thumb and index finger and laid it on his tongue. He worked it around in his mouth and chewed. He offered a piece to Sharp. "I grow these hydroponically," he said. "Very sweet."

Sharp ignored the offer. "What else? What is your point here, Bolnoy?"

Bolnoy flipped shut the tin and slid it into his coat pocket. He rolled the mint around on his tongue. "There were elevated, pale spots," he said. "They remind me of organisms growing in culture dishes. They were clustered on the parietal pleural surfaces and on the blackened visceral. Both of the pleural cavities contained 100cc of serous fluid."

"The serous fluid is normal," said Sharp. "That doesn't tell me anything."

Bolnoy tongued the mint between his front teeth and nibbled.

"I'm trying to answer your question. Unlike a bureaucrat, I like details. I like knowledge at the microscopic level."

Sharp dragged her fingers under her eyes and outward along her cheeks. She pursed her lips.

The Russian's thick eyebrows arched like caterpillars above his eyes. "You have, how do you say? Screwed the pooch. You have created something here for which there is no predator. You have no control of it now. This is a mean thing you have made."

"And?"

"And it does not matter how quickly these subjects die. If you sprinkle enough of them, some will sprout. They will spread like weeds. Those weeds will strangle everything."

Sharp's nose wrinkled as if the Russian suddenly smelled bad. "We are preserving the species," she said. "Plain and simple. We need the riches south of the wall. The oil, the natural gas, the farmland, the water. Without it, our society won't be able to function much longer."

Bolnoy chewed on the mint. His silence judged her.

"I don't need your approval," she said. "You, a Russian of all people, should understand the sacrifice of the individual for the betterment of the state."

Bolnoy stuffed his hands into his pockets.

"I'm doing my job," she said. "All of us are doing our jobs."

"CV-02 and the other four had weaker immune systems," said Bolnoy. "This is obvious. Their bodies could not fight the dual infection. It is possible also that the viral pneumonia causes a bacterial infection in lungs. Add a secondary viral influenza, and the body cannot fight both. The same mechanisms that fight viruses make fighting bacter—"

"I know the science," Sharp snapped. "I know how it works."

Bolnoy shrugged. "Then you should have no more questions for me. You already have answers."

The Russian brushed past Sharp, disappearing down a long

corridor that led back to the anterior rooms of the BSL 3 autopsy lab. Sharp fought the instinct to watch him walk away from her and marched in the opposite direction.

She wound her way to an elevator that descended two levels to her private office and living quarters. She completed the triple authentication with her card, fingerprint, and facial recognition, and entered the cool, dark space in which she spent very little of her time.

Sleep was a stranger. Personal connections were alien. From the minute her Army husband had left her side to help build the wall separating Texas from everyone else, she'd retreated into a hardened shell. When he'd died during its construction, that shell thickened into something impenetrable.

Sharp waited for the door to slide shut behind her, for the motion-sensitive overhead lights to awaken, and she slinked to her desk. She tapped a large tablet tilted vertically on the white laminate surface and rolled her chair close.

With her elbows on the desk, she tapped a series of commands into the tablet. She bounced slightly against the ergonomically designed mesh back of the chair, swinging the seat from side to side with her heels. A pleasant-sounding, asexual voice purred from an overhead speaker connected wirelessly to the tablet.

"Good evening, Dr. Sharp," said the artificial intelligence programmed to assist her in using the complex's vast computing power. *"How might I assist you?"*

"I'm looking for all deployed non-security tracking implants not located at coordinates 33.7993 degrees north, 84.3280 degrees west. Please advise with display."

"Searching for all deployed non-security tracking implants not located at your current location, is that correct?"

"Yes."

"While I calculate the data for you, I'd like to inform you there are fourteen deployed tracking implants at your current location, 33.7993 degrees north, 84.3280 degrees west," said the AI. *"There are an additional thirty-five non-*

deployed tracking implants that, as of the gathering of this information, are nonfunctional. There are four additional tracking implants that are deployed but nonfunctional because the host shows no life functions."

The information was displayed on her tablet as a spreadsheet. The tracking implant identification numbers correlated with their subjects. There was latitudinal and longitudinal information as well as length of service and basic biometric intelligence for each of the associated subjects.

Sharp twisted the chair, the pale blue glow of the screen holding her attention. "Thank you," she said.

The tablet's display refreshed with the latest information and the AI narrated the new data. *"I've located the following tracking implants and their locations,"* it said. *"All are north of the series of coordinates identified as 'the wall.' There is one exception, however."*

The screen changed again, revealing a single set of data for a tracking implant associated with subject CV-01. Sharp stopped twisting and focused on the numbers displayed on the screen. They didn't make sense. The biometric data was offline and the location for the tracking implant was inconclusive in real time.

"Have we lost the tracking data for CV-01?" asked Sharp. "I don't understand what I'm seeing. Is CV-01 deceased?"

"I'm running another diagnostic, Dr. Sharp," said the AI. *"I should have that information in a moment."*

The display dissolved into another screen with another set of numbers. They also didn't compute. They showed the tracking implant at her current location.

"I'm running a time lapse from the moment of injection through the point at which the data transmission was halted," said the AI. *"Please stand by, Dr. Sharp."*

The numbers fluctuated, the geolocator's coordinates shifted, and the biometric data reflected Lomas's body temperature and heart rate. After several hours, his temperature spiked, his biometrics collapsed to zero, and then his body temperature spiked again in the seconds before the tracking implant ceased transmitting data.

"Is that an external spike in temperature?" she asked the computer.

"Yes," said the AI. *"The measurement is nine hundred degrees Fahrenheit, which is consistent with a fire."*

"What is the location?"

"The last transmission location was 32.476171 degrees north, 98.594055 degrees west."

"Which is where exactly? Is that Abilene?"

"No, Dr. Sharp," said the AI. *"The location is east of Ranger, Texas, on Interstate 20."*

Sharp's muscles tensed. She flexed her fingers and balled them into fists, planted her feet flat on the floor, and slid to the edge of her chair. She stared at the numbers on the screen. Her first test subject had not made it to his location. For some reason, the courier hadn't delivered and Blankenship hadn't done as he was assigned.

She lay back in her chair, releasing the tension and relaxing her posture. This was a setback. She knew this wouldn't be easy. Nothing worth having ever was.

She told herself this was only one subject, only one of many. It was minor. Inconsequential. If she repeated it enough, she hoped she'd believe it. However, something deep within her, something that clawed at the back of her mind, told her this was much more than a simple failure. It wasn't an anomaly. An overwhelming feeling of dread suggested this was, in some way, catastrophic to all they had planned.

CHAPTER 16

Grissom slid uncomfortably from his horse. He held his shoulder and stumbled toward the center of the camp where the other men were loading up. They were ready to go. Nobody paid attention to him until Bumppo stopped him short of reaching Junior.

His face etched deep with concern, Bumppo grabbed Grissom's collar and tightened his fist around the sweat-stained cotton. "Where's Whisper?"

Grissom shook his head. "He's dead. Battle got 'im."

The lines in Bumppo's forehead shifted from anger to worry. He loosened his hold on the shirt. "What do you mean? How? Where?"

"I dunno," said Grissom. "It was dark. He was waiting for us. He had to be waiting for us."

"Why didn't he kill both of you?"

Grissom swallowed hard. He couldn't look Bumppo in the face. "He wanted me to warn you."

Junior marched toward them from his horse, rubbing his hands on his shirt. With his chin up, he called to both, "Warn who?"

"Whisper's *dead*," Bumppo told him. "Battle killed him."

Junior motioned with his chin toward Grissom. "He's dead and you're here?"

Grissom's dead arm hung limply from his dislocated shoulder. His face was stretched with the thumping pain that radiated from the misaligned joint. He nodded.

Junior shook his head. "Ain't that something," he said, unfazed by the revelation. "Go ahead and learn us about what happened."

"He came from nowhere," Grissom said with a shaky voice after taking a deep breath. "Just popped up on the road. Cut us off."

"He killed Bumppo's best man?"

"Something like that," said Grissom. "He claimed he was lost, needed help. Said he'd been wandering. We didn't know who he was. Then his horse shows up."

"Shows up?" asked Junior, his voice sharp with incredulity.

"I don't know where it was," said Grissom. "Maybe he'd tied it somewhere, I don't know. But it shows up and that's when we know he's lying. Like a flash he draws and fires, shoots Whisper dead. My horse spooked and threw me off."

"Why didn't he kill you?" interjected Bumppo.

"He told me to deliver a message."

Bumppo and Junior exchanged glances. Junior stepped closer to Grissom and lowered his voice. "What message?"

Grissom's mouth opened and closed again with the hesitation of a messenger who knew better than to deliver. He closed his eyes. "Battle said it doesn't matter whether you got nineteen men or nineteen hundred. He said if you come to Baird, it's where you'll die."

Junior gently put a hand on Grissom's good shoulder. "Anything else?"

Grissom swallowed hard. "He also said…"

"What?" Junior prompted.

Grissom's eyes fluttered and he looked at his feet. "He also said he's going to let the same dog that killed your dad chew on your carcass until all he has to bury are the bones the dog doesn't want."

Junior's hand gripped Grissom's shoulder, his nails digging through the thin fabric of the shirt. His eyes narrowed and twitched. He stuck out his tongue and licked the corner of his mouth.

Grissom flinched like a dog expecting a backhand to the head. But Junior released his hold and backed away. He wasn't looking *at* Grissom anymore, he was looking *through* him. His hand slid to his holster at his hip and he took another half-dozen steps backward until he stopped. He stood there for more than a minute. He didn't speak. He didn't move.

Grissom held his breath. Bolts of pain pulsed from his shoulder, drawing an ache in his neck, but he too was cemented in place. He swallowed hard. His throat was dry. So dry. His tongue was thick in his mouth. He tried to avoid making eye contact with his boss. He knew he shouldn't.

Bumppo cupped his hands over his mouth and dragged his fingers downward, as if wiping away the tension. He started to speak, but he was interrupted by the loud crack of gunfire.

Without saying anything, let alone changing his expression, Junior drew his weapon from his holster, pulled back the hammer, leveled it, and pulled the trigger. With smoke trailing from the end of the barrel, he mindlessly spun the weapon forward and backward on his finger and slid it back into his holster.

Startled, Grissom jumped at the blast. It didn't register at first that Junior had fired at him. Then he felt the heat at his gut and looked down at himself.

There was a small hole torn near his navel. A spot of blood bloomed into something larger, something monstrous, and Grissom knew what had happened.

He clutched the wound with his good hand and lurched forward. His eyes drifted lazily from the deathblow to the man who dealt it. Tears welled in his eyes and then drifted down his cheeks. The heat became cold, a cold that spread like frost from his core to the rest of his body, and his legs weakened.

"W-w-why?" he stuttered.

Bumppo moved to Grissom's side and helped lower him to his knees. He cried out, "What are you doing?"

Grissom's vision blurred, the edges darkening. The pain was gone. His pulse slowed. The conversation between the man holding him and the one standing over him was mumbled gibberish. He tilted back his head and through the haze saw the watercolor shape of a large black bird circling overhead. Its wings were extended, slicing through the air, buoyed by the breeze. He accepted his fate. The man whom he'd served faithfully for much of his adult life, the only one in the post-Scourge world he considered family, had done him a favor.

* * *

Junior watched Grissom take his last breath. It was a rattle, a ragged breath that struggled to leave his lungs. The color changed in his friend's face, the tension floated from his body. He ran his tongue across his teeth and turned his attention to the sallow-faced Bumppo, who was sitting on the ground with Grissom's head in his lap. He shrugged.

"He delivered the message," said Junior.

"And you shot the messenger," said Bumppo. "You literally killed the messenger. I've never—"

Junior crouched down, balancing his weight on the balls of his heels. He pointed at Bumppo's face and sneered. "You've never had a man tell you that the dog who ripped apart your father is coming for you? Is that what you were about to say?"

Bumppo shook his head. "We need every man we got. We're down two now and you killed one of 'em. You killed your own man."

Junior circled his finger, referencing the men now surrounding them, obviously curious as to what had just transpired. His focus, however, was squarely on Bumppo. "That should be a warning to you and yours, then, shouldn't it?" he asked rhetorically. "If I'm gonna kill the man I trusted most, what am I gonna do to those I paid as hired guns? You best not run. You best not flake. You best not give me no bad news. You understand me?"

Junior slid his hand to his holster until Bumppo nodded silently. He took a final look at Grissom's body, spun on his boot heel, and marched, arms swinging, toward the water. He reached the edge, ignoring the crescendo of murmuring behind him, and dipped his hands into the pond. He cupped them together and drew enough of the cool water to splash it onto his face. He watched the concentric ripples dissipate until his reflection reappeared.

Junior didn't recognize the eyes staring back at him. They were feral, searching for prey. He understood the task ahead, what he'd sacrificed to satisfy the consuming rotgut called revenge. As he stared, searching for familiarity in his face, the image morphed into something softer. It was Grissom's face.

Grissom, the willing manservant who'd done whatever Junior had asked of him. He'd cooked, cleaned, bartered, hauled, listened, and advised. He'd lost his father too. An orphan of the Scourge, he'd found shelter with Junior's family by accident. Two years younger than Junior, he'd always looked up to him. He'd followed his every move, mimicked him, worked hard to please him. Junior knew these things about Grissom. He knew that the boy who'd come to them— seeking moldy bread, fetid water, and a manure-soiled mattress in a barn—had given so much more than he'd taken. Grissom wasn't like anyone else he'd known. In Junior's world, men were raiders and conquerors. They ruled with fear and lived to satisfy their most basic instincts: power, money, and sex.

Grissom lived to help. He lived for others. He sought only companionship and acceptance. Junior admired him for it. He also hated him for it. Grissom had served, unwittingly, as Junior's conscience, a balance to the scale. He was innately good and ran afoul only in an effort to please his one friend.

Regret swelled in Junior's chest. His chin quivered. As quickly as he let his humanity return, he quashed it by punching the water with his fists. He waited for the wash to clear, the ripples to settle, and his reflection to reappear. It was his face again, his lupine features staring back at him with eyes that were at once dead and wild with the anticipation of coming violence. Grissom got what was coming. He never should have let Battle get the best of him. He shouldn't have let him escape. He'd failed. He'd gotten another man killed and returned without the intelligence they'd sought. A bullet was the best thing for him, no doubt.

"I don't need your judgment," he quavered. He blinked back tears and bit down hard on the inside of his cheek. Warm, metallic-tasting blood filled his mouth, flooding the spaces around his tongue. He slid his tongue to the rough wound in his cheek and sucked his cheeks inward. He took a deep breath through his nose and exhaled. He swallowed a mouthful of blood and balled his hands into fists.

Junior stood. He wiped his face with the back of his hand and drew snot into his mouth with a loud snort. He spat the gritty, bloody wad into the water and his boots crunched their way back to the waiting posse. His red, swollen eyes floated across the men mounted on their horses. He waved dismissively at them.

"What are you waiting on?" he asked. "We got a town to kill."

In a single, smooth motion, he swung himself into his saddle and looped a hand into the reins. He adjusted his boots into the iron stirrups he'd stolen weeks earlier and kicked his heels into his ride. The horse responded with a grunt and picked up its hooves, moving back to the highway and leading the cadre of mercenaries toward Baird, toward Junior's destiny.

CHAPTER 17

"It's noon," said Lou. "They gotta be coming soon. Everyone who's anyone knows the bad guy rides into town at noon."

Dallas shook his head. "I ain't never heard that."

"Guess that means you ain't anyone, then?" Lou snipped.

She was perched atop a flat-roofed building in the middle of town between Fourth and Fifth Streets, which ran through the center of Baird. Fourth Street doubled as Interstate 20 Business, running parallel just south of the highway. The former government building itself was two stories plus a basement, and at one time was the county courthouse. It equipped him with the best crow's nest view of the town.

Lou was absently twirling her knives in her hands. She was slightly less disappointed about her assigned position than she was about having to share it with Dallas.

"Why noon?" he asked. He was armed with a rifle and was braced against the two-foot brick lip that ran around the top of the two-story structure as a decorative ledge. "Why not before sunup when everybody's sleeping?"

Lou rolled her eyes, which otherwise were pinned to the eastern horizon, looking for advancing enemies. She adjusted her cap on her head, straightening the tattered bill. She thumbed a worn spot on the front and rubbed the stitched *H* emblazoned to represent the Houston Astros.

"It's a myth, you know," she said.

"What?"

"The Old West duels that we have now never happened a hundred fifty, two hundred years ago. What's going on now is an apocalyptic approximation."

Dallas looked at her like a confused dog, as if the context made no sense to him. He rubbed the sweat from under his eyes with his knuckles.

"This world we live in south of the wall is like a parallel universe or something," Lou said. "Everyone likes the pretense that this is 1870s Deadwood, and we're all gamblers, gold-seekers, whores, and heathens. But what we're living is like some twisted version of that."

"How do you know that?" asked Dallas. "Everything I heard is that the Scourge sent us back to the Old West. That aside from the occasional lightbulb, automatic weapons, and some working cars, we're pretty much living in the Old West."

"Duels didn't happen except by drunk men fighting over money or women," she said. "I mean there was Wild Bill Hickok. He shot and killed Davis Tutt in a duel, but Hickok got tried for murder."

"What about the shoot-out at the O.K. Corral?"

"That wasn't a duel," she said condescendingly.

Dallas shook his head. "No," he said, "but neither is what's about to happen here."

"Fair enough," Lou conceded.

"You're smart, huh?" asked Dallas. "I mean, you like to act smart at least."

Lou bit her lip, considering how to respond. It was a backhanded compliment. But it was a compliment, so she wasn't quick to snap at him. Nobody had ever called her smart. Her father had called her inquisitive and a book-sponge, he'd never called her smart. Neither had Marcus. He called her deadly and sarcastic. He called her deadly sarcastic too, but never smart.

Even Rudy and Norma, who'd been generous and kind with their home and their love, hadn't expressed their views of her obvious intelligence. She was sweet, she was funny, she had a good wit, she was generous, she was good with Fifty. But never smart.

She smiled demurely, her eyes locking with his. She'd never noticed how blue they were, like icy pools of glacier water. Blue like the sky on the morning after a bad storm when the clouds cleared out.

"I just read a lot," she said. "Well, I used to. When I was with my dad, we'd both read a lot. I guess you learn stuff when you read."

"Your dad die in the Scourge?"

She looked away from him, back to the east. "No."

"Oh," said Dallas. "Sorry."

The hazy, warbling horizon dissolved in front of her and Lou pictured her dad sitting at a long study table in the library, his legs crossed at the ankles and resting on the pressed wood tabletop. He'd have a stack of three or four books next to his feet, another in his lap, and one in his hands. He'd occasionally chuckle or sigh or curse. Sometimes he'd call out to Lou, his voice reaching her in some far-flung aisle of children's fiction or biographies. She'd snap shut her book, her thumb holding her place, and bounce along the well-trod paths in the industrial Berber carpet and sidle up next to him so he could read aloud a particularly interesting paragraph, page, or chapter.

She could smell him in her memory. The oily musk scent that made her feel safe. His features had muddied with time. She recalled his skin. It was smooth and brown, with waves of thin black hair across the backs of his forearms. She could picture his pronounced nose and wide nostrils. He'd joked he could suck in a bird like a jet engine if he inhaled deeply enough.

His eyes were sad. No matter how much he smiled or laughed, his eyes revealed a melancholy he'd done his best to hide.

His shoulders were broad. She could sit on them when she was much younger and bounce around from spot to spot, reaching the books on the highest shelves.

These days, she couldn't put all the pieces together. Like a puzzle missing its middle, she couldn't see his face. When she tried, it only angered her.

Dallas nudged her from her daydream. "Hey," he whispered. "I see them."

Lou blinked and refocused. On the horizon was a plume of orange dust rising like smoke following a moving fire. They were coming. Fifteen of them, maybe more. They were galloping toward town on Fourth in a posse wide enough to stretch beyond the edges of the road.

She reached next to her and picked up a purse-sized rectangular mirror. The plastic frame was warped and the glass featured a large spiderweb crack running from one edge to the other. Lou rubbed her thumb across the fracture and then dropped her arm over the edge of the building, facing west. She tilted the mirror, the sun glinting off the mirror with bright streams of light. A flash responded from a building a half block away. She rolled onto her other side and repeated the signal to the east. Four streets away, between Lou and the approaching gang, a flicker of light acknowledged her signal.

"It's happening," she said to Dallas.

When she pushed herself to her feet and started to move, Dallas caught her wrist and held it. "I'm sorry," he said. "I shouldn't have asked about your dad. It's none of my business."

Lou sighed and sucked in a pensive breath. "It's okay," she said. "When this is over, I'll tell you about him. He might have liked you. Or he would have acted like he did, at least."

Dallas let go of her arm, rose to his feet, and followed Lou to the narrow staircase leading them down the building and to their next position.

* * *

Norma Gallardo slid the mirror into her dress pocket and opened the front door to the long U-shaped building in which she was holed up. She'd been there since prior to sunrise and her eyes were heavy with sleep. She could feel the swell under her eyes when she blinked, and the taste of last night's dinner was on her tongue.

It hadn't been easy to sleep knowing what today might hold. She'd tried. Lord knew she'd tried. But the more she'd thought about her lack of sleep, the harder it was to doze off.

Rudy had awakened her before dawn. They'd ridden to town together and then split up as Marcus had instructed. Although she had protested, she'd lost.

It wasn't that she didn't agree with Marcus's plan, as it were. It was that she didn't like being separated from her husband, and neither was she thrilled about being alone.

The two women who boarded in their home had stayed behind. They were taking care of the property and, in the event everything went to pot, they'd keep it. Rudy was with Marcus; Lou was with the stranger, Dallas; and a couple of Marcus's neighbors who volunteered to help were elsewhere in town, readying for the coming storm.

Norma held the door open for a moment, standing on the uneven threshold while she soaked in the midday sun that shone directly overhead. The breeze fluttered a tattered nylon Texas flag on a pole across the street. The rusted pole was mounted to the façade of a one-story house and hung at more than its intended forty-five degrees. The white star at the center of the flag was rust colored and the edges of the banner were frayed and torn.

Norma stepped from the doorway and south along the walkway that led to the street. The breeze whipped past her, blowing her hair across her eyes, and she combed the strands off her face with a rake of her fingers. When she reached the street, she stepped to its center and straddled the single yellow line. There was a dark red splotch on the asphalt between her feet. She stared at it for a moment and thought about the duel Marcus had won five days earlier.

Was the stain from that fight or another? Was it a few days old, a few weeks, a year? She couldn't know. There were too many fights to count, too many dead to remember.

She swallowed hard, enjoying for a moment the cool swirl of air on her face and neck. The chill was refreshing and life-affirming. Her hands rested on her hips above a thick belt that hung loosely on her trim waist.

On one side, the wide, worn saddle-colored leather held a nine-millimeter. The other holster contained a solar-powered handheld transceiver. Norma adjusted the buckle below her navel and narrowed her gaze east along Fourth Street. Above, she heard the echo of a trapdoor slamming shut on the roof of the old county courthouse. Beyond the buildings at the far end of the street, where it curved gently north toward the highway, were puffs of orange dust.

Norma glanced over her shoulder and beyond the U-shaped building in which she'd spent her morning. There were crops of dead scrub oaks and mesquite. The trees resembled zombie hands reaching toward the sky from their graves. Dotting the spaces between the tress were modest homes. Some of them, maybe one in every five or six, was occupied. The rest were in disrepair and home to whatever rodents managed to eke out a subsistence. The square grid of streets wrapped boxes that all looked the same to Norma. Each of them featured the dead or dying trees, knee-high weeds whose color varied between pale green and wheat, and eight to ten of those single-story houses.

Baird was on the verge of being a ghost town. A couple of hundred people were all that stood between its place on a withered map and extinction. Yet none of them, save a couple, were willing to fight for it. They were tucked in their houses, hiding from the advancing army.

This wasn't about them, they'd said defiantly as she worked to recruit them. This was about Marcus Battle. This was his fight. He'd brought it on himself, they'd said. A life of violence begot violence.

Norma hadn't disagreed with them. They'd been right, of course. Marcus was a violent man who'd invited as much gunfire as he'd deterred. He was outlaw and lawman at the same time. While the townsfolk were happy enough to hide behind his bullet-riddled body for protection, they weren't about to join him and stand by his side.

Maybe if Rudy became the sheriff, it wouldn't be so bad. He didn't have the territory-wide reputation Marcus had. He didn't court duels with fame-seekers or revenge-minded sociopaths. He was a quiet family man who might be exactly what her town needed.

The thoughts chased each other through her mind as she stood there, her arms folded across her chest. Marcus was a man who couldn't know peace, no matter how much he claimed to want it. As long as he was here, nobody in Baird could sleep easy. It was a paradox, of course, too much to process with armed horsemen on their way.

A wisp of wind danced across her face. It was coming. If Marcus's plan worked the way he'd designed it, she'd be the one to end it.

* * *

Marcus lay flat on the red roof of a single-story house, his belly on the mildew-stained shingles. It was noon. Somehow, he'd known the man who called himself Junior would be coming at noon.

He and Rudy were four blocks east of Lou and Dallas. Rudy was on the ground in front of the house, Fifty lying at his feet, his big head resting on his meaty paws. They were on a dirt road that ran perpendicular to Fourth Street. A gust of northerly wind chilled the air. Marcus pulled his jacket collar up around his neck and flexed his fingers to fight off the stiffness that came with the chill.

Rudy craned his neck to look up at Marcus. "Except for the fellas on the overpass, we're all lined up along the same corridor," he said, "and our lookout just left her post."

Marcus picked up a canteen from the roof and popped its top with his thumb. He slugged a long pull of warm, metallic-tasting water and wiped his mouth with the back of his hand.

"Is that a question or an observation?" he asked, and tossed the canteen to Rudy.

Rudy caught it, brought it close to his lips, and held it there. "Both," he said, and took a healthy swig.

"Yes. We know they'll ride into the middle of town. It's what everybody does. This guy, Junior, isn't going to be any different."

Rudy poured some water into his cupped hand and offered it to Fifty. The dog greedily lapped it up. Rudy offered him another taste. Fifty wagged his tail as he drank.

"We know they've got three times the people," said Rudy. "They're on horses; we're on foot. You still haven't told me why that is."

Marcus took the canteen and capped it. "We're easier targets if we're on horses. Plus, we know this town; they don't. We have the advantage."

Rudy frowned. "It's three to one."

"Yeah," said Marcus. "But I think we're all good for three kills."

"Even Norma?"

"Especially Norma."

Marcus craned his neck past Rudy and motioned toward the overpass beyond their line of sight. "Those guys are going to be a big help."

"I hope so," said Rudy.

"This is going to be over fast," said Marcus. "I'm telling you."

Rudy smiled nervously. "Lou kindly reminded me last night that the shoot-out at the O.K. Corral only lasted thirty seconds. I doubted her. She put me in my place with some inconvenient facts she had stored in that mind of hers."

Marcus chuckled. "She tends to do that."

Both men laughed for a moment. It eased the tension. Marcus flexed his fingers again and readied his rifle.

"Is this plan of yours going to work?" asked Rudy.

"Yes," Marcus said. "I've made a lot of mistakes in the last five years, I'll admit that. My soldiering isn't gonna win me any medals. But this time I'm on point. I think the plan gives our people the best chance of living."

Rudy's features hardened. His muscles visibly tensed. His voice flattened with an unfamiliar tone.

"It better. My wife is alone. I know she's the last line of defense, but if your plan doesn't work, she's exposed. If anything happens to her, I might be the one who puts a bullet in you, friend or not."

Marcus nodded. "Fair enough. But if I'm wrong, you might be shooting my corpse."

Rudy's eyes shifted to the east. The rumble of the horses was audible now.

* * *

Neither Blake Peele nor Aaron Cay were fighters. Both were better with wrenches and screwdrivers than with mechanized weapons. But they were willing and they were available.

When Marcus plotted his defense, he decided to place Blake and Aaron on the Interstate 20 overpass that ran north of town. They'd be in a perfect position to snipe the advancing menace as it veered from the freeway and traveled the business extension on to Fourth Street.

Even if their shots missed every one of the possible targets, they'd be both a warning and a distraction to Junior and his men. If they managed to hit any of them, all the better. Plus, being farther away from the action minimized the chances of them getting shot and killed.

"Are these sniper rifles?" Aaron had asked when Marcus tutored them on the particulars of their weapons.

"Any rifle in the hand of a sniper is a sniper rifle," Marcus had replied. "Since neither of you are snipers, no. But they'll do the job."

Two days later the men found themselves lying prone on the overpass, wanna-be sniper twins, rifles pressed to their shoulders, sweat beading their foreheads, their mouths dry, their hearts pounding.

"You saw the signal?" asked Aaron.

"Yeah," said Blake. "She flashed it. I saw it."

Aaron lifted his head from the scope and panned the horizon with his eyes. "They're coming. Do you see them?"

Blake lifted his head and silently searched for the bad guys. His eyes moved past trees and across rooftops. Nothing at first. Then he pointed. "There," he whispered.

Aaron followed Blake's finger to a hazy cloud of orange dust. It reminded him of smoke from a slow-moving locomotive.

Neither said anything. Both fidgeted. Blake kept checking and rechecking the magazine in his rifle. Aaron was chewing on a weed, twirling it around in his mouth with his fingers.

Blake exhaled loudly, as if blowing the puffball free of a dandelion. "Okay," he said resolutely. "This is it."

The orange locomotive moved westward, closer to the edge of town. Both men knew when they were to open fire. Both men were to pick off men at the back of the group first, make them scatter.

"On three," said Aaron.

"On three," Blake echoed.

The amateurs did what Marcus had taught them. They didn't worry about scope adjustments other than focus, they didn't account for wind speed or slope. They aimed, they pressed their fingers to their triggers, and prepared themselves to apply pressure.

"One," said Aaron.

The posse was clearer to both. They could make out horses, men bouncing in their saddles.

"Two."

The posse slowed. The men kept their crosshairs on their chosen targets.

"Three."

Then the targets did something they didn't expect. They headed north.

"Hold," said Aaron.

"What are they doing?" Blake wondered aloud.

Aaron lifted his head. "I don't know. What do *we* do?"

A bead of sweat thickened and ran the length of Blake's nose. "I don't know."

Aaron lowered his head again, holding his eye to the scope. "I say we shoot at 'em anyhow."

"Which group?"

"Does it matter?"

"I don't know," said Blake, exasperation in his voice.

"The ones coming at us," said Aaron. "The guys coming north. I say we hit them."

* * *

Junior Barbas sat high in his saddle, his body bouncing rhythmically with the gallop of his horse. There was a breeze at his face that numbed his cheeks and dried his eyes, but he was barely conscious of it. His eyes and his mind were focused on the narrow, rutted street ahead. It led straight into the heart of Baird and to the place where he would avenge the wounds inflicted on him and the death of his father.

He could picture Marcus Battle's face. It was plastered in his mind. He could feel the unexpected punch and burn of the shots to his arms, smell the sour odor of his father's decomposing remains. He could taste the briny sweat that dripped into his mouth as he pushed his body past what his muscles and nerves told him was possible.

He tightened his grip on the reins and surveyed the landscape ahead of them. Bumppo rode at his side, his horse keeping pace. Another hired gun rode to his other side. Behind them, the remaining fifteen mercenaries galloped in an amoebic, undisciplined blob.

Junior had instructed them to kill anything or anyone they saw. Men, women, children, horses, goats, dogs. They were all fair game.

"Makes it easier if you ain't gotta guess about what to shoot," he'd said.

As the southwesterly running road curved straight west, Junior raised his hand above his head and slowed the horses to a walk. He signaled for the men to arm themselves and pointed. A group of men rode north. He pointed to the left and another posse rode south.

"They won't expect us to split up," Junior said to Bumppo. "They'll think we're all headed straight up Main Street."

"You want me to lead one of the other groups?" asked Bumppo. "We can meet on the other end of town and—"

"Naw," Junior said and then winked. "You stay with me. I wanna keep an eye on you."

Bumppo frowned. "Whatever you want," he said disapprovingly. "You're the money man."

"Damn straight," said Junior. "Now let's do this."

The moment he turned his attention to the road ahead, the crack of rifle shots echoed. A second volley of shots, one after the other, snapped and reverberated like rolling thunder.

Junior yelled at Bumppo, "You and me! Now!"

He ordered the remaining four men to hold their position and kicked his horse into a gallop. Another thunderclap of shots ripped across the sky as he rode quickly to his men. Not seventy-five yards ahead, he spotted two of them bleeding out in the street. Neither of them moved and their horses were gone. A third was sitting awkwardly in his saddle, grasping his neck. Blood leaked and sprayed with the dying man's pulse.

The three that had moved north were off their horses and hiding behind the façades of buildings on either side of the street. Junior drew his rifle from his scabbard and slammed it against his shoulder. He scanned the distance as a round zinged past him an instant before he heard the percussion of the shot.

"There," he said, nodding with his head and directing Bumppo to their targets. "On the overpass. You see 'em?"

Junior narrowed his eye at the targets, a pair of men lying low on the overpass north of them. Neither presented an easy shot. He drew in a deep breath, settled his boots in the stirrups, and picked the one to the left.

"You take the one to the right," he said to Bumppo.

Junior put his finger on the trigger, centering his aim on the target. He applied pressure at the same time he saw a muzzle flash fill the optics. The rifle blasted its round, the butt kicking hard against his shoulder. He kept his eye to the scope, watching for the result. Then he saw it, a spray of pink, and the target slumped forward, flattening its profile against the road. The shot from the target rumbled across the sky.

"Gotcha," he murmured to himself and turned to Bumppo. "Your turn. Why ain't you—shoot—"

Bumppo was grabbing at his chest. His rifle was on the ground. His face was devoid of color, his eyes wide with fear, his brow crinkled in pain. His mouth was moving, but all Junior could hear was the sound of leaking air. Junior's eyes zeroed in on Bumppo's chest and saw the dark spreading stain from beneath his hands.

Junior took his rifle in one hand and used the other to dismount. He moved the short distance to Bumppo but didn't reach him before the hired gun fell from his horse. His face slapped against the road with a crack. He was gone.

Junior slapped the back of Bumppo's horse and the animal bolted north. He picked up the dead man's rifle and scurried for cover to the side of the street opposite the three other men still alive.

He pressed his back against the building and pulled Bumppo's weapon over his head, positioning it behind his shoulder. He pulled at the sling across his chest and grabbed his own rifle with two hands. His eyes found the hired guns hiding across from him and addressed them with a sweeping gaze. "There's only one of them. There's three of you. Take him out."

* * *

Blake gagged on the sudden rise of thick, stinging bile in his throat. He'd never seen a man killed before, let alone someone he knew. He'd seen people die from disease, come across dead bodies peppered with bullet holes or shredded with blades. He'd helped wheel them to the graveyard near town. He'd buried them, prayed for them. But to watch the life ooze from a man was something altogether different.

One moment Aaron was healthy and breathing, raining hellfire on the invaders below. The next he was gargling and seizing, his eyes fixed and his tongue hanging to one side of his gaping mouth.

Blake swallowed the acid and bit down hard on his lower lip. He lowered his head, fighting the flood of tears he knew was coming. His heart raced and he found himself catching his breath as it tried to run from him.

Time slowed while Blake gathered his wits. The exhaustion of hours shrank into mere seconds while he regrouped and tried to focus on the task at hand.

He shouldered the moisture from his eyes, blinking away the fog, and tried finding new targets. He looked south, hunting for the men who had hidden behind a building. He didn't see them. Nor did he see the man on the horse whose shot killed Aaron.

There were four bodies in the street, tumbled chess pieces knocked from the game. Each scan inched farther left and then farther right.

Nothing.

And then something.

His peripheral vision caught the flash of a man between two buildings.

Blake positioned his body to face the threat. He lowered his head and held his position. The man was two or three blocks closer. He held steady, as steady as he could. The wind swirled and traveled up his back, chilling the sweat on his neck and behind his ears.

Another flash of movement.

This one was to the side of the first, and closer. It was a different man too. Blake was pretty sure of it. The shape of the blur was bigger, more lumbering, and less certain of its movement.

A third now, closer still. They were advancing quickly.

Blake pivoted. His pulse pounded in his neck and at his temples.

Were there only three? Were there more? Where was the man on the horse?

Blake stayed put. He couldn't chase shadows, wisps of men. He needed a solid target.

And then he spotted it.

One of the men stumbled as he moved into sight. It slowed him enough that Blake had time to adjust and pulled the trigger. He pulled again and again. Three shots in rapid succession. The first whizzed past the man's head. The second hit him clean in the side at his ribs. Already off balance, he toppled over onto the street and skidded into a curb. The third shot missed high.

A fourth shot reverberated in Blake's ears. A fifth. Both zipped past him, humming in the air, and the bullets tore the air above their intended target. Blake tried adjusting his position to respond, but a sixth shot punched him in the top of his shoulder. His arm went numb and he dropped the front end of the rifle onto the gravelly overpass.

He grunted and gasped for air while the muted sound of a seventh round erupted and the bullet found his side, boring through muscle to nestle in his lung. Blake's vision clouded and blurred. His pulse slowed and weakened. His short breaths became useless puffs.

He was dying. He closed his eyes and welcomed what was coming.

* * *

"They're doing what Marcus said they'd do," said Lou. She was leading Dallas through the maze of low-slung buildings south of Fourth Street. "You hear those shots?"

"They're coming from the north." Dallas's long strides made it easy for him to keep pace with Lou, who bounced along a path only she'd memorized. "Why didn't we stay and wait for them at the courthouse? We had a great perch up there. We were safer there."

"Marcus said he had his reasons. He wanted us gone once we spotted the posse."

"Okay. I guess we do whatever Marcus says."

"Yep," she said. "That means we're gonna have a meet-up somewhere on the south side."

Lou had knives in both hands and a rifle strapped across her back. She moved with purpose off Market, onto East Third Street and Chestnut, then past the old Parker Funeral Home.

"Where are we headed?" Dallas asked.

"South of the railroad tracks," Lou replied. "They won't go south of the tracks. From there we can come up behind them if we have to."

The tracks were only a couple of blocks ahead of them. Dallas was breathing heavily as they reached East First Street, cutting between a wide metal building and a slew of rusting silos.

"You're out of shape," Lou remarked.

Dallas shook his head as they dipped past the silos and stopped at a fence that separated First Street from the railroad easement. "No," he said. "I'm in good shape. I'm just nervous, you know. I'm anxious about the fight. I feel like my heart is going to explode out of my chest."

Lou peeked through an opening in the fence. She looked both ways and pulled back inside the fence line, winking at Dallas. "That's not the fight, Dallas," she said. "It's me. I'm the one who's got you flushed and nervous."

Dallas's already pink face reddened further. He looked away from Lou and kicked his foot in the dirt.

Lou was flirting with him, but it wasn't because she was attracted to him. The way he moved told her he was about to puke. She wanted to distract him, get his mind off the coming violence.

"No," he finally said. "I'm not...you're not...never mind."

Lou giggled. She winked again and motioned for him to follow her south past the fence. No sooner had they reached the tracks than they saw the enemy.

"Whoa," she whispered. "Get down."

She tugged at his shirt and the two of them flattened themselves in the knee-high brown weeds that grew along the edges of the thinning ballast. Neither of them moved. Lou listened for any signs the enemy had seen them. Nothing.

"They're maybe a half mile ahead," she whispered in Dallas's ear. Their bodies were pressed side to side, hidden in the weeds. She could feel his pulse coursing through his body, smell the dirt mixed with sweat on his skin.

"What do we do?" he mouthed. His eyes told her he was frightened more than anxious.

Lou wanted to give him the right answer. She wanted to offer some sage advice that would calm him, make him valuable. As it was, he was trembling. He was pale. He was useless.

"Stay here," she said. "Don't move unless you hear me call your name. If I do, you pop up and open fire."

"Marcus said we only hit them if they hit first. We're just supposed to do recon and then head back, get a handle on the numbers."

"Recon can get messy," Lou said. "If I call your name, open fire."

"What if I hit you?" he whispered, his breathing shallow and fast. "What if I kill you by mistake?"

"Then I'm not as smart as you think I might be." She raised her finger to her lips, took off her baseball cap and lifted her head above the top of the weeds. She zeroed in on the spot she'd seen the men on their horses. They were closer now, six of them.

"Six," she muttered and lowered her head. "Six men."

She shrugged her shoulders to adjust the rifle sling, which threatened to blister her at the bottom of her neck, and removed the rifle. She placed it in the dirt beside Dallas and nodded at it to make sure he noticed it was there. She picked up her hat and pulled it on her head sideways.

She raised herself on her elbows, crawled a few body lengths ahead of Dallas, and rolled north toward the fence. Staying low, she found another gap in the aging chain-link and crossed to the other side.

Staying low, Lou quickly traversed the mostly dirt road that was First Street. She hustled, breathing evenly in through her nose and out through her mouth until she reached the end of the street at Lombard. She was farther from the tracks at this point, elevated four feet above them, and had the cover of thick tangles of brush.

Lou held both knives, one in each hand, and moved south back to the tracks. As she stepped quietly through the brush, searching for spots that wouldn't rustle and give away her location, she peered through the foliage to the spots of daylight that shown through like yellow panes of stained glass.

When she reached the edge of the brush, she squatted onto her heels and listened. At first all she could hear was the thump of her own pulse in her ears, but as she focused on the sounds around her, she could make out the breeze brushing against the brittle limbs of the yaupon, enticing them to scratch against one another. The approaching horses clopped on the tracks. There were men's hushed voices and the subtle rattle of the large weapons in their hands or on their hips. She could even make out the squeak of leather from their movements in their saddles.

To her left was a break in the brush, an opening through which she could clearly see the first of the riders. They were riding two by two and three deep. Lou bounced the knife in her hand. She rolled her thumb across the grip of the other blade.

Two knives, six men. That would be tricky. But she knew what to do.

As the last of them passed her, Lou scurried to the opening and emerged through the opening into the daylight. There was a thin ridge at the edge of the ledge on which the foliage grew. She took two broad steps and then jumped, her legs spread and her blades aimed at the back of the man on the horse closest to her. She landed awkwardly on the back of the horse and drove the knives into either side of the man's spine to keep her from falling. The man grunted and cried out in pain, his back arching as he let go of his horse and teetered to one side.

As quickly as she'd slammed the cutters into the man's back, she withdrew them and kept her balance on the horse long enough to throw one of them at the target. His eyes were still narrowed with confusion when the blade sliced deep into his neck.

Without waiting to see that man fall, she tumbled from the horse, pushed herself free, and flung her other blade. It hit the man in front of her squarely in his spine. He went limp as if someone had flipped a switch on his nervous system, and he slid from the horse to the tracks, his boot catching in the stirrup and his horse dragging him along the rails and rocky ballast.

When she hit the ground, landing hard on her shoulder, she yelled,

"Dallas!" All of it happened within seconds and before the other three men had time to react.

Dallas popped up to unload his weapon. A flurry of shots reverberated like firecrackers, one after the other.

Lou stayed on the ground, given cover by the horses, until she found the man with the neck wound, crawled the short distance to him, and pulled his body over hers.

The three men around her were returning fire. She could hear their frustration in their voices as they tried to control their nervous horses. One scream followed a grunt.

Lou lay under the dead body of the malodorous hired gun on top of her. His odor was somewhere between corn mash, urine, and vinegar. She caught whiffs of all three in varying strengths. She tried holding her breath as she listened to another volley of gunfire followed by a silence interrupted only by the clops and snorts of horses.

"Lou?" Dallas called from far away.

"Looouuu?" he called again, closer this time. His voice was filled with rising urgency.

Despite her aching shoulder protesting, Lou pushed the man from atop her body and rolled free of him, gasping for clean air. "I'm here. I'm okay."

Holding the rifle like a grunt picking his way through a minefield, Dallas cautiously made his way toward her. He had the rifle pulled to his shoulder, ready to fire again if any of the dead men so much as twitched.

As he reached each of the men he'd gunned down, he lowered the barrel in a cursory safety check. He sidestepped them and headed for Lou. She was on her feet when he got to her. One boot was pressed on her second victim's neck so she could pry the blade free. She wiped both sides of the bloody steel clean on the dead man's shirt.

"You okay?" asked Dallas. His eyes were wide as he surveyed the damage she'd done in the blink of an eye.

Lou rolled her shoulder and squeezed it. She winced. "Yeah. Bruised my arm pretty good. I'm fine though."

"Good," Dallas said with obvious relief. "I think I got three of them. How'd you get the others?"

Lou stepped over a body, and another, then found her second knife, prying it loose with a grunt. "Knives," she said without looking at Dallas.

"Right," he said, ignoring the sarcasm. "But how? Three men, two knives."

She tucked both knives in her waistband and adjusted her ball cap, spinning the brim to the front. "I've done this before," she said. "A lot."

Dallas gulped. "Oh. I guess you couldn't just observe and report?"

"I told you, sometimes recon gets messy. We need to head back and get my rifle. Then the plan has us hustling back to the courthouse."

She stepped closer to her new friend and only then did she notice the bloodstain on his shirt. It was below his ribs. She stood directly in front of him and stared at the wound. She reached out her fingers as if to touch it, but stopped short. "You're bleeding," she said, worry creeping into her voice. "You got hit."

Dallas touched his hand to his shirt and looked down. "Oh, that. It's a nick. Grazed me. I'll be okay."

"It could get infected," she said. "We gotta do something about it."

"When this is over," he said, motioning toward her rifle and taking a step in that direction, "you can get me fixed up. Deal?"

Lou looked up from the blood. It looked worse than a nick. But he was right, they had work to do. "Deal," she said, and followed him back to get her gun.

* * *

Fifty bared his teeth. The hair on his neck and back stood on end. He snarled, the muscles in his legs and shoulders tensed.

Rudy stood behind him. "He's ready to go. I think he senses it as much or more than we do. Something big is coming for us."

Marcus eyed the dog and then Rudy. "You heard those shots north and south. We'll know in a minute how big that something is going to be."

The three were at the edge of Fourth Street, awaiting the inevitable confrontation. If there were nineteen men coming, they'd likely split into fairly equal groups. Even if the splinter groups were smaller, they had to have taken some casualties.

"I'm gonna guess at least a few of theirs are gone," Marcus said, trying to convince himself as much as Rudy. "Our odds are better now than they were a few minutes ago. That's my guess."

"Odds ain't better if the boys up north are dead, and Lou and Dallas are—"

Marcus shook his head. "Don't say that. Lou can handle herself. You've seen it. Plus, she was only supposed to do recon and report the numbers."

"That's not what happened," said Rudy. "You heard the gunfire."

Marcus scowled. "She's coming back. So's Dallas."

Rudy's eyes suddenly reflected a sadness Marcus hadn't seen in his friend since Norma was missing more than a year earlier. Rudy nodded. "You're right," he said softly.

A swell of guilt flooded Marcus's chest. Again, he'd managed to drag others into his fight, risking their lives on behalf of his own. He pushed the thought from his mind. Now wasn't the time for apologies or self-reflection.

"Remind me why we stayed here while everyone else left their positions to fight up close?" asked Rudy, a hint of accusation in his voice.

"Because," said Marcus, his eyes training east, "if I was wrong and everyone came up Main Street, they'd be clear of a battle we can't win."

"You were in the Army?" asked Rudy.

Marcus ignored the question. There was no easy answer strategically. "I think it's time," he said, pushing himself from the wall. He marched out onto Fourth Street and glanced over his shoulder at Rudy. "You ready?"

Rudy made a clicking sound and Fifty followed him into the street. They stood there for a moment and Marcus nodded at Rudy, who jogged backward two blocks and took Fifty with him around a corner.

Marcus shouldered his weapon. Through the scope, the men approached. Five men on horseback rode toward him, all of them armed. None of them were ready to fire.

When they were maybe two hundred yards from Marcus, two more men joined them from the north. There were seven now. The seven horsemen of the apocalypse. Only seven. But now they were galloping.

Marcus slowed his breathing, controlling his heart rate, and focused on the rider closest to him, a man in the front on the side of the street. He was still several hundred yards away, but Marcus tracked him with the rifle until the right moment. He pulled the trigger.

His rifle powered the round eastward until it hit its target. Through the scope, the man seized, clutched his chest, and slumped forward on his horse.

He quickly adjusted his aim and pulled the Springfield's trigger again. A second shot met flesh and dropped another rider. They were down to five.

"Like shooting fish in a barrel," he murmured. He turned the gun to a building on the opposite side of the road. It was close to the road, a one-room shack with windows but no front door.

He looked up from the scope to watch the coming quintet. Two of the men rode close to the house and he quickly lowered his eye to the scope. He found a rectangular black box sitting atop a quartet of bricks wrapped in brown paper inside the open doorway and fired a single shot.

The resulting explosion evaporated the building and the two men closest to it.

* * *

The ground under Lou's feet rumbled. She crossed Fourth Street near the old courthouse, and the billowing black smoke and remnant flames caught her attention.

"One down," she said. "We better get moving."

The two of them hurried to the courthouse, quickly climbing the stairs to the roof. They rushed to the ledge and against the low red brick that encircled the top of the building.

Both worked to catch their breath. Lou gingerly pulled the rifle sling over her head and leaned the weapon's barrel over the ledge. She rubbed her shoulder with her thumb and winced but nodded at Dallas she was okay.

Dallas moved away from her toward the eastern corner and readied himself there. He checked the magazine and swapped it out for an extra, fully loaded one he carried in his jacket pocket. He slapped the mag into the rifle and aimed the barrel toward the smoke. It was still thick, but had quickly dissolved from black to gray.

Lou looked west and saw Norma standing on the path between the street and the U-shaped building in which she was supposed to retreat if necessary. She had her hands on her hips, one resting on a handgun, the other on a radio.

The radios didn't work well. Only two of them functioned at all. Using them was a risk. Lou had told Marcus that. He'd told her it was a backstop, a last resort if everything else failed. He told her he'd tested them and they'd been okay. Lou knew that if their lives depended on those radios working, they were as good as dead. All of them, even the two guys who had nothing to do with anything, Blake and Aaron.

Wait…Blake and Aaron.

Lou picked up her rifle, bent over at her waist, and scurried across the rooftop to the rear northeast corner. That position gave her a better vantage point of the overpass. She dropped to one knee and aimed her scope toward the spot Blake and Aaron were supposed to be.

She scanned from west to east until two motionless heaps on the shoulder of the road came into view. She couldn't be certain the bodies belonged to Marcus's neighbors, but she was pretty sure.

That meant five of them remained. And that was if Rudy was okay. She hadn't seen him as she and Dallas bolted to the courthouse roof. Only Marcus had been exposed in the middle of the street.

She cursed under her breath and moved back to her original spot. "I think Blake and Aaron are dead, Dallas," she said. "I don't know about Rudy."

Dallas rolled onto his side to look at Lou. "I can't tell how many there are, but they're coming fast."

Lou pressed her eye to her scope. "Do you have a shot? I don't have a good angle."

Dallas rolled back into firing position and nodded. "Yes, I have a shot."

"Take it," said Lou. "Don't wait. Take it."

* * *

Despite having the cover of the building, Rudy instinctively ducked and lost his balance when he felt the surprise, percussive blast of the explosion. His ears ringing, he got back to his feet. Fifty's ears were pinned back and his tail was tucked. Rudy unsuccessfully tried shaking the dull tone from his ears. Then it hit him. The explosion was his signal to move again.

Rudy blinked his eyes to clear his head. He took another deep breath and ran into the street. Fifty hesitated but followed him. He spotted Marcus standing in the middle of the street, inviting his own death, it seemed, and saw his body jerk with the recoil of the Springfield. A moment later another explosion followed.

Rudy had worried the detonators wouldn't work. Marcus knew that firing a round directly into the C-4 they had stored on the second floor of the jail wouldn't do much, but hitting an active detonator could trigger the explosive.

It did work. Twice. Though from his vantage point, which wasn't great, Rudy couldn't tell whether the blasts had done anything to diminish the advancing threat. The building straight ahead of him was the courthouse. He stood in its shadow next to the jail and ordered Fifty to sit at his side. The dog obeyed and they waited.

Rudy peered around the corner, looking toward the U-shaped building where he knew his wife was holed up. He couldn't see her, but getting a glimpse of the building was satisfying enough.

He peeled back into the shade, where the temperature was noticeably lower. He flexed his hands one at a time to ward off the stiffness that came with winter. He was younger than Marcus, but everyone who met them thought them the same age. Somehow, he'd aged faster than a man who'd seemingly lived a thousand lives.

Rudy envied Marcus in some ways: his skill, his confidence, his indifference to death. In other ways, he pitied the man others called Mad Max. To Rudy, Marcus frequently teetered on the edge of sanity. It was evident in his eyes, in the occasional mumbling in which he appeared to be carrying on a conversation with someone inside his own head.

He was a walking oxymoron, a man who fought to live but gave his own life and that of those around him so little consideration. He was a decorated war hero who made the careless mistakes of a man who'd never picked up a gun, let alone used it on the front lines in a foreign land. He was sullen and withdrawn, but could fill a room with his company.

Rudy shook his head, thinking about the risk he was taking, the risk they were all taking to fend off yet another ne'er-do-well who came seeking Marcus's head. A wave of anger washed through his body and he tightened his grip on his weapon until his knuckles lost their color.

What had he allowed Marcus to do to his hometown, to his family and friends? Marcus wasn't their savior, he was their undoing.

As much as he cared for his friend, as much as he was indebted to Marcus for helping rescue his wife from the Llano River Clan, Rudy couldn't allow this to be the end. He couldn't let Marcus's narcissism win the day.

He clicked at Fifty and the dog's ears pricked. "Let's go," he said, and marched out into the street with his rifle drawn. Marcus was off to the side of the street, using the smoke and debris for cover while three men, now on foot, fired at him.

Rudy heard shots from overhead. Without looking back, he knew they were coming from Lou and Dallas. None of them were finding their mark. Three men were closing in on Marcus. The large piece of truck-sized plaster that stood as a crumpled barrier between Mad Max and the enemies wouldn't hold for long.

"Sic 'em," Rudy hissed. While Fifty leapt forward, galloping toward the trio of threats, Rudy took aim and fired.

The first shot clinked off a piece of metal roof and missed. The second was true. It hit its target in the arm, knocking the weapon from his hands at the moment Fifty pounced.

Still advancing, Rudy moved to a second target and fired. The man was preoccupied with Marcus and never saw the bullet that drilled a hole through the side of his face. He stumbled, fired a reflexive, errant shot into the air, and dropped to a heap on the street.

Fifty was tearing through the first man when the final target turned his attention away from Marcus and toward the dog. The man was tall and lean, with a shaven head. He was muscular and his face carried with it the scowl of revenge. Rudy was certain the man still standing was the one called Junior.

The man swung one hundred eighty degrees and took aim at Fifty. He tightened the rifle to his shoulder and lowered the barrel at the dog. The rest of it unfolded in slow motion.

In the instant the man pulled his trigger, Marcus put a bullet in the back of his thigh. The man hitched at the impact of the wound and the shot sailed harmlessly off target.

Marcus pulled his trigger again, but he was empty, having used the five shots preloaded into the weapon. Off balance, the man managed to level the weapon again. He pressed it against his body.

Without hesitation, Rudy applied pressure to the trigger. He pulled it repeatedly. Twice, three times. Four.

They sliced through the air and into the man's body. Punch after punch, the shots knocked the man to one knee. He dropped his weapon.

Rudy rushed to the man's side and kicked the weapon away, arriving there a beat ahead of Marcus. Fifty, blood dripping from his jaws, climbed across the bodies and debris to stand next to his master. He was panting and his tail wagged in large arcing sweeps.

The man was on his back. His chest heaved. His eyes were wide and stared blankly toward the cloudless sky.

Marcus stepped in front of Rudy, patting his friend on the shoulder as he straddled the dying man and squatted over him. He poked a finger at one of the bullet holes and twisted it.

The man wailed and his eyes squeezed shut in agony. He coughed and blood leaked from the corner of his mouth.

"You Junior?" asked Marcus.

A wide smile eased across Junior's face as he reopened his eyes, blood framing his teeth. The grin answered Marcus's question. He wiped his finger on Junior's shirt and gripped a fistful of the fabric to pull the man's torso toward him.

He lowered his face closer to Junior and sneered. "This the revenge you were planning?"

Rudy inched closer. Fifty jumped a body and sniffed at Junior's dying body.

Junior's eyes fluttered. Garbled air leaked from his lungs.

Marcus yanked on the shirt. "Answer me," he said through his teeth. "Is this what you came for?"

Rudy put his hand on Marcus's back. "He's dead, Marcus."

Marcus shoved Junior backward and let go of the shirt. Junior's head slapped against the road, his neck twisted to the side. Blood drained from his mouth and pooled on the asphalt. Marcus stared at it leaching outward.

"It's over, Marcus," said Rudy. "You beat him."

Marcus used Junior's corpse to push himself to his feet. He lifted his eyes and surveyed the damage. Smoke rose from the buildings he'd blown up. Parts of men, their horses, and splintered debris were strewn onto the street as if washed ashore and abandoned as a swollen tide retreated into the sea. He faced Rudy and struggled to look him in the eyes.

"Thank you," he said. "You're the one who ended this. You, Lou, Dallas, the boys from next door, and Norma. You're the ones who ended it."

Rudy nodded faintly, looking at his boots. "Yeah," he said. "It was a team effort. But it doesn't matter. We did it. Like I said, it's over."

Marcus shook his head. "It's never over, Rudy. Not as long as I'm around. I put all of you at risk. All of you."

Rudy didn't disagree with Marcus. He didn't reassure Marcus everything was copacetic. He didn't offer sympathies or gratitude. The only thing breaking through the suddenly uncomfortable silence was Fifty's rhythmic panting.

CHAPTER 18

FEBRUARY 10, 2044, 2:00 PM
SCOURGE + 11 YEARS, 4 MONTHS
BAIRD, TEXAS

Rising twin plumes of smoke bloomed toward the early afternoon sky south of the interstate. Taskar tried to eyeball the distance. Not far, he deduced.

He eased the car toward an approaching exit and accelerated along the ramp. A folded, greenish sign pitched at forty-five degrees announced the location.

"Baird?" he questioned aloud, his voice echoing inside his mask. "Population one thousand five hundred and thirteen."

He chuckled at the number. He doubted Baird had seen that size population in more than a decade. He'd driven past the town countless times and never noticed it. He never even knew it was there, frankly, which would have led him to believe it was abandoned.

The twin towers of smoke told him otherwise. Someone was there. Good or bad, there was a human presence. There was someone he could warn, someone he could enlist to sound the alarm in Abilene and beyond.

His focus shifted between the smoke and the road directly in front of the hearse. Then a real alarm sounded.

The oxygenator at his chest was beeping. It was running low, the internal lithium ion battery signaling a low charge. He sucked in shallow breaths to conserve what was left. He had no clue how much longer the filter giving him clean, unspoiled air would last. At that point he'd have to remove his suit.

The first beads of nervous sweat populated his temples and between his nose and mouth. The back of his neck was damp again. He didn't think he had any fluids left in his system, let alone enough to produce an intensifying case of flop sweat.

He was nearly drenched inside his suit by the time he reached Fourth Street and approached the burned, smoking hulls of buildings that signaled him into Baird. There was one on either side of the street. Between them was the result of what he presumed to be explosions. Debris, body parts, and other unrecognizable things littered the narrow street.

Beyond the mangle stood five people, all of them armed. Two of them were aiming their rifles straight at him. Taskar pressed the brake, slid the hearse into park, turned off the engine, and sat motionless with both hands on the wheel.

He was trying to sip the air in the suit as the incessant beeping warned him of the failing air supplier. With the weapons pointed at him, and the motley crew of men and women marching toward him suspiciously, Taskar found it increasingly difficult not to swallow large gulps of air to calm his nerves. Other than that, he didn't move until the gruffest looking of the group approached the driver's side window. There was something familiar about him.

The man was tall, his sinewy muscles straining against the tight fabric of his worn, life-stained shirt. His broad shoulders made him appear taller than he probably was. His face was the roadmap of a hard life. There were wrinkles within wrinkles.

His brow appeared tattooed with worry lines that stretched in deep parallel lines from temple to temple. Thin crow's-feet fanned from the corners of his sad, deep-set eyes, white-radiating traces of the spots the sun hadn't reached. The sandpaper scruff that framed his mouth, chin, and jaw was a patchwork of brown, red, and white. His close-cropped hair was cut in the same severe manner he'd seen on the mercenaries that roamed the border.

The man tapped on the glass. "Roll down the window."

Taskar lowered the glass, then put his gloved hand back on the wheel. He could only imagine what this familiar-looking stranger was thinking—a hazmat-suited driver of a hearse in a nothing town ten years after the apocalypse.

The man narrowed his eyes, the purplish circles underneath them flattening. "Do I know you?"

That was not the question Taskar had expected. "Maybe," he said. "I think I've seen you somewhere."

The man stepped back and studied the hearse. Then his eyes widened with recognition. "The border. You were at the wall. Six or seven years ago. I saw you there."

Taskar still couldn't place the man, but he was likely right. Lots of people had seen Taskar at the wall. He'd seen lots of people too. During the final days of the Cartel, the few crossing points were teeming with those looking to leave and those looking for whatever meager existence they could eke out.

"Could be," he said. "Probably."

The man poked the barrel of his rifle at the beeping oxygenator. "What's that?"

Taskar swallowed. He could taste the air now. It was thicker and laden with the plastic of his hazmat suit. The others outside his hearse had drawn closer. A young woman with a sideways baseball cap twirled a knife on her fingers. A middle-aged man with a round, kind face stood with his rifle in one hand. There was a tattoo on his forearm Taskar couldn't read.

A woman who was likely his wife was at his shoulder. A young man who didn't seem to fit with the rest of them stood awkwardly off to one side. His weapon was shouldered and aimed through the windshield.

"What's that?" the man at the window repeated. "Why are you wearing that suit?"

The plastic of the suit crinkled and sweat traced Taskar's spine from his neck to the small of his back. "It's an oxygenator," he said. "It supplies filtered air into my mask. This suit…I'm…it's—"

"What are you protecting yourself from?"

"My name is Timothy Taskar."

"I didn't ask your name."

"I'm a courier," said Taskar. "I drive people where they need to be. Sometimes I take them from one side of the wall to the other."

The man took another step back and adjusted his rifle, nestling it against his shoulder. His eyes danced along the length of the hearse. They settled on Taskar and he shook his head. "You're not transporting anyone," he said, his pleasantly inquisitive tone gone. There was urgency and suspicion now. "You're alone. What. Are. You. Doing?"

The quartet in front of the hearse took another collective step closer. The man at the window held his ground.

"Get out of the vehicle," he barked. "Open the door and get out."

A well of nausea swelled in Taskar's gut. "Okay, but please don't shoot."

He shouldered his way out of the hearse and raised his hands above his head. The oxygenator was beeping faster. Clearly, it was almost out of air.

Taskar's knees were knocking. "I'm not sick."

"Where are your passengers?" asked the young woman with the knife. She was holding it by its grip now.

"They're dead," he said. "I killed them."

"I think you should shoot him, Marcus," said the young woman. "This whole thing stinks."

Taskar shook his head inside the hooded mask. "I had to," he said. "I didn't want to kill them. I did it to save lives. I came here because I need your help. I came here to warn you."

"Warn us about what?" asked the man named Marcus.

"The Scourge is back," he said. "And it's worse than it was before."

CHAPTER 19

Dr. Charles Morel stood in the control center with one hand tucked under his arm and the other scratching his chin. His eyes were glued to a pair of monitors, both displaying the interiors of holding rooms. Like all the others, the subjects inside those rooms were strapped to stainless steel examination tables. They were CV-18 and CV-19.

CV-18 was a man; CV-19 was a teenaged girl. Neither of them had come to the facility willingly. There weren't enough volunteers, so Dr. Sharp had ordered the "involuntary retrieval of noncompliant subjects."

Both subjects were injected with the YPH5N1 virus. Neither of them were showing symptoms anymore. Neither of them were sick, even though others would have been by now.

Morel picked up his tablet and tapped a combination of icons. An array of biometric data appeared on the monitors in front of him. Their eye patterns were normal, their glandular secretions appeared within range, and their heart rates, brain activity, and oxygen levels were all negative as far as an infection was concerned. He smiled to himself.

There had been other subjects who'd been slow to develop symptoms and hadn't yet become irretrievably ill. None, however, other than CV-18 and CV-19, were asymptomatic.

His stomach churned at the thought of having to explain it to Dr. Sharp. He reminded himself he knew the day would come where he'd have to answer for what he'd done, what he hadn't told Sharp about his work.

He rechecked the data. His eyes scanned the other monitors. They revealed the silent agony of the subjects inside their rooms. Some writhed in pain, others lay virtually lifeless, their arms and legs occasionally twitching.

Behind Morel, a series of clicks told him someone was coming in the lab. "Speak of the devil," he mumbled to himself.

He didn't have to look over his shoulder to know it was Sharp. She announced herself with a string of expletives.

"You better have good news for me," she warned. "I've had nothing but issues today."

Morel quickly tapped on his tablet and switched the monitor displays. CV-18 and CV-19 were replaced with cameras in the autopsy room. "What issues?" he asked, deflecting.

"We've managed to get one subject past the wall," she said, taking her place next to him in front of the monitor wall. "But it's dead. I've got no tracking on him. Even if we infect thousands with its rotting corpse, we'll never know about it. So, at least for testing purposes, it's a failure."

Morel raised an eyebrow. "Is that it?"

"No. We've got fourteen implants working here."

"Correct."

"And thirty-five more that we haven't inserted into a subject?"

Morel checked the tablet. "Yes."

"We've deployed how many into the field?"

"One," said Morel. "CV-01."

Sharp bristled. "I thought there were others," she snapped. "You told me there were others. The AI told me there were other trackers in the field north of the wall."

Morel shook his head. "No. The plan, as you explained it, was to deploy CV-01 and CV-02. CV-02 died. We've not readied any of the other subjects for deployment."

"Then why are there trackers in the field?"

"We injected trackers into the general population months ago," he said. "We needed to test the tracking programs and the injectables themselves. They've been active for at least ninety days. Don't you remem—"

"Of course I remember," said Sharp with a look that told Morel she'd forgotten. She cursed and narrowed her eyes. "What's with those monitors?"

Morel rubbed his chin. "What about them?"

"Why are we looking at the autopsy rooms? I've had my fill of Bolnoy."

"I—they..."

Sharp glared at Morel. The tight bun at the top of her head pulled her eyes outward, as if she were a large cat. "Change the monitors," she hissed. "Show me something I care about."

Morel switched the screens back to the only options he had. CV-18 and CV-19 reappeared. Morel kept his eyes on his tablet, pretending to be engrossed in something.

"They don't look sick," said Sharp. "Are they sick?"

"Let me check their vitals."

Morel punched the tablet. "They appear normal."

Sharp was uncomfortably close to Morel. "What do you mean normal?" she asked. "Were they injected? Have we followed the protocol?"

Morel nodded but kept his eyes on the tablet. "Yes. We followed the protocol. Both subjects are carrying the virus."

Sharp took a step closer to the monitors, forcefully brushing against Morel. "Yet they're asymptomatic? No fever? No elevated heart rates? No elevated leukocytes?"

"No."

"How long since they were exposed?"

"Five days."

"Five?"

Morel nodded. "Yes. They appear…"

"Appear what?"

"Immune."

Sharp sucked in a deep breath. "I guess we knew we wouldn't have one hundred percent efficacy. Still, I would have preferred not to have two seemingly healthy people unaffected. That doesn't bode well."

"It's only two," said Morel.

"Yet it's two," she said. "Not one. Do we know why yet? What makes them special?"

"We haven't started on that."

"Get started on it, then," said Sharp. "Euthanize them and send them to Bolnoy. We need to know ASAP where the weakness is. Then we can further enhance the virus."

Morel looked up from the screen. "Euthanize them?"

Sharp shrugged. "How else did you think we would isolate their defense mechanisms? Their immunity?"

"I didn't—"

Sharp cackled. "Of course you didn't. For as brilliant as you are, Morel, you're an absolute moron. Euthanize them, get them to Bolnoy, and deploy another subject south of the wall. In fact, deploy three."

"That will take a few days. It took us four days to ready the deployment for CV-01."

"Do it in two," she said. She waved at the monitor wall. "Get those two to Bolnoy before the end of the day."

Morel sheepishly nodded again. Sharp grumbled something about his intellect and marched off. The door buzzed and clicked behind her. He exhaled as if he'd been holding his breath underwater for too long.

He'd always been afraid of Sharp. It wasn't because of her acerbic personality or her aggressive scientific pursuits, which were often in direct contrast to his beliefs. It was because of the sway she held over him, the ways in which she held his life in the palm of her bony, icy hands.

Morel, like most of the people working for the government after the Scourge, did so because of the benefits it provided their families. For years, those living outside Texas had trouble maintaining a subsistence level of survival.

As the government regrouped, as it rebuilt or reengaged a virtually abandoned infrastructure, more and more jobs became available. They were, however, mostly connected to the government itself. It was a post-Scourge new deal that saw men and women fixing roads, manning power plants, and ultimately building the wall. Using the model designed and constructed a quarter of a century earlier, more than a thousand plague survivors erected the wall around Texas in eighteen months. In some places it was a solid, twenty-foot limestone edifice. In others, it was a patchwork of metal, wood, and concertina wire. It kept the Cartel inside, for the most part, and prevented able-bodied men and women from abandoning the new order of things on the outside.

Charles Morel wasn't a prepper. He hadn't had the foresight to anticipate the coming end-of-the-world-as-he-knew-it. There was no compound in the Smokey Mountains. He didn't farm or know how to make candles out of beeswax. He wasn't an expert marksman.

He was like most of the survivors. He needed work. He needed running water and electricity. He needed food. He was dependent on others. A job with the government, no matter how distasteful it might seem, was the best path toward that end.

Thus, when an opportunity to work for the CDC in Atlanta came available, he took it. He moved his depressed wife and four surviving, emaciated children to Atlanta, Georgia, from Raleigh, North Carolina.

He'd worked for a biotech firm in what had been the Research Triangle Park. It, along with every other job in the RTP, had evaporated. Companies that might have been able to isolate and eradicate the Scourge, as they had so many other diseases, folded when most of their leadership died. Morel had no choice but to move.

The change in their lives was immediate. The CDC had sent them a large hydrogen-fueled van in which to transport themselves and their belongings to a new home in Atlanta. They were given a spacious loft in Buckhead five miles from Morel's new job.

There was electricity. Hot and cold water flowed from the faucets with a wave of their hands. They had a large refrigerator and freezer stocked with fresh fruits and vegetables.

"I haven't seen a fresh peach in two years," Morel's wife had said. A smile had shone across her sullen face for the first time since they'd lost their twins to the Scourge.

In the bedrooms there were clean linens on the queen-sized beds. Clothing, in the right sizes, hung in the walk-in closets. The toilets flushed.

In the coming weeks and months, his wife returned to the happy, show tune-humming woman with whom doctoral student Charlie Morel had fallen in love so many years earlier. His children put on weight. They slept without nightmares. They read books and played chess.

Morel went to work each day with the belief he was working on a vaccine for the Scourge. He was part of an elite team of researchers who'd come from across the country to prevent another outbreak of the disease. They'd gotten close. Building upon German research, the team, led by Dr. Gwendolyn Sharp, had managed to incorporate modular nanoparticles into what they called an "adaptable vaccine." As a disease evolved, the vaccine would learn and adapt to the changing viral structure. It seemed to have worked. Then the focus changed.

Sharp had come into the lab and told her team they were shifting the focus from vaccination to enhancement. She'd told them that using their nanotechnology to take the existing virus and make it more lethal was a more urgent goal than preventing the existing virus from reemerging. She'd also told them it was none of their business, yet, as to why the shift was occurring.

Some on the team quit. They refused the new assignment. They were stripped of their jobs, their homes, their refrigerators stocked full of chilled produce, and their flushing toilets.

Morel had gone home more than once to explain to his wife he couldn't keep his job. He couldn't do what they wanted him to do. He couldn't create a monster worse than the one he'd spent so much time seeking to destroy.

He also couldn't bring himself to tell her.

Life was difficult enough in a rebuilt world. Remove the trappings of a government job and it would have become unbearable again.

Night after night, week after week, he prepared himself to drop the bomb. He'd invariably failed to deliver. Then one day he was in his lab, taking his time with a new batch of samples, when Sharp marched in and ushered his assistants out of the space.

"I know what you're doing," she'd said flatly.

Morel had looked up from his microscope and squinted at her. "You mean epithelial analysis?"

She'd slithered toward him. "No. I mean I know you're dragging your feet. You're here, true. You didn't leave like the others with your skills. But you're not engaged. You're not proceeding with the enthusiasm needed for our project."

Morel had squeezed his eyebrows, hoping to convey some sense of confusion, some nonverbal denial of her accusations. He'd shaken his head. "Of course I am," he'd said. "I'm here all the time. We've made excellent progress and I—"

Sharp had raised her hand to stop him. "Save it. I looked at your work. I've seen the retardation of your *excellent* progress. If this is the best you can do, then you might as well pack up your boxes. You might as well tell your wife what you've been dreading."

Morel had sat up straight in his seat. He'd pulled back his shoulders and swallowed hard.

The corner of Sharp's mouth had curled up into a nasty half-smile. "We know," she'd said, "because we track you. We track everyone. That inoculation you got when you first arrived here? It contained a biometric tracker with satellite mapping."

The color had drained from Morel's face. What else did they know? What else had they surveilled?

"Every night since we first told you about the enhanced mission, the importance of this new direction, you've walked your five miles home and then traveled around your building for another hour before heading up to your home. You pace back and forth. You start for the entrance, pause, and then retrace your steps to the sidewalk."

"You're tracking me?"

"Of course. We also have cameras in your building, on your building, on the street corners. Dr. Morel, let me be clear. We don't invest in people the way we've invested in you, and your delicate wife, and your young, now healthy children, without insurance. Without having the ability to track our investment. I'd hate to think we'd need to sell short your stock."

Morel had scratched his head and rubbed the back of his neck. The tension in his muscles had built like a rubber band stretched to its limits.

"Do you understand?" she'd said. "Do you think your wife would understand, should I have the same conversation with her?"

Morel had clenched his teeth together. His fingers had curled on the table, his nails scratching at the cold black granite surface. He'd nodded his understanding and Sharp had left him alone. When his team had returned to the lab, asking him questions, he hadn't answered them and had implored them to work harder.

He'd wondered so many times since that day if he'd made the better decision by staying. Would they have been better off taking their lumps and moving on to something else, to somewhere else? Now he knew, despite what it meant about his morality and the eternal destiny of his soul, he'd made a good choice.

"Euthanize them," she'd said to him.

Euthanize them.

CHAPTER 20

FEBURARY 10, 2044, 3:45 PM
SCOURGE + 11 YEARS, 4 MONTHS
BAIRD, TEXAS

"Keep him back," said Norma. "If he's taking off that suit, I don't want him anywhere near me or Rudy."

The hearse-driving, hazmat-suit-wearing stranger who called himself Taskar had already removed his hooded mask.

Everyone else save Marcus was thirty yards from him. Rudy and Dallas had their weapons leveled at Taskar. Lou was picking her fingernails with the sharpened tip of one of her knives.

Marcus figured the suit was more dangerous than the man. He'd been breathing filtered air. The bloodstained suit was exposed to the elements, though.

"Take your gloves off last," Marcus warned. "Don't touch anything with your bare hands. Otherwise, I can't help you."

The stranger removed his suit methodically, if not with difficulty. It took several minutes for him to disrobe. Marcus watched to make sure Taskar didn't touch the exterior of the suit with his bare skin.

When the visitor was finally down to his sweat-soaked boxers and undershirt, he shrugged. "What now?"

"We gotta burn that suit," said Marcus. "Then we gotta take you to get some clothes. You got any matches?"

"In the hearse," he said. "On the passenger seat."

"Probably should have thought of that before you took off the suit, genius," said Lou.

Marcus shot Lou a glance. "All right, then," he said. "You can use a stick or something to dump the suit in the building over there. There are hot spots that'll burn it."

Taskar nodded, his teeth chattering, and walked over to the char of debris half a block away. His boxers hung low on his narrow hips, his thin shirt flapped against his skin in the slight breeze that threatened to strengthen in the late afternoon.

He picked up a shard of the splintered pine framing stud and dragged it back to the hazardous suit. Using the wood, he managed to fish the crumpled, potentially infectious plastic from the road, carry it over to smoldering cinders, and fling it onto a healthy flicker of remnant flames.

He repeated the journey two more times and then heaved the wood into the hot mess. He crossed his arms over his body, cupping his elbows with his hands. Marcus motioned to him and led him toward the jail.

The others kept their distance. Norma held Rudy's free hand. Rudy whistled at Fifty to stay at his side. Dallas strode alongside Lou, his long legs not having to work hard to keep pace with her. All of them watched the stranger with suspicion.

Marcus moved closer to Taskar. "So you're telling me they've concocted some mega virus and they want to release it here? They want to kill everybody south of the wall?"

Taskar, his teeth chattering and his skin goose pimpled, nodded. "It's awful. It's worse than the Scourge. I've seen it. They call it YPH5N1. I think it's the plague mixed with swine flu."

Marcus rubbed his hand along the back of his head. The others pretended not to pay attention to their conversation. They maintained their distance, but each of them carried their heads to one side as they walked, as if to inch their ears closer to what the visitor said.

Taskar described the bloody deaths, the mortality rate, the high-tech labs, the snipers on top of the CDC headquarters, the evil woman in charge. He stopped walking when he explained how he'd put Lomas out of his misery. His chin quivered, but not from the cold.

"I've seen a lot," said Taskar, his voice quavering. "I've never seen anything like that. There was so much blood."

Marcus stepped close to Taskar and put his hand on his cold, damp shoulder. Behind him, Norma gasped. Taskar's eyes fluttered and looked at Marcus's hand.

"You're touching me?" he asked.

Marcus squeezed Taskar's shoulder. "I figure if it's my time, it's my time," he said. "I survived the Scourge. If I'm meant to survive this new thing, I will. If I'm not, then God actually likes me."

Marcus smiled. Taskar's eyes twitched and the vertical lines that ran between his eyebrows above his nose deepened with confusion.

"C'mon," Marcus said. "We need to get you dressed."

* * *

Taskar was wearing an oversized Dallas Cowboys T-shirt and a pair of loose-fitting Dickies. The shirt, faded and bleached free of its original blue color, hung below his elbows and low around his neck. The pants were rolled over at his ankles. He held them up at the waist with one of his hands as he stepped from the jail and stood on the low stoop facing the street.

Inside, Marcus stood opposite Lou. She was against a wall, one foot flat on the floor and the other crossed in front at her ankle.

"Why can't I go with you?" she asked. "You know as well as I do you'd be dead five times over if it weren't for me."

"I'd suggest poor marksmanship is more likely the reason I'm alive," Marcus said with a wry smile. "If any of those men could shoot, I'd be buried in our version of Boot Hill."

Lou searched Marcus's eyes. He could tell she wanted to tell him something that would change his mind. They were both certain there was nothing she could say.

"You really think you and that weird chauffeur dude can stop some big army up there?" she asked with a tone that suggested she knew he couldn't. "Really, Marcus? You're not Superman."

"Superman, huh?"

"There was a comics section in the library," she said.

"Not a Wonder Woman fan?"

"She's okay," said Lou. "But her whole origin story doesn't match with the history of the real Amazons. I couldn't buy into it."

"But an alien from a pretend planet is believable?"

"You're trying to change the subject."

"Maybe."

"You're going to die, you know."

Marcus sucked in a deep breath. He was her mirror image against the wall and he looked her in the eyes. "I've been dead a long time," he said. "Lola tried to resurrect me and I suppose it worked for a little while. But like Frankenstein, all I tend to do is cause havoc. I bring death with me. I'm selfish in that pursuit too."

"Marcus, you—"

"Let me finish."

Lou tightened the fold of her arms across her chest.

"In trying to save my own hide, I've seen too many others risk their own lives," he said. "You included. Rudy, Norma. It's as plain as day. Everybody here is better off without me."

Lou opened her mouth to speak. Marcus raised an eyebrow. She scowled.

"I'll be fine," he said. "A man knows when it's time, when he's reached the place where he lets go. I've been holding on too long."

They stood there in silence for a moment. "Go ahead," said Marcus. "Your turn."

"First of all," she said, "I wish we still had Google, because I'd type in that speech of yours word for word to find out what lousy movie you stole it from. And second, Frankenstein was the scientist not the monster."

"What?"

"You said you were like Frankenstein. You're not. You're like the monster. Frankenstein's monster. I read the book. Mary Shelley wrote it."

Marcus smirked. "Al Pacino isn't anywhere in it, is he?"

Lou raised a snarky eyebrow and smirked. "Who?"

"Never mind. Bottom line is, I'm leaving. Once I stop the people who want to rain down a plague on us, I'll send word I'm okay. If you don't hear from me…"

Lou uncrossed her ankles and looked at her feet. "You're leaving me here, then," she said. "I don't get a choice."

"You've got too much to live for. Besides, Rudy can't be sheriff without you."

Lou walked away from Marcus, her hand trailing along the wide wooden door frame as she stepped out into the sunlight.

Marcus followed. Taskar was standing on the stoop outside the open door. Marcus brushed past him, patting him on the back, and eyed the twenty-five people now standing in a loose semicircle on the opposite side of the road. Along with Norma, Rudy, Lou, and Dallas, nearby residents had come out of hiding to survey the carnage on their Main Street. Marcus recognized every one of them. They stood as if waiting for the preacher to take the pulpit.

He scanned the crowd, pausing on those closest to him. Lou was standing beside Fifty, her eyes narrowed. She was fidgeting with her hair, adjusting her ball cap.

"Here's the long and short of it," Marcus said to the group. "I'm leaving."

Murmurs of discontent rumbled through the assembly, though Marcus noticed Norma didn't react. Lou lowered her hands to her knives, rubbing her thumbs along the grips.

"Taskar here tells me they're sending more sick people this way," he said. "They want to thin the herd, so to speak, and make the land ripe for the taking. I'm going to stop them."

"How do you know he's telling you the truth?" asked Dallas.

"Same reason I figured you were," said Marcus. "Anyone who comes here with bad intentions tends to let that be known straight up."

He nodded toward the still-smoldering heaps of debris several blocks east, the acrid smell of which had drifted westward with the breeze. The gathered crowd followed his eyes toward the thinning, upward trails of smoke then drifted back to him.

"They want to kill us," said Marcus. "They want our land, our resources. We can't let that happen."

The crowd grumbled again. Husbands and wives exchanged concerns. Children clung to their mothers' legs. Teenagers cussed.

"Taskar's going with me," said Marcus, silencing the group. "He knows the ins-and-outs. He's got the fuel. We've got explosives we didn't use. We've got the radios. Only thing we need is a vehicle that works. Can't take the hearse."

"Are you coming back?" asked an American Gothic-looking man wearing overalls and a straw hat. His hands were dipped into deep pockets at his hips. He wore snakeskin boots that narrowed into points at the toes. Marcus couldn't remember his name. Jim? Tim? Tom?

He glanced at Lou. "No," he said. "It's a one-way trip for me. If it all works out, Taskar here will likely head back. If nothing else, he'll tell you what's what."

JimTimTom leaned back on his boot heels. "If you're not coming back, then I got a Ford F-150 you can take. Should run okay. I got it from a man who smuggled it from north of the wall two years ago."

"Thank you," said Marcus.

"No need to thank me," said JimTimTom. "If you taking the truck means you take your violence with you and don't come back, it's a more than even trade."

"Sounds fair to me."

Lou laughed and muttered something under her breath.

"You got something to say?" asked JimTimTom.

Lou shrugged. "Yeah." She pointed toward Marcus. "That man over there kept you safe for more than a year. He ended the Cartel. He—"

"He nearly got all of us killed today," said the farmer. "And last week. And the month before that." He stepped from the crowd and then faced them. "We only asked him to be sheriff 'cause we were afraid of what might be coming. We should have been afraid of *him*. If he leaves, the never-ending rot in my gut leaves with him. I'd give him ten trucks if it meant he didn't come back."

Rudy stepped forward, letting go of Norma's hand. "That's a bit much, Harold," he said, getting the man's name right. "Marcus saved my wife. That's why I wanted him here. He's a man who won't stop until the bad men are dead and gone."

"Really?" asked Harold.

"Really."

"Who's to say *he's* not a bad man?"

Rudy tightened his hands into fists. "Marcus Battle is a good man," he said through his teeth. "Not a one of you people got kidnapped or robbed or killed while he ran this town. Not a one."

"Not a one of us could sleep sound neither," Harold countered.

Rudy started to step aggressively toward Harold, but Norma caught his arm and stopped him. He looked back at her and she seemed to calm him with her eyes. Rudy's shoulders relaxed, his hands unwound.

Norma looked across the street at Marcus. "I don't know what we're fighting about," she said. "Marcus is leaving. Harold is giving him his truck. It's been decided. I think Marcus knows his value here, and he knows his value elsewhere. Don't you, Marcus?"

In that moment, Marcus knew the choice to leave wasn't really his. Even if he'd chosen to stay, to fight the next threat and the one after that, the people of Baird wouldn't have wanted it. He'd told Lou he was a walking plague, a man whose worth was measured by the number of graves he dug and the bodies he dumped into them. He hadn't stopped to consider that everyone else felt that same way.

Lou had agreed with him, except to correct his literary reference. Rudy had defended his choice to invite Marcus into town, he hadn't defended Marcus. And Norma, the woman who he'd left alone that morning with nothing more than a handgun and a radio transceiver, the woman who had reluctantly agreed to be the backstop, the emergency failsafe should everything go wrong, was looking at him with eyes that told him he was loved but no longer welcome.

He looked at Lou and smiled. "At least everybody is on the same page. We best get that truck and head out. Who knows how long it'll be until they send the virus south again?"

* * *

The sun was low on the horizon, casting varying shades of orange and deep reds that colored the thin clouds building in the west. It looked like the sky was on fire.

Marcus studied the palette and tried to freeze the memory in his mind. A gentle breeze brushed past him and he blinked. It was time to go. The truck was fueled up, and there were extra tanks strapped to the roof. They had food, water, and plenty of ammunition for their rifles.

He stood between the door and driver's seat, one foot on the running board, the other in the dirt driveway in front of Harold's ranch-style farmhouse. The window was down and Lou had her fingers curled over the door frame. Rudy was beside her and Norma beside him. Fifty was sitting patiently behind the trio. The dog yawned and licked its chops.

"You're driving?" asked Lou.

"At first," said Marcus. "Taskar needs some sleep."

"You know where you're going?" she asked.

"Roughly."

"We'll take good care of her," Rudy said. "She'll be okay."

Marcus chuckled. "She's more likely to take care of you."

"Thanks for everything," said Rudy. "I mean that."

"I know," said Marcus.

Norma stepped forward and put her hand on Marcus's. She rubbed it with her thumb. "I do owe my life to you. You know that."

Marcus nodded.

"You were right," she said.

Marcus tilted his head to one side. "How so?"

"Rudy is the best man for the job," she said. "Lou will help him. Dallas too."

"Good," said Marcus. "At least *somebody* listens to me."

Norma slid her hand from his and led Rudy away from the truck. "You need a moment," she said.

Lou adjusted her ball cap then took it off. She scratched her head, raked her fingers from the front to the back of her tangled mop, and puffed her cheeks. Her saucer eyes blinked a couple of times. They were glossy.

She held the cap in her hand, bending the brim into a curve. It was stained with sweat, dirt, and blood that had faded to brown.

Marcus pushed himself from the door and eased around to stand in front of Lou. She looked up at him, thin pools of tears welling above her lower eyelids. She let the air out from her cheeks with a popping sound.

"I was going to give you the hat," she said, her voice soft and unsure. "Something...to remember me by."

"You don't have to do that," said Marcus.

Lou smiled through her tears. "Oh, I'm not."

Marcus smiled. He fought hard against the thick knot swelling in his throat. Lou twirled strands of hair around her index finger.

"My hair's too much to handle," she said. "Plus, the hat was my dad's. He loved baseball. Loved the Astros. Hated the designated hitter, whatever that was. Thought artificial turf was blasphemous."

"I don't like goodbyes," said Marcus. "I'm not good at them."

Lou shrugged. "I think anyone who *is* good at them is a raging jerk."

Marcus stuffed his hands into his pockets. "I should be good at them, then. I'm not the—"

"Stop. Enough with the 'woe is me' baloney. We all know you're mentally disturbed. We all know deep down you like killing people to settle some score. It's okay, Marcus. I love you for who you are."

Marcus bit the inside of his cheek. He tried swallowing past the lump but couldn't. His eyes burned and the tears came streaming down his cheeks. He pulled his hands from his pockets, stepped forward, and wrapped his arms around Lou. He squeezed her into his chest and put a hand on the back of her head, his fingers spread wide.

"I love you too, Lou," he said, his voice cracking.

With the hat still in one hand, Lou reached around Marcus's back and hugged him. He could feel her quietly sobbing through the rise and fall of her back. They stood there for what felt simultaneously forever and not long enough.

Marcus pulled back and slid his hands to her shoulders. "Be good." He winked. "Do good. Start every day with those two goals and you'll be set."

Lou wiped her nose and then her eyes with the backs of her hands. She put the hat on her head and straightened it, reached into her waistband, and pulled out one of her knives. She balanced it in her palm and then spun it around to hold the blade between her thumb and fingers.

"Here," she said. "Take it."

Marcus shook his head. "No. Those knives mean everything to you."

Lou extended her hand, jabbing him in the chest with the butt of the grip. "Take it," she insisted.

Marcus gently wrapped his fingers around the grip and took it from Lou's grasp. He tried forcing a smile, but it felt awkward on his face.

Lou tipped her cap. She walked away from Battle, her boots crunching on the thin, uneven layer of crushed granite that mixed with the dirt. Fifty shifted his weight from one paw to the other then bounded toward Lou. He eased alongside her as she walked, herding her toward the paved road at the end of the driveway.

She turned onto the street and then disappeared behind a barn that blocked Marcus's view. He slid into the driver's seat of the Ford and placed the knife in the center console beside him.

"That was uncomfortable," said Taskar. He was reclining in the passenger's seat. The oversized shirt was bunched around his waist underneath the seatbelt he'd already pulled across his chest. He had one eye closed. The other looked warily at Marcus.

"For you and me both," said Marcus. He pushed the ignition and the engine whined. He slipped the truck into gear and eased it along the driveway, adjusting the side-view mirror. When he reached the end of the drive, he slowed and turned left onto the street. He accelerated onto the pavement and fought the urge to look in the rearview mirror.

It was many miles to Atlanta. With luck they'd be there by nightfall the next day.

CHAPTER 21

Gwendolyn Sharp pressed her face against the cold glass of a floor-to-ceiling window in what used to pass as a conference room on the third floor. The lights were off, and she was alone. For the first time in weeks, it was raining. The drops were large and slapped against the glass. Strobes of lightning flickered in the distance, momentarily lighting the thick, dark clouds.

From her vantage point, the remains of the city spread out toward the horizon. There were clusters of streetlights marking the areas where people lived and worked. There were the pockets of black where others, the undesirables with little skill or ingenuity, huddled in ramshackle leftovers devoid of basic creature comforts.

Sometimes, when she stood with her face or hands touching the smooth pane, the orange flicker of barrel fires or outdoor pits glowed where the "less-thans" cooked their food or boiled their water.

She imagined those dark patches as the whole of the area south of the wall, the place once called Texas. Despite her husband's job on the wall, she'd never been south, not since the Scourge.

Her husband had taken her once to a Department of Defense

conference in Dallas. They'd visited the spot where President Kennedy had been assassinated. She'd stood on the knoll, looking up at a sixth-floor window in the old book repository. She'd wondered how a conspiracy so vast could work, how the many moving parts all had to work together, like one gear grinding into the teeth of the next and the next.

Wide-eyed, wiry-haired theorists had stood on the corners outside the repository, spouting their versions of the events that had changed the course of the nation. Some had believed the government was behind it. Others had proclaimed it was the Russians. Still more had blamed the mob. One of them had proudly displayed color photographs of the dead president's flayed scalp, which he'd insisted was proof of more than one shooter.

Of course, she now knew, all of them were right. And none of them were. Conspiracies were everything and nothing all at once. They were complicated webs more than machines, she'd come to learn. She rolled her cheek on the glass and caught another flash of lightning. A bolt forked from the clouds and shot toward the ground along the horizon. She waited for the distant roll of the thunder across the sky and then felt it vibrate the glass against her cheek and it rumbled.

The people living south of the wall, from everything she'd heard, were savages. Every last one of them.

They lived on canyon floors, battled like gladiators in a football stadium, and killed each other for sport. They ran drugs and women, sought vengeance with impunity. Only some had electricity, and fewer had access to the working fuel refineries just outside the wall in Louisiana. Their food was what they caught in traps or with bows and arrows. They were lawless and uncivilized.

"They don't deserve what they have," she muttered. "They're better off dead."

She was doing them a favor, she rationalized. Her new hybridized virus was their salvation. It was putting them out of their misery.

Who would want to live south of the wall? That wasn't living. It was Hell. She was sure of it.

Sheets of rain were blowing diagonally in the wind in a streetlight almost directly below her. They strummed against the glass at her face.

Sharp envisioned her husband overseeing the construction of the wall. She imagined him directing the digging and trenching and stacking. She could hear his deep, resonant voice in her head.

"Texas is overrun by gangs," he'd told her when she'd protested his leaving. "They're going to come north and destabilize what little control we've got. Troops are spread thin. Supplies are scarce. People need work; they need security. We've reached a deal," he'd said. "We keep them inside and they stop people from coming north, taking what few opportunities we've got. Texas is full of desperados, pure and simple."

He'd died six months later when he'd offered his evening rations to a seemingly needy family looking for help. They'd taken his food, thanked him, and then shot him dead. They stole his clothes, his boots, his sidearm, and his watch. Sharp had given him that watch.

Savages. Every last one of them.

Her husband vanished as a phone on the conference table warbled its electronic tone. An accompanying red light flashed in the darkness. The AI voice announced the caller. It was a superior. He wanted an update.

"Hello, sir," she said, clearing her throat.

The responding voice was hollow, as if in a tunnel. *"Sharp,"* said the man, *"I've got the senior team here. You're on speaker. Everyone has clearance. The line is secure. Answer my questions freely. Understood?"*

"Yes, sir."

"Where are we? I need a sitrep."

"We've deployed the first subject," she said, stepping closer to the table at the center of the room.

"Without success, I understand," said the superior. *"Is that correct?"*

"That's correct," she admitted, "but we expected setbacks. That's why we are set to deploy another ten within the next forty-eight hours."

Another voice from the call, one farther from the phone, chimed in. *"We've seen the video of those fully infected. Impressive. These are people who were immune to the Scourge and yet succumbed rapidly to your YPH5N1. Are there any subjects who are not susceptible?"*

"Yes," Sharp replied. "We hypothesized the mortality rate at seventy-nine percent, which is some thirteen percent greater than the Scourge. We've seen two who are currently asymptomatic. We've also had some who deteriorate very quickly, faster than expected."

"It's a work in progress, then?" asked the superior.

"Yes."

"How much of the hybrid virus do you have? That is to say, is there any redundancy?"

Sharp paused. There wasn't any redundancy. There was the one lab, the one freezer full of viral samples, and there were those infected. Until they were released into the wild and the disease spread, their years of work were housed in a single secure location.

"All of the samples are in-house, sir," she said. "That was the protocol. You wanted to contain the threat. No need to risk infecting innocents."

"Yes," he said. *"Very good. We'll check back in twenty-four hours once you've deployed the additional subjects. We're anxious to learn about the field tests. We need Texas back. We need the land, the oil, the gas. We can't do it without significantly depleting their population."*

"Yes, sir."

The phone chirped and the call ended.

Sharp walked back to the window and touched it with her fingers. The rain was inaudible now, the strain of the wind against the window gone. Faraway clouds strobed. The storm was moving away.

"Dr. Sharp?"

She looked into the glass at Morel's reflection. He was standing in the doorway, his hands folded in front of him. He was wet.

"What?" she asked over her shoulder.

"Three transport drivers have arrived," he said. "And I have teams loading the patien—er, subjects into their vehicles."

"Good," she said. "They have fuel?"

"Yes."

"Suits?"

"Getting them fitted now."

"Any of them having second thoughts?"

"No," he said. "They're excited about the opportunity to deliver weapons of mass destruction."

She looked at Morel. "You were outside?"

He looked at his soaked lab coat. "I was. I helped with intake for the drivers. Each of them is assigned an armed guard, by the way. The vehicles, one of which is a hearse, are located in the sally port."

"What are their destinations?"

Morel counted them out with his fingers. "One of them is going to Houston, actually an enclave north of Houston called The Woodlands. They have some high-density housing we think will spread the disease quickly. Plano, that's near Dallas. The last one is going to San Antonio. A lot of the former Cartel members are there. It's also a population center, relatively speaking."

Sharp nodded. "Houston, Dallas, and San Antonio," she said. "Exactly what I would have done."

"Thank you," said Morel.

"What about the subjects who aren't sick?"

"What about them?"

"Did you do as I asked?"

Morel used one hand to brace himself against the door frame. He looked down and nodded almost imperceptibly. "They're with Bolnoy. He's doing as you asked. He complained about the added work, but he's doing it."

"Good," she said. "When are the drivers leaving?"

"Before midnight. The front should be moving out and the skies should clear soon. They'll get something to eat and then head out."

"Thank you, Charles," Sharp said. "I'll see you downstairs."

Morel started to back away from the doorway.

"Charles?" she called.

"Yes, Dr. Sharp?"

"How is your wife? Your children? How are they? Do they need anything extra? Toilet paper? Soap? Toaster pastries? I know your children like toaster pastries."

Morel stuffed his hands into his lab coat pockets and drew them together, closing the jacket at his waist. The look on his face, his skeptical scowl, told Sharp he didn't believe she was sincere.

"I mean it," she added. "Anything they need."

He shook his head. "We're fine, Dr. Sharp," he said flatly, without a hint of gratitude. "We have everything we need."

She smiled. "Fine then. I'll see you downstairs. Let me know when the teams are ready to depart. Don't hesitate to involve me if we have issues, as we did with the one who drove the hearse."

"Of course," he said. "I won't hesitate."

CHAPTER 22

Marcus took a swig of water and wiped his mouth with the back of his arm. Although the rain had lessened to a drizzle, he'd kept the wipers working against the windshield. There was something about the rhythm of the rubber blades swiping on the glass that kept him focused, though in the back of his mind, he kept trying to place where he'd seen Taskar before. He knew the man was somehow familiar, he just couldn't place it. It was like a word on the tip of his tongue. He was even sure he'd seen the hearse before too.

He'd driven the majority of the trip. Taskar had handled the tricky part crossing the wall. The rest of it was easy. Marcus was surprised by the condition of the roads north of the wall. They weren't racetrack smooth, but they were light years better than the rutted crumble of highways that crisscrossed Texas. Still, a trip that shouldn't have taken much longer than sixteen or seventeen hours had taken more than twenty-four.

They'd stopped three times to refuel. Each time Marcus restarted the truck, he held his breath until the engine stopped coughing and purred. Taskar didn't talk much. Marcus couldn't tell if he was the quiet type or if he'd been through something he didn't want to relive. He figured it might be a little bit of both, so he didn't push.

The first sign of real civilization, with electricity and traffic, was Birmingham, Alabama. Military convoys had passed them, some SUVs too. A couple on a motorcycle had whirred past along the shoulder. It wasn't rush-hour in pre-Scourge Los Angeles by any means, but given the horse-and-buggy life south of the wall, this was gridlock.

Birmingham was nothing compared to Atlanta. The city, its blacktop highways glistening from the rain, and its pockets of yellow and white lights dotting the high-rises that rose above the invisible parks below, was magnificent.

Marcus gripped the wheel with both hands, his eyes scanning the spires of the tallest of the buildings. He hadn't seen anything like it in a long time. He couldn't actually remember how long it had been.

"Wow," he said under his breath, his eyes skittering from one side of the highway to the other and back.

"It's not as impressive as it seems," said Taskar. He yawned, stretched his body like a cat, and pulled up his seat back.

Marcus shifted lanes. "How so?"

"There's every bit as much poverty and crime here as there is south of the wall," Taskar said. "It's just disguised by all the nice shiny things that still work."

"Maybe," Marcus said, "but they have power. They have an infrastructure. There are jobs."

"Only if you're connected," said Taskar. "The government is a monopoly. If you're in with them, you can live decent. I had no connections for the longest time. Being a former Dweller, it wasn't easy. I might as well have been a farmer in…where are you from?"

"I'm from outside Rising Star," said Marcus. "But you're talking about Baird. The town is called Baird."

"Baird," Taskar repeated.

Then it hit Marcus. Taskar. A Dweller. He *had* met him.

"You were a Dweller?"

"Yeah, but I left. I didn't agree with the politics of where they wanted to take things."

"You've been a transporter for how long?"

"Seven, maybe eight years," he said. "Could be nine. I've lost count."

"Where'd you live?"

"North of the wall. Different places. I'd make trips back and forth. That's how I made money, you know, smuggling people from one side to the other."

"Did you ever transport a woman named Ana? She had a baby named Penny."

Taskar shrugged. "Could be. I moved a lot of people. A lot of babies."

"We've met," said Marcus. "Wichita Falls. You were in that hearse. You'd moved Ana and Penny to the wall. There was a backlog. They made us cross together, but you stayed behind."

Taskar moved his body to more directly face Marcus. His face contorted such that Marcus could almost see the sparks in his memory trying to fire.

"I remember you," said Marcus. "It was after the Cartel fell to the Dwellers."

Taskar shook his head. "It sounds familiar," he said. "And I recognize you, but I don't remember that woman and her kid. Sorry. I'm guessing you didn't make it, since you're here with me now?"

Marcus gripped the wheel with both hands. A vision of Penny's lifeless body flashed in his head. He shook his head. "We made it," he said. "But Ana drowned. My friend Lola and I adopted her kid. We went back to Rising Star. We raised her."

"Whoa," said Taskar. "That's crazy. How is she now? How old is she?"

"She's dead," Marcus said flatly.

Taskar stared out the window, his hands flat on his lap.

They traveled another few minutes in silence, the wipers squeaking against the glass, until Taskar pointed. "You're going to exit here. That's the best option. We're not going to be able to drive all the way up to the front door."

Marcus eased toward the exit. "Why not?"

"They've got snipers on the roof and cameras everywhere. I know we've come a long way, but this is beginning to feel like a bad idea."

"I've survived every bad idea I've ever had," said Marcus.

"It only takes once."

"People keep telling me that. I tend not to listen to them."

Marcus slowed the truck, but kept driving. The compass on the dash told him they were heading southeast.

"Keep going this way," said Taskar. "You'll come to an intersection up here. Turn right. Go a little farther to another major intersection. It's probably a good place to stop. If I remember correctly, there's a parking lot, and we'll be a little more than a mile from the CDC."

Marcus followed the instructions onto Briarcliff. Unlike in Texas, the street signs were upright and accurate. In a few blocks he came to a parking lot in front of a large single-story building. It looked like a grocery store, but it was obvious nobody had used it for anything in a while. The lot was speckled with weeds and littered with trash. The truck's headlamps were the only illumination.

"This it?" Marcus asked, applying the brake and stopping.

"I think so," said Taskar. "This is good. I know we're not far."

"Let's load up, then."

Marcus elbowed his door open and planted his boots on the ground. His legs were stiff and his old wounds ached. He stretched his neck and back and squatted on his heels to ease the pain in his thighs. It didn't help much. He limped, more noticeably, to the back of the truck and lowered the covered tailgate.

"You're hurt?" asked Taskar.

"Soreness from an old injury," he said. "Got it from a bad idea."

Taskar grimaced, apparently unamused. He reached into the back of the truck and pulled out a backpack loaded with bricks of C-4 and detonators. Marcus removed a pair of rifles. He took his Springfield and an AR-15, which he offered to Taskar.

"It's only got one extra mag," he said, handing over a curved, fully loaded magazine. "So be judicious with the trigger."

Taskar took the rifle and checked the attached magazine. He pulled the weapon to his shoulder and eyed the sights, aiming the barrel at the ground.

Marcus slung his Springfield over his shoulder. He then pulled another pack from the truck's bed and withdrew his handgun. He checked to make sure it was full of cartridges, which it was, and then he slid it into a holster he wore at his hip.

While Taskar readied himself, Marcus walked back to the driver's side. He drew Lou's knife from the center console and tucked it into his waistband at the small of his back. He pulled up his pants and limped back to Taskar, who was still playing with his new weapon.

"You comfortable with that rifle?" Marcus asked.

"Yeah," said Taskar. "I've been in tight spots before."

"Bad ideas?"

Taskar smirked. "Maybe."

CHAPTER 23

FEBRUARY 12, 2044, 11:00 PM
SCOURGE + 11 YEARS, 4 MONTHS
ATLANTA, GEORGIA

The rain had stopped. The air was damp and colder than before the storm. Standing in a sally port on the back side of the facility, Dr. Morel's breath bloomed in small puffs of vapor. He was standing amongst the trio of drivers who'd volunteered for the transport jobs. They were suited up in matching hazmat suits. He was wearing a less-restrictive version of the suit and hadn't yet affixed a locking hood and mask at his neck.

A technician from Bolnoy's team was checking the oxygenators affixed to their chests. None of them looked worried or anxious, in sharp contrast to Timothy Taskar.

They'd made a mistake with that one. Morel was sure of it, and he was glad.

They were awaiting the arrival of the subjects. All of them were exhibiting the early signs of the disease. When Morel had last checked, they suffered from high fevers, lung infections of varying degrees, and visibly swollen submandibular lymph glands.

Morel had assured Sharp that they were sick enough to infect others but not far enough along to die in transport. He hoped he was wrong. He was counting on it.

For months, he and his team had done just enough to advance the program. They'd conducted accelerated rat and dog trials. They'd completed their early human tests. They'd even sent the first subject into the wild. All of it was made to appear as though he'd done as he was told and had achieved what Sharp liked to call the endgame.

But there was something about the illness he hadn't told her. Half the samples contained what he'd termed a "suicidal component." That was what he'd injected into the three subjects about to go to Dallas, Houston, and San Antonio.

When Sharp had changed the directive and then threatened his family, Morel had secretly undertaken an ancillary project that he developed in parallel to the new YPH5N1. It was a virus that, after producing signs of infection, would fight itself until the virus was eradicated and the body's lymphocytes healed the infected cells.

He'd done it by taking the Scourge vaccine they'd come so close to completing and binding it to the H1N1 component of the disease. The live attenuated Scourge vaccine was essentially a significantly weakened version of the deadly YP strain. It might produce some symptoms, but wasn't fatal.

Under the microscope, it was indistinguishable from YPH5N1, intended to induce seventy percent mortality. Neither Sharp nor her superiors would know the difference unless they knew exactly where to look. And they wouldn't.

The flu virus attached to the vaccine, as it would the plague. Since the body developed antibodies to fight the plague, it could also have enough strength to beat back the flu. It could take days or weeks, and it hadn't always worked. But in two cases, CV-18 and CV-19, it had. This was true science fiction. And Morel had made it happen.

Bolnoy's team might discover it in their postmortem analysis of CV-18 and CV-19. They'd likely find the antibodies and wonder how the pair developed them so quickly instead of succumbing to the lethality of the Swine Scourge. It wouldn't matter. Bolnoy didn't like the mission either. He didn't like Sharp. He wouldn't tell her.

Morel regretted what he'd done to CV-18 and CV-19. He regretted what he'd injected into rats and dogs and other humans. They were the sacrifice he'd made for his family, for the countless thousands of lives he'd ultimately save by murdering a few.

There would be more sacrifices. When the trio of subjects failed to produce the expected infections, they'd be euthanized. There would be more tests, more subjects, more transports. People would die from the virus. It would spread. But not like Sharp and her superiors had planned. A Texas takeover wouldn't be as easy as they'd like to think. The military was still a shadow of its pre-Scourge self. From what he'd heard, they weren't as proficiently violent as the amoral cowboys south of the wall.

Ultimately, Morel believed he would lose his own life. Sharp wouldn't put up with the failures.

By then, he hoped to have moved his family somewhere safe, somewhere with all the trappings of a government job but without the Faustian contract. He didn't know where it might be, but he would do it. He'd talked with Bolnoy about it. The Russian had connections everywhere.

The vapor of his breath plumed and dissipated in front of his face. The transporters were ready. One of Bolnoy's men tapped a square display on his wrist and the electronic doors that led from the sally port into the building buzzed and clicked.

The twin doors opened mechanically outward and Sharp appeared alongside three gurneys and their escorts. She and the escorts were in biohazard suits. She looked at Morel and pointed to her head.

Morel nodded and, from a rolling cart next to him, picked up his hooded mask. He affixed it to his modified hazmat suit by twisting it until it locked and sealed in place. He reached around to the back of the hood and fixed a quarter-inch flexible tube to the oxygenator at his chest. He sucked in his first breath of filtered air and tasted the charcoal and plastic mixture on his tongue and in the back of his throat.

"Let's load them up," Sharp said. "I want them on the road within the hour."

The hazmat-suited aides guided the gurneys from the large double doors to the sally port floor. They rolled them down a ramp and then maneuvered each to its assigned SUV.

One of the subjects—an older, feeble-looking, white-bearded man—groaned as they lifted the gurney into the back of the vehicle. His mouth was swollen and cracked, his nose draining snot. His eyes were bloodshot and swollen underneath thinning brows. His cheekbones were exposed like ridges on his sunken face, and his sinewy arms strained against the leather straps holding them in place. "You'll all rot," he moaned. "Every last one of you will spend eternity in Hell for this."

Coughing, he disappeared into the SUV's bed. The aides shut the door behind him. His groaning curses and promises of damnation were muffled but still audible as the aides loaded the other two subjects.

Once the doors were shut, Sharp placed a gloved hand onto an iron railing and marched down the steps from the landing at the double doors to the bay floor below. She watched her booted feet as she walked.

Morel suppressed a smile. It was the first time he'd ever seen her unsure of herself. He moved toward her. He watched her, uneasy in her suit. She'd been in a suit countless times. Though, Morel reasoned, she'd always been in a lab, in a controlled environment. This was different. As soon as the bay doors opened, she was exposed to the outside world.

He knew she didn't care for anything beyond the walls of the headquarters. She worked there, she lived there. It had taken an act of what remained of Congress to get her to meet with Taskar offsite. A team of guards had accompanied her on the journey and stood by, ready to act if needed. Maybe her dislike of those south of the wall wasn't entirely wrapped in her husband's death. Maybe, Morel thought as he stood next to her, watching the massive bay doors open on the back of the sally port, she disliked them because they were comfortable with the freedom and the risk that came with being in a wild, lawless wilderness. She was envious more than angry, frightened more than vindictive.

Morel could feel the door rumbling open in the fabric of his suit. It vibrated against his skin. Sharp glanced at him and offered an awkward smile. He was convinced she didn't know how to smile, that she'd viewed a demonstrative video from the AI system to explain how to do it.

When the doors finished opening, the drivers started their engines and the SUVs rolled out one after the other. Sharp led Morel to the edge of the sally port and they stood there until the caravan's red taillights dimmed as they drove away.

"One big step forward," Sharp said to Morel.

"One step," he replied.

"Let's go find Bolnoy," she said. "I want answers about CV-18 and CV-19."

Morel drew a deep breath of artificial air and sighed. "After you," he said, motioning her back toward the double doors.

* * *

Marcus heard the engines before he saw the SUVs. They were loud. There was certainly more than one of them.

"You hear that?" he asked Taskar.

"Yeah. Sounds like a convoy."

"Coming from the CDC?"

Taskar nodded. "Could be. We're only three blocks from them. I don't remember much else being operational in this area."

Marcus thumbed the sling off his shoulder and gripped the rifle.

Taskar did the same. They were positioned on a street corner, multistory buildings on all sides. Marcus crept to the edge of one of the buildings and motioned for Taskar to do the same on the opposite side of the street.

The engines grew louder. The LED headlights' glare intensified on the road in front of him. They were close now.

He readied himself, bracing his side against the building. He took slow, measured breaths and took note of his pulse. His hands were steady. He wasn't sure what was coming at him, he wasn't certain he'd open fire, but he had to be ready.

The first SUV passed him. It wasn't traveling fast, no more than twenty-five miles an hour, Marcus guessed. Despite the lack of light, he could see two people in the front seat. Both were wearing large angular biohazard suits.

The second vehicle passed close behind the first. It too had two people in the front seat, wearing protective suits.

Above the hum of the engines, Taskar yelled across the street to Marcus, "That's them!" he called. "They're taking sick people south."

Even in the dim ambient light of the SUVs, Marcus saw the panic in Taskar's eyes and heard the desperation in his voice.

"They've left!" he yelled as the third SUV rolled past. "We're too late!"

Marcus ignored him. He dropped to one knee, found his target, and drilled a round through the front tire of the lead SUV some fifty yards up the street. The tire popped and hissed. The SUV swerved and stopped suddenly, its brakes squealing and the antilock mechanism grumbling loudly.

Taking a cue, Taskar unloaded a pair of shots into both driver's side tires in the third SUV, while Marcus worked the bolt and plowed a bullet into a rear tire of the middle vehicle.

The third driver didn't stop in time and skidded at an angle into the rear of the SUV in front of him. Marcus had three rifle shots remaining and moved toward the collision, intent on using them. He chambered the next cartridge.

On the opposite side, Taskar mirrored Marcus. "The subjects are in the back!" he called. "They're innocent. The guys in suits work for the CDC."

"Got it," Marcus replied. His finger was on the trigger, ready to fire, when a hazmat-suited passenger climbed out of the third SUV. Marcus caught the glint of a weapon in his hand. He applied pressure to the Springfield's trigger and zipped a bullet through the man's mask. The man spun wildly, spasming and grasping at the shattered visor before crumpling to the ground.

Marcus loaded his fourth round and inched forward, scanning the street with the barrel. On the opposite side of the collision he heard a burst of AR-15 pops. Then a second as the door of the middle vehicle opened and a hazmat-wearing passenger dropped out and hit the ground. At the same time, a rifle shot zipped past Marcus's head. He instinctively crouched low, hurried behind the wreck for cover, and dropped to the ground. Another shot dinged the open SUV door in front of him and a third ricocheted off the street.

In the dark and the glare of the headlights, Marcus had trouble locating the source of the gunfire. He knew it was the passenger in the first vehicle, he just couldn't see him.

He inched his pack from his shoulders, heaved it to the ground, and laid it in front of him. He rested the Springfield's barrel on the pack and panned the area, searching for the enemy.

On the opposite side of the wreck, out of his field of view, another volley came from the AR-15. It was at his ten o'clock. Taskar had advanced beyond his position. Another double shot from Taskar at the same time incoming shots ripped through the air overhead. Marcus caught a muzzle flash to the right of the first SUV, beyond the reach of the fan of the headlight. Marcus held his position and waited.

"C'mon," he muttered. "One more shot." The muzzle flashed and Marcus adjusted his aim as a round slammed into the dead, hanging body of the passenger in the second SUV. He pulled the trigger, quickly cranked the bolt, and fired again.

In the echo of the gunfire, Taskar called out, "You got him! You got him!"

Marcus pulled back onto his knees, still holding the rifle.

Taskar appeared around the front of the second vehicle. "We're good," he said breathlessly. He was clearly amped. "All six. You got three, I got three. That was quick thinking. Shooting the tires. I didn't think of that. Pretty smart. Good job."

Marcus stood and popped the five-round internal magazine from the Springfield. He reloaded it one bullet at a time, pulling the cartridges from his pants pocket. Then he wiped the rivulets of sweat from his forehead. His fingers were getting stiff and his back ached. "It's cold here," he said. "Colder than Texas."

Taskar shot Marcus a confused look. "That's what you're thinking about?" he asked. "The weather?"

Marcus shrugged. "Yeah. I don't like the cold. It messes with my joints."

Taskar stood there dumfounded. He slid a thumb inside the shoulder strap on his pack and shrugged it higher.

Marcus nodded toward the dead men in the street. "You said six are down. What about the patients? Where are they?"

Taskar's face stretched with recognition. "I forgot about them," he said, his cadence still spiked with adrenaline. "They should be in the backs of the SUVs, strapped to gurneys."

Marcus slid the bolt to chamber the first round. He moved slyly toward the back of the third SUV and pressed his face close to the glass to peer inside, but as soon as he saw what was inside, he stumbled backward with shock.

"What?" asked Taskar, who'd taken his place to Marcus's side. "What is it?"

"I think he's dead," said Marcus. "Or she. I can't tell. Whatever it is, it looks like someone hung skin on a skeleton."

Taskar tentatively stepped forward, cupped a hand around one eye, and looked into the SUV. He held his gaze there for a moment. "He's not dead," said Taskar, "and this is nothing. There's no blood or anything. Did you ever see anyone die from the Scourge? I did. If you didn't, this is what it looked like."

Marcus thought about telling Taskar the image reminded him of his wife, Sylvia, on the day she died, emaciated and pale. She was a ghostly doppelgänger of her healthy self. He decided not to offer an explanation. It wasn't any of his business.

"What do we do with him?" asked Marcus. "And the others, assuming there are similar people in the other two SUVs?"

"I don't know," Taskar said. "We can't leave them here, but I don't think we want to be touching them."

"Do we put them out of their misery?" asked Marcus. "Like you did Lomas?"

Taskar frowned. "I don't know if I can do that again."

Marcus chuckled. "You just shot three men in cold blood."

"That's different. They had it coming. We killed them to save a lot of other lives. I don't want to kill these people," said Taskar. "Not yet. And we're wasting time by standing here arguing about it."

"Okay then," Marcus said and started walking. He stooped to pick up his pack and slung it over his shoulder. His limp was increasingly pronounced as he moved south toward the CDC.

Taskar caught up a half a block later. "You gonna make it?"

"Don't have a choice now, do we?"

* * *

"Position One, this is Position Two. Did you hear gunfire? Over," said the sniper at the northwest edge of the CDC's roof.

He was speaking into a voice-activated microphone pressed to his neck. He'd heard the easily recognizable pops of semiautomatic gunfire, but he'd seen no evidence of it. He couldn't tell how far away it was or in which direction. The other large buildings made it difficult to isolate the original sound from the echoes.

"Copy that, Position Two," said the sentry atop the roof above the plaza at the entrance. *"I heard it. You spot a location? Over."*

"Negative," said Position Two. "Audible confirmation only. Over."

The sniper moved along the edge of the building's roof, searching the streets below for any indication of a threat. Gunfire was not uncommon, especially in the nongovernment neighborhoods that surrounded the CDC. They were dark places, many of the buildings abandoned or inhabited by squatters.

"Position Three," squawked his earpiece, *"this is Position One. Do you have confirmation? Over."*

Position Three was above the sally port. He'd watched the SUV's caravan beyond the tall cluster of buildings nearest the CDC, ensuring nothing happened to them as they left the secure perimeter surrounding the headquarters.

"Affirmative," he said into his mic. "Copy that. I did hear the shots. AR-15 and something else. A single-shot maybe. Over."

"Visual? Over," asked Position One.

"Negative that," said Position Three. *"No flash. Nothing. Over."*

"Stay frosty," said Position One. *"All positions report anomalies. Over. Out."*

Position Two patrolled as close to the edge of the roof as he was comfortable. The soft gravel crunched under his jackboots. The damp wind blew at his back and his face as he made his way back to the corner, retracing his area of responsibility.

The wind was biting and stung his earlobes and the tip of his nose. It dried his eyes and mouth. He sniffed back the chill and edged close to the corner, peering over the edge. He scanned the streets below. Nothing. As he was about to turn, a flash from the border of his peripheral vision caught his eye and he heard a pop. Then the world went black. His body stiffened and slapped onto the gravel.

* * *

"One down," said Marcus. "How many are there?"

"I don't know," said Taskar. "I didn't get a good look around the perimeter of the roof. I do know there are at least two or three. I saw them by the front entrance when I parked there."

Marcus lowered his rifle. "Let's find the next one, then, before they notice one isn't communicating."

He led Taskar around the corner of the building, staying a block away. A sharp, burning sensation radiated from both knees as he moved. One of his ankles felt weak. The cold sucked.

They reached the next corner and Marcus pointed toward the roof. There was another sentry armed with a rifle. He was dressed in black, but a hint of moonlight glimmered off the man's bald head.

Marcus dropped to one knee, a sharp jolt of pain firing through his thigh, and he winced. "Spot me."

He drew the rifle to his body and placed his eye to the scope. He eased his finger onto the trigger and applied steady pressure. Kill shot.

"That's two," said Taskar. "Next corner is the front plaza. There will be more than one there."

Taskar motioned where they should go. Marcus slung his rifle over his shoulder and limped onward.

* * *

"This is Position One to Positions Two and Three," said the patrol commander. "Radio sitrep ASAP. Over."

It was the fourth time he'd tried to hail them on his comms. They hadn't answered, but he'd distinctly heard a single-shot rifle report twice since their group discussion. He scanned the roof as best he could, but it was dark. The roof was expansive, and much of it was obstructed by HVAC equipment. He turned to his subordinate at the plaza position and pressed the mute key on his transmitter.

"We've got a problem," he said. "Head downstairs and communicate my concerns directly to Dr. Sharp. I don't want this going over the radio."

"Yes, sir," said Richter, the sentry. "What do you want me to tell Dr. Sharp, sir?"

"Tell her we have a threat. We'll contain it before it breaches the building, but she needs to be aware. Understood?"

"Roger that, sir."

Richter sprinted toward the roof access door. There'd been an armed threat only once in the five years the commander had been assigned to the CDC. It was random. Somebody lost their mind and haphazardly opened fire on everything he saw. This didn't feel like that. He knew, without having to see their bodies, that two of his men were dead. This was a deliberate attack. It was systematic and executed with precision. He inhaled a deep breath of the moist February air, the icy chill filling his lungs. The smell of tar lingered in his nostrils after he blew it out. He backed away from the ledge, treading as softly as he could on the gravel.

* * *

Richter keyed the coded elevator and pressed his eye to the retinal scanner. A red light turned green and he pressed the car button. Seconds later he was whooshing downward, the numeric display above the stainless doors descending rapidly until he reached SUBFLOOR 2.

The elevator jerked to a stop and the doors slid apart. Not waiting for them to fully open, he slid sideways between them and hustled along the hallway to the next set of coded doors. He repeated the identification procedures and hurried through to a series of rooms where he knew he'd find Dr. Sharp.

He slid on the floor as he tried to stop his momentum at the last set of secured doors. Once inside, he breathlessly told a man he recognized, but whose name he didn't know, he urgently needed to speak with Dr. Sharp.

The man tapped on a tablet, asked, "Is something wrong?"

"I can't discuss that with you, sir," said Richter, gulping air between words. "I have orders to speak with Dr. Sharp."

"How do you have clearance to be in here?" asked the man. He was tapping on the tablet hastily now. "Who gave you permission?"

Richter puffed his chest and raised his chin. "I'm with the security detail," he said. "I'm an assistant to the commander. I've got the highest level clearance, sir."

"She'll be here in a moment," the man said. "She's changing clothes."

Richter stood with his hands behind his back and, for the first time, took notice of his surroundings. He was in a laboratory, but on one wall was a bank of large flat-screen monitors. A couple of them displayed the images from exterior surveillance cameras. Others were trained on empty rooms. Some of the monitors were dark.

There was the click and hum of the door behind Richter. He caught a whiff of perfume and a woman brushed past him and then stopped to face him.

"Who is this, Dr. Morel?" she asked of the lab-coated man behind her. "Why is he here?"

Richter started to speak, but Dr. Sharp stopped him. He closed his mouth and swallowed hard. "I asked Dr. Morel," she said, her eyes fixed on Richter's.

"He's security," said Dr. Morel. "Works for the commander. Says there's something urgent. He wouldn't tell me—"

"I only asked who he is, Charles," Sharp said. "I didn't ask for your doctoral dissertation."

Dr. Morel rolled his eyes behind her back.

"Why are you here?" she asked.

"We have a potential security breach," Richter said. "There's an issue with the perimeter. The commander asked I inform you immediately."

Sharp scowled. "What is a *potential* security breach?"

"We have two positions not reporting, ma'am."

Sharp tilted her head to one side, her tight bun threatening to topple from her crown. "What am I supposed to do with this information?"

Richter flinched. "I'm not sure what—"

"What would you have me do? You've given me information. How does it affect me? Where should I go? Do I worry? Do I grab a gun? Do I run for my life?"

Richter's eyes flittered. "I can't answer that, ma'am. I'm a messenger."

Sharp rolled her eyes. "Then I'll do nothing. Go tell your commander you've delivered the message and I've heard you."

Richter nodded, backed away from Sharp, and hustled toward the door.

* * *

"Do nothing?" asked Morel. "I don't understand. He just said somebody's coming for us."

Sharp weaved her way through the desks toward Morel. She adjusted her bun, touching the array of bobby pins with her index finger.

She took the tablet from Morel. "He didn't say that. He said there was a *potential* breach. I'm not worried about it."

She tapped the tablet's icons, working through a series of command pages.

"He said there were two men who weren't responding," Morel said. "That's not *potential*, it's actual. The commander wouldn't have sent him down here otherwise."

Sharp's eyes moved between the tablet and a pair of monitors on the wall. The displays flipped from ground-level surveillance to roof-mounted security cameras. The first revealed nothing. The second, an image of the northwest corner of the building, was different. On the side of the screen was what appeared to be the bottom of a boot and part of a leg.

Sharp stepped closer to the monitor. "Is that…?"

"A body," said Morel.

"It's not moving, is it?"

"It doesn't look like it."

Sharp blinked and looked away from the display. She shook her head. "It doesn't mean anything," she said, trying to convince herself.

"Check the AI," suggested Morel. "Don't all of the guards have tracker implants?"

"Some of them," she said, "not all."

"Still…"

Sharp pressed an icon on the tablet. "Okay."

"Good evening, Dr. Morel," said the AI voice through an overhead speaker mounted above the monitor wall. *"How might I assist you?"*

"It's Dr. Sharp."

"Please accept my apologies, Dr. Sharp. You are utilizing Dr. Morel's access tablet. I'll refresh the system with your settings. How might I assist you?"

"Please locate all security trackers at 33.7993 degrees north, 84.3280 degrees west."

"I'm locating all security trackers at 33.7993 degrees north, 84.3280 degrees west," replied the AI. *"While I analyze the data for the requested subset, I can tell you there are seven registered security trackers in the system."*

"Thank you," said Sharp.

"I can also tell you there are fifteen registered security personnel. Eight of those registered personnel do not have positional biometric trackers."

"Thanks for the simple math," said Sharp. "Do you have the data?"

"You're welcome," said the AI without a hint of sarcasm. *"I'm*

compiling the information now. Would you like an update on your biometric data, Dr. Sharp?"

Sharp bristled, and her grip on the tablet tightened. "What data?"

"From your tracker, Dr. Sharp," said the AI. *"I'm happy to report to you that your oxygen levels are normal despite an elevated heart rate. More exercise could—"*

"I don't have a tracker," she snapped.

"I have the data you requested on the security trackers, Dr. Sharp," said the AI. *"I have located all seven security staff. Three, however, are reporting no data. It's possible their life functions have ceased."*

"Wait," said Sharp. "I don't have a tracker."

"Is that a question requiring an affirmative response?"

"Yes," said Sharp.

"Very well, Dr. Sharp," said the AI. *"You do have a tracker. It's located between the hypodermis and the gluteus medius. Your tracker became active seven months, three days, fourteen hours, thirty-two seconds ago."*

Sharp's eyes danced around the room as she searched her memory. Seven months ago. What was seven months ago? Then it hit her. She raised her head and anger surged through her body from her gut to her legs and arms. She felt it rising in her throat like bile. Through her clenched teeth, she calmly addressed Morel.

"You did it," she said. "You injected me with the tracker during our annual vaccinations, didn't you?"

Morel didn't respond.

"Answer me," she snarled.

No answer.

Sharp spun around to face her subordinate. He wasn't there. She balled her fists, digging her nails into her palms as she marched from the lab and out into the hall. She'd been preoccupied with the AI such that she hadn't heard the security door click and buzz open. She was so incensed by her perceived betrayal, she didn't recognize the AI had told her three security guards were dead.

* * *

Marcus took out the commander with a shot at the neck above his nano-fabric vest. He was positioned on the second floor of a four-story parking garage across from the CDC plaza.

"There should be another one," said Taskar. "I remember there being two of them."

"I don't see a second man up there," said Marcus. "I do see two men inside the front doors. Both are armed."

"I can take them out," said Taskar. "I've got a clear shot through the glass."

Marcus shook his head. "If they've got this much external security, that glass is probably bulletproof. You'd be wasting ammunition."

"What do you suggest?" asked Taskar. "How do we get inside?"

Marcus rubbed the scruff on his chin and neck. It itched. He needed to shave.

"Ideas?" Taskar prompted.

"I'm thinking," said Marcus. He sighed. "Okay, here's the plan. We draw them outside. Once they're exposed, we have access into the building."

"Not necessarily," said Taskar.

"What do you mean?"

"The doors are coded. I think they use fingerprints or eyes to open them."

Marcus shrugged. "Not an issue. Take my rifle and my Glock."

"What?"

Marcus stood up and handed Taskar the Springfield. Then he drew the handgun from his hip and placed it on the concrete pony wall that surrounded the garage on each level. "Spot me," he said. "If it looks like I've got trouble, fire away."

Taskar nodded. "Then what?"

"When it's time, you're gonna bring my guns and join me in the lobby."

"How will I know when that is?"

"You'll know," said Marcus. He shrugged his pack from his back and dropped it to the floor. "Bring this too."

He untucked his shirt, adjusted his pants, and descended the nearby staircase to the street level. He limped across the plaza toward the front door with his hands above his head. In his mind, he pictured Penny's dead body. He imagined Sawyer falling from the treehouse. He envisioned himself on his knees at the graves in his backyard.

He felt Sylvia's hand lose its grip on his and her fingers go limp as she took her last breath. He smelled Lola's sweet scent as he held her on the floor of the garage, strands of her red hair finding their way between his lips as he whispered into her ear how much he loved her.

Tears welled in his eyes. He blinked to loosen them, making them drip onto his cheeks. By the time he reached the doors, he looked like the wounded, frightened man he wanted them to think he was.

Before he could knock on the glass, both of the guards were on him. They ordered him to step back as they exited the building. The stocky one had his pistol trained on Marcus. The other, with a well-trimmed mustache, had his hand on his unsnapped holster, ready to draw.

"Who are you?" snapped the stocky one. "Identify yourself."

"I-I-I..." Marcus sobbed.

"Spit it out," said the stocky one, jabbing his weapon toward Marcus's chest. "This is a secure facility."

"My name is Junior Barbas," he said, whimpering through a Southern-stained accent. "My wife is starving. She's sick. I can't work on account of my leg. I just need some help for her."

"We can't do that sir," said the mustached one. "This isn't a public building."

The stocky one pressed a button at his neck. "This is Position Five," he said. "We have a visitor in the plaza. Over."

Marcus dropped to his knees, pain exploding in both of his legs, and clasped his hands together in prayer. "Please," he begged through real tears, "I just need some medicine. Some pills to help her sleep. To help with the headaches."

The radio squawked. *"We have three nonresponsive positions. There is an active threat. Repeat. Active threat. Search the visitor. Over."*

The one with the handgun stepped forward. "I need to see your hands. I'm going to search you."

Marcus did as he was told. He kept his eyes on the hands of the guard with the mustache. They weren't anywhere near his holstered weapon.

"Do you have any identification?" asked the guard. "Any proof of who you are?"

Marcus shook his head. He was gasping for air as the stocky guard cautiously stepped behind him. He noticed neither guard was wearing a protective vest.

"Stand up," the stocky guard ordered. "Keep your hands away from your body."

Marcus struggled to his feet and held his arms outstretched. He kept them there as the guard used one hand to grope him. They were idiots, Marcus thought. Neither of them was in a position to use their weapons.

The stocky guard reached around Marcus, and at the moment he touched his back, Marcus tensed. He gripped the guard's weapon with one hand, twisting it away from his body, as he pulled the man's girth into him and used the other hand to draw Lou's blade from his waistband.

He swung the blade in an uppercut, jamming it into the guard's neck and up through his jaw, thrusting it as hard as he could. The guard's face contorted unnaturally and his eyes snapped wide with surprise, freezing with the shock and pain of his final moment alive.

As quickly as he'd driven the blade to the hilt, he withdrew it and, amidst the violent spray of blood, cast the man aside with a shove.

While the other guard struggled for his gun, Marcus threw the knife at his chest.

Marcus, however, was not the skilled thrower that Lou was, and the handle hit the guard instead of the blade. It bounced harmlessly to the ground. When the guard looked at his chest, surprised he was unhurt, Marcus leapt forward and tackled the guard to the ground.

The guard's head snapped backward as they fell, slapping off the concrete plaza and dizzying the man. He groaned. His eyes open and closed with confusion. Marcus pulled the man's gun from his holster and pressed it to his forehead.

"What's the code?" he asked.

The guard mumbled gibberish and drool leaked from the corner of his mouth. Marcus grabbed his jaw with both hands and drew the man's attention to his eyes.

"What. Is. The. Code?"

The guard mumbled again then spat out the numeric sequence for the electronically coded doors.

Marcus thanked him and pulled the trigger, then rolled off the mustached man and onto his back to catch his breath. Looking up at the black Georgia night, he waved his hand in the air to signal Taskar it was safe to join him.

* * *

Sharp burst into Bolnoy's office. Morel was standing in front of Bolnoy's desk. The Russian was sitting in his high-back leather chair. Both men ignored her when she demanded an answer.

"Did you hear me?" she snapped. "Why did you inject me with a tracker?"

Bolnoy's eyes looked into hers as he spoke. "It's always good to know where the rats have been," he said. "That way you know what is spoiled and what is not."

Sharp seethed. Her face reddened with the heat of unreasonable anger and she marched across the sparsely decorated room to Morel. She balled her hands into fists and punched him in the shoulder, leading with the knuckle of her middle finger.

Morel cried out in pain and grabbed his arm. "Are you kidding me?" he asked, turning to face her as she swung again.

The second punch landed on Morel's jaw and knocked him off balance. A third grazed his chin.

Bolnoy stood from behind his desk, shouting at Sharp to stop. She ignored him and swung again. Morel blocked the throw and backed away.

"What is your problem?" he asked, rubbing his reddened face with his hand.

Sharp stomped her feet as if the floor were Morel's face. A long vein bulged from her slick hairline down the length of her brow. "You violated my privacy!" she said, shaking her fists. "You had no right."

Bolnoy chuckled. "Do you think the irony of this is lost on her?"

Sharp scowled at the Russian. "You're no better. You knew about this?"

"Everybody knew about this," said Bolnoy. "The information about who is tracked and who is not is in the system. It's a couple of taps. It's not his fault you never looked."

"I never gave my permission!"

Morel held his hands in front of his face. "Actually, you did," he said apprehensively. "It's in the vaccination documents you signed."

Sharp's face twitched. Her eyes searched for a reason she wouldn't have known that. "Still," she spat, "you didn't tell me. You didn't want me to know, did you? That's why you ran from the lab."

"That's not why—"

"Whatever," she hissed. "You're done. After these three test subjects are in the wild, I'm replacing you. You and your codependent wife and your sickly little brats can fend for yourselves."

Morel lowered his hands. His eyes focused over her shoulder on the wall behind her. Bolnoy's narrow gaze was also fixed on the wall.

Sharp cursed. "What?"

Morel motioned to the wall with his chin. "I think we have more pressing concerns than whether or not you knew you were being tracked."

Sharp turned around and saw a quad-display monitor mounted flush to the wall. It displayed security camera video at the entrance to the facility.

"Is that live?" she asked.

"Yes," Bolnoy replied.

Sharp cursed again and drew her hands to her mouth. "Mother of—"

"I know," said Morel. "I know."

On the monitor were four different angles of the same macabre scene. A broad-shouldered man wearing a T-shirt and cargo pants was holding a severed hand to the biometric finger scanner. A companion was holding something in between his fingers up to the retinal scanner.

Sharp's hands dropped to her sides. "Is that…?"

Bolnoy finished her sentence. "An eyeball."

Morel stepped to the monitor and pointed at it. "I recognize him. The one with the…eyeball…he's the driver. Timothy Taskar."

"That's impossible," said Sharp. "He's dead."

Morel looked at her. "How do you know that?"

"AI confirmed tracking information."

"He didn't have a tracker," said Morel. "You were in a hurry to get him out the door. He was already waffling. You didn't want to spook him even more. He didn't have a tracker."

The three of them looked at the monitor and watched as the two men unlocked the doors, swung them open, and marched into the lobby. Whatever it was they wanted, they were now that much closer to getting it.

* * *

"What do I do with the eye?" asked Taskar as he followed Marcus through the rows of large white plastic tents that filled the three-story atrium.

Marcus was carrying a severed hand, its fingers laced in his as if he were being cute with an invisible date. "Keep it," said Marcus. "We're going to need it again."

They moved past the computer terminals and exam tables Taskar remembered seeing the last time he was there. Unlike his previous visit, there were no people in colored, full-body protective suits. There were no guards either.

At the far end of the atrium, they found the elevators. Marcus stopped and squinted at the control panel above the floor indicators.

"This one needs a badge," he said. "You have the badge?"

Taskar used the hand not holding an eye to fish one of the guards' badges from his pocket. He swiped it across the panel. The light switched from red to green.

"Down?" Marcus asked.

"Yes."

Marcus pressed the button. A minute later the elevator buzzed and the twin stainless steel doors slid apart. They stepped into the car and the door slid shut behind them. Taskar pressed the badge against the panel. Nothing happened.

"Finger," he said to Marcus.

Marcus twisted the hand in his and pressed the index finger to a pad. The light turned green again and Marcus pressed the button Taskar said was the right one.

The elevator shuddered and then whooshed downward. Taskar felt the familiar loss of gravity in his feet and his stomach lurched. It reminded him of his prior visit and bile crept up his throat. The elevator slowed and an artificial voice announced their arrival at their destination floor.

"This is the observatory lab," said the voice. *"Please watch your step upon exiting."*

The doors whooshed apart and an armed guard was standing there, his nine-millimeter handgun aimed at Marcus, moved to Taskar, then back at Marcus. All three of the men stood frozen for a beat.

Without reflection, Marcus gripped the severed hand by its wrist and swung it at the gun, slapping it free from the guard's grip. It rattled across the hallway floor, the shocked guard watching it skitter out of his reach.

Marcus then pistol-whipped him with the butt of his handgun. The guard stumbled to the side and collapsed to the floor, unconscious, a swelling lump already forming on his forehead.

He shrugged at Taskar. "I can't kill everyone."

Taskar shook his head and led Marcus into the hallway. It forked in three directions. Marcus dragged the unconscious guard into the elevator and sent him up.

"I think we go left," Taskar said. "But it could be right. I don't remember."

"Go left," said Marcus.

"Really?" asked Taskar. "I'm not sure."

"It was your first guess. Go with it."

They moved left, walking deliberately along the concrete flooring. Marcus was limping, but kept up with Taskar.

"This is right," Taskar said. They passed an intersecting hallway and reached a coded door. "We're here."

The two of them opened it through a multistep process using the key card, the manually entered code they'd used at the front door, the finger, and the eye.

Marcus dropped the hand onto the floor and gripped his pistol with both hands. The door clicked open and Taskar pulled it toward himself. As he did, Marcus moved into the doorway, sweeping his weapon across the space. Other than a loud hum, banks of computers, and a large monitor wall, it was empty. Nobody was home.

* * *

"This is where we need to be," said Marcus. "It gives us the best shot of hitting everything with one explosion."

He was standing at the door, tracing his finger along a wall-mounted schematic map of the building's layout. He pointed to a spot on the map and tapped it with his finger.

Taskar motioned with his chin. "What is that?"

"It says it's the specimen storage room," said Marcus. "If they've got samples of the bigger, badder virus, they'll be in there. At least that's what I think."

Taskar scanned the map. "It's close to the rooms where they keep the patients too."

"Exactly," said Marcus. "There's a closet between the storage room and one of the patient rooms that contains elevator mechanics. It's got a lot of wiring in it. Might provide us with our best shot. And it's on the same level. We don't have to change floors."

"Still, getting there could be tough," Taskar argued. "Even with the key card, the body parts, and the code, it's a lot of doors. That area is secure. See the thickness of the walls?"

Marcus smirked and shrugged the pack on his shoulders. "We have a lot of C-4."

He ran his finger along various routes through the building. Taskar agreed with some of them, disagreed with others. Together they concocted a path. Both men checked their weapons. They were ready to go. And then the door opened.

* * *

Charles Morel froze with his hand on the door handle. In front of him were the two men he'd seen on the security monitors. They'd beaten him to the lab and had their weapons pointed at his chest.

"Don't shoot!" he pleaded. It was the only thing he could think to say. "We're unarmed."

Sharp and Bolnoy stood behind him in the hallway. Neither of them moved, and Morel wondered why they didn't make a run for it. His body provided more than enough cover for them to have sprinted from the hallway and toward the elevator. Maybe they were frozen too.

"Dr. Morel?" said Taskar.

"Don't shoot," he said again. "I can…I can help you."

"What?" Sharp shrieked from over his shoulder and he felt the hard jab of her elbow into his spine.

Morel screeched, arched his back in pain, his face cringing, and dropped to one knee. That left Sharp exposed to Taskar's aim.

"You," said Taskar, his anger sparking. "Sharp."

"These the people who sent you south?" asked the man with Taskar, the same man on the monitor holding a severed hand.

Taskar nodded. He stepped forward, keeping his aim on Sharp. "You okay?" he asked Morel.

Morel coughed and rolled to one side. "Yes," he rasped. "I'm fine."

"We can help you," Bolnoy said. "What do you want?"

Sharp's face reddened. She gritted her teeth. She did not, however, take a swing at the much larger Russian.

Morel pushed himself to his feet with the help of the open door. "I have a wife and children."

Taskar narrowed his gaze. "We want to end this place," he said. "We want to destroy whatever it is you're making here."

"That's not happening," Sharp said defiantly with two weapons pointed at her. "Nobody's ending anything. We're just starting. You'll destroy what we're doing over my dead—"

A loud, percussive blast knocked Morel off balance before he understood Bolnoy had pulled a handgun from his back and fired.

The single shot echoed loudly in the small space as it punctured a round hole in the back of Sharp's head. She stood there for a moment, blinking, her mouth agape, her sentence unfinished; then her chin dropped and she collapsed to the floor in a heap.

* * *

Bolnoy took his finger off the trigger and placed the weapon on the floor. He took a step back. "I couldn't listen to her anymore," he said. "Take the gun. It's yours."

"I've been there," Marcus said. "If you hadn't pulled the trigger, I might have done it."

"I was about to kill her," said Taskar. "He beat me to it."

There was a ringing in Marcus's ears that muted the discussion, but he could hear. Still, he kept his weapon on the one with the Russian accent.

"Any more weapons we need to know about?" Marcus asked.

Both men shook their heads.

"What are you going to do to help us?" he asked.

Morel looked at the Russian. "We can help destroy the samples," he said as if asking the Russian for permission.

"Who is that?" asked Taskar. "Who's your friend? I don't remember seeing him."

"You didn't," said Morel. "He does autopsies."

"I am Bolnoy," said the Russian. "I do more than autopsies."

"You are willing to help us destroy the virus?" asked Marcus. "We have explosives."

Bolnoy nodded. Morel nodded in compliance.

Marcus nudged the men back with a motion of his rifle. "Let's go, then. We think the elevator mechanical room will be the best point."

Bolnoy nodded his approval.

The men led their uninvited guests through the maze of the sublevel. At each door they gave the information needed to pass.

They'd gone through three of them when Morel explained they had reached their intended destination, just outside the mechanical closet.

"If you do it here, it will kill the subjects too," said Morel.

"That's part of the plan," said Marcus. "Whoever is infected needs to die. They're unfortunate casualties of this."

"Some of them aren't that sick," explained Morel.

He told the group what he and Bolnoy had been doing. That many of those who'd been injected would recover.

"Some won't," said Marcus, "and we can't take that risk."

Morel raised a finger. "I've been thinking about this," he said. "What if we didn't kill the subjects? What if we only destroyed the samples, got rid of all the virus, but we kept the subjects alive until we know if they'll be okay?"

"What do you mean?" asked Taskar.

"I mean that we keep an eye on these people who are sick," said Morel. "We keep them here. If they are sick, they will die. If they are not, they will go free."

Bolnoy shook his head. "That's no good," he said. "Superiors come. They see what happened. They blame you. They kill whoever stays. We cannot stay."

"I say we blow the whole thing," said Taskar. "All of it."

"We do need to hurry it up," said Marcus. "The closer we get to daylight, the closer we get to people coming back to work, creating problems for us."

Morel stiffened. He pulled his shoulders back. "I'll stay," he said. "I owe it to the people I infected. I'm the one responsible. I'll stay."

When Bolnoy started to protest, Morel cut in, "Just promise me two things. Watch over my family if I can't?"

"Of course," said Bolnoy.

"And destroy every last bit of the virus in the sample room," added Morel.

"What does that mean?" asked Taskar. "Are we doing this?"

Bolnoy nodded. He smiled at Taskar and started to lead Marcus,

Taskar, and the backpack full of explosives into the sealed sample room.

Marcus caught his arm. "Hold up," he said. "How do we know this isn't a ruse, that you're not just going to release sick people into the world after we leave? How can we trust you?"

Bolnoy shrugged. "You can't. But I did kill the woman who started the program."

Marcus smirked. "Good point."

* * *

The explosions were violent, quaking the building as they incinerated the entirety of the YPH5N1 cache in the sample room. Because the room was secured and had its own dedicated air circulation, the blast was contained.

Morel provided all four with hazmat suits and freshly charged oxygenators. Together they marched to the three transport SUVs a couple of blocks away, retrieved the subjects one at a time, and moved them back to their rooms within the facility.

It was three o'clock in the morning by the time they were finished and had removed the suits. Morel again promised to cope with whatever consequences might befall him for his betrayal. It was his penance, he'd explained, and apologized to Taskar.

"None of us is all bad," Taskar said. "None of us is all good either. It's not my place to judge you. Someday I might even forgive you."

Marcus left Morel with Bolnoy's gun. Just in case.

Bolnoy agreed to collect Morel's family and move them to a more secure, hidden location. He'd communicate its whereabouts in the event Morel was able to join them once the subjects were either healed or dead.

Marcus and Taskar thanked the men and then slogged the long walk back to the truck. Once they'd reached it, Marcus told Taskar he wasn't going with him.

"What?" asked Taskar. "I don't get it. Why would you stay here?"

"I don't belong anywhere," said Marcus. "I think I'm destined to roam, to travel."

"Like a hero saving the world?"

"Hardly," said Marcus. "Like a man trying to survive."

Taskar pointed back toward the CDC. "You saved the world back there."

Marcus laughed. "You think we saved the world? We didn't. We stalled the inevitable."

Taskar frowned. "You're damaged."

Marcus looked up at the moon, which had appeared from behind the silvery clouds moving fast across the dark morning sky. He closed his eyes as if in prayer.

"I'm working on it," said Marcus.

Taskar climbed into the truck and pulled the seatbelt across his chest.

"You gotta hold up your end of the deal," said Marcus. "I helped save the world; now you have to go back to Baird and tell Lou I'm okay. Maybe I'll see her again someday."

"I thought you didn't save the world."

"*You* thought I did," said Marcus. "Promise me you'll tell her. She's as close to family as anything I've got."

"I'll tell her," said Taskar. "But if she's family, you—"

"I don't deserve a family," said Marcus. "Not now. Maybe not ever."

Taskar offered his hand. Marcus took it and shook it firmly. Then he closed the driver's side door and Taskar drove off. The red taillights dimmed in the distance and the truck vanished into the night.

CHAPTER 24

Lou stood on her porch in the darkness against the roughhewn cedar railing, which framed the small rectangle at the front of her house. She looked at the thin wisps of clouds that sailed past the countless stars dotting the expansive black sky.

She wondered if Marcus could see the same stars, if he might look at them and think of her. A breeze swirled around her and she tilted her cap back on her head. The chill was refreshing, renewing. She inhaled and relished the chilly air, which smacked of dry grass and dirt, with hints of mesquite.

Lou wanted to think that Marcus would ride back on the breeze someday. Whether he was on a horse or in an SUV, or magically appear by clicking his ruby slippers, he'd find his way.

She knew, though, he wasn't returning to Baird. He'd said as much with the way he hugged her goodbye. He'd suggested as much by making Rudy the sheriff. Rudy had disagreed.

"He's not gone forever," he'd tried to reassure her as they walked back to his property. "He can't be alone. If I know anything about Marcus, it's that he's a people person."

"I think that's an exaggeration," Norma had argued. "If he's a people person, then Lou is as fragile as a dandelion. And we both know that's not true."

Lou had picked up a stick from the side of the road and chucked it ahead for Fifty. The dog had bounced on his back feet and exploded forward, racing for the stick. He'd grabbed it in his teeth and pranced back to Lou, his tail wagging. He brushed the stick against her thigh, asking her to toss it again.

"We'll be fine," Lou had told them. "We all got along in our own ways before we met Marcus. We'll get along now."

"I suppose," Rudy had said. "It won't be the same though."

Lou had tossed the stick again and Fifty bolted for it. He picked it up and shook it in his jaws.

Norma took Rudy's hand with both of hers and held it to her chest. "If by 'not the same,' you mean less violent, I agree."

Rudy had glanced at his wife and smirked. Lou had been able to tell they'd talked about it. They'd probably wanted Marcus gone. They'd wanted him to take his issues with him. Lou didn't agree he was a danger to everyone around him. At least he wasn't any more than she was. But she couldn't blame them for feeling the way they did. Marcus did let a lot of blood on the streets of an otherwise quiet town, enough that they needed a new cemetery for all the bodies.

The wind shifted. The dark outline of the Gallardos' house was visible. She imagined Rudy and Norma were getting a good night's sleep. The two whispering women probably were too, unless they were up early, gossiping to themselves.

Lou chuckled at the thought and looked to the ground at the foot of the two steps leading to her porch. Fifty was there, curled into a ball. He was dreaming. His back legs twitched and kicked. He whimpered.

Lou wondered where Fifty traveled in his dreams. His feet padded across imaginary ground. Could he be dreaming of some place without gunfights, without the need to attack enemies at their necks, a greener Eden full of sticks and girls to throw them? Or was that a dream, a subconscious reliving of the only reality he'd ever known—the dry, cracked, and cragged, wall-enclosed post-Scourge world?

It didn't matter. He was sleeping. That was something. Lou hadn't had a good night's sleep in years, only stolen minutes here and restless hours there.

When she'd lived on her own, after her father and before Marcus, she couldn't sleep. It was too dangerous for a young girl to let down her guard long enough for dreams.

With Marcus, life had been frenetic. It was uncertain. There was always a coming storm or one from which they'd need to clean up. Being Marcus's friend didn't lend itself to lazy Sundays or long, comfortable nights tucked under a down comforter.

Lou yawned. Maybe Rudy and Norma were smart to celebrate Marcus's departure, however long it might be.

She thought about what the day would hold, what she'd have to do once the sun peeked above the horizon. She pinched the bridge of her nose and tried to formulate a mental to-do list. She couldn't.

There were bodies to bury, but Dallas would help with that. *Dallas.*

Lou smiled thinking of him. He was a nice guy. He was soft spoken and considerate. He thought she was smart.

Lou stretched her arms above her head, arching her back. She softly whistled to Fifty, who rolled over and groggily climbed the steps to her side. She rubbed his head and led him through the front door. Its rusty hinges creaked and the thin wood door slapped shut behind her.

The two of them padded their way on the dusty wide-planked oak floors to her bedroom. It was in the back at the end of the hallway that split the middle of the single-story clapboard house. The thin, dust-stained sheers fluttered at the open window.

Lou sat on the edge of the cinderblock-mounted mattress in the corner and patted it with her hand. Fifty hopped onto the bed and chased his tail into a ball. He lowered his head onto his front paws and licked his chops. Lou rubbed his hindquarters, her fingers raking through his fur.

She bent over and yanked off her boots, tossed them across the floor, reached across to a wooden pine crate that doubled as a nightstand, and retrieved her knife. She held its cold handle in her palm and turned it over, rubbing her thumb along the worn grip. She ran the index finger of her other hand along the top edge of the blade, tracing it lovingly.

She sighed and put the knife back on the box, took off her hat and laid it next to the knife, and spun her feet from the floor onto the bed. She drew back the rumpled cover and drew it across her body, sinking her head into a thin feather pillow.

She drifted to sleep thinking about *The Wizard of Oz*, picturing L. Frank Baum's description of the glimmering road of yellow gold bricks that paved the way for Dorothy Gale to find her way home. She could hear her father's voice reading the book to her, the texture of his voice adding to a magical adventure that saw good triumph over evil, even if it was only a dream.

CHAPTER 25

FEBRUARY 13, 2044, 7:24 AM
SCOURGE + 11 YEARS, 4 MONTHS
ATLANTA, GEORGIA

Marcus Battle stood on the arching overpass of an empty freeway. His pack was at his feet and his rifle was against the concrete guardrail. It was a Saturday and the sun was warming the horizon. Every part of his body was sore, and his knees and fingers throbbed. A chill ran along his spine and he shuddered involuntarily.

He stood against the guardrail, looking east. The sky was melting from purple to red to orange. It was a new day.

His breath, visible in thick puffs, ballooned outward. He stuffed his hands into his pockets and put his weight on his good leg. Eleven years and four months after the Scourge first started picking off people and changing his world, he felt like he was back to square one.

He was alone. He was without purpose. He didn't much care for living in a world without the people he'd loved.

He turned to the southwest and gazed past the clusters of buildings and the fog settling into the thin valleys between the gently sloping hills. He could go back. He could find his way past the wall again and make his way to Baird.

He could go somewhere else. Houston maybe? Galveston? He'd

heard the island was enjoying a renaissance, relatively speaking. There wasn't much violence there.

He laughed at the thought of that. Not much violence.

He looked north. It might only take a couple of weeks to reach Canada. Canadians were good people. He'd met a few before the Scourge. They were polite and self-deprecating. But he couldn't take the cold. One blizzard and his knees would shatter. His arthritis would immobilize him. Not an option.

"East, then," he mumbled and faced the sunrise. It was climbing fast above the horizon. Savannah? Charleston? Hatteras? All of them sounded appealing. Lazy towns, he'd always heard, with a warm Southern charm. That was a possibility.

He struggled on his bad leg and turned his back to the sun. West. West might be the best choice. It was an endless sea of prairies and mountains. At the end there were rocky coastlines that ran from Mexico to Alaska. There were so many more spots in the west from here. Kansas City or Denver, Phoenix, or Los Angeles. There was even Baja, Mexico, and the San Juan Islands near Seattle.

Marcus took a deep breath, listening to the wind whistle its way through buildings and rustle the tall Georgia pines that speckled the highway esplanades.

He picked up his pack, bending at his aching knees to save his stiff lower back, and slung it over his shoulder. He reached inside the other strap and shrugged the pack into place, positioned the padded straps equidistant from his neck, and snapped the plastic buckle at his chest. He reached down and picked up the Springfield.

Without knowing where he was going, he knew what he was doing. He was starting fresh. He was wiping clean his bloodstained slate.

He might find what he was looking for in a few days. It might take him years. He might never make it there. But he'd keep moving until he did. He'd travel until he felt at home.

Marcus wiped the sheen of cold sweat from his forehead and

smiled. He thought of those he loved, considered those he'd killed. The latter took longer than the former. And then he started walking. It was fitting that he'd narrowed his choices to the places where the sun rose and where it set. It was a calling.

"As far as the east is from the west," he whispered to himself, "so far has He removed our transgressions from us."

Sign up for Tom's Preferred Reader Club.
It's free and you'll be the first to learn about
upcoming releases and promotions.

eepurl.com/bWCRQ5

LOOKING FOR YOUR NEXT READ?
EXPERIENCE THE APOCALYPSE
AS NEVER BEFORE
IN
RED LINE: AN EXTINCTION CYCLE NOVEL

EXCERPT FROM *RED LINE*

Chapter 1

Near Son La, Vietnam
April 1, 1980

Lieutenant Trevor Brett nibbled on the woman's ear, paying special attention to the lobe. He'd first seen her weeks ago and there was an instantaneous, animal attraction. Her musk was intoxicating and narrowed his fractured mind to a single focused thought.

He had to have her.

His memory flashed to that moment. Her smooth skin looked delicious. Her silky black hair framed her features in a way that made her all the more inviting. She was thin, which wasn't necessarily good. Lieutenant Brett had long ago given up being picky about those upon whom he'd set his sights.

The woman had had no choice but to succumb to his advances. She was like the others before her. The initial fear and pulse pounding gave way to resignation and acceptance.

So Brett nibbled. It wasn't flirtation.

No.

He was *chewing* on the ear, rolling the chunks of cartilage around his tongue and between his jagged yellow teeth. He held it between his gnarled, clawlike fingers for leverage. It was the newest addition to the necklace he wore around his neck. Like a piece of sugary sweet candy on an elastic string, he couldn't keep it out of his mouth. He couldn't resist the urge to gnaw. His thickly rounded sucker lips popped and slurped.

There was little satisfaction from the gristled piece of skin, but it kept his mind from fixating on the relentless hunger that fed at his gut. The woman, as he'd suspected despite his attraction, wasn't enough to satiate the hunger for long.

Women often weren't enough. Men, thick and greasy men, were the prize. He needed another man.

Brett was perched fifteen feet off the ground on the gnarled limb of a tamarind tree. His clawed feet gripped the knotty wood with calloused, elongated toes that had the appearance of vulture's talons.

He suddenly stopped chewing and held the snack against the roof of his mouth. He tilted back his head and closed his eyes. He inhaled through his nostrils, first with a long pull of air and then with short quick bursts. A slow, rounded grin crept across his face. The odor was unmistakable. It was thick and greasy.

Filtered through the scent of rotting vegetation and mildew was the sweet smell of Brett's favorite prey. He took another quick suck of air in his nose. The odor was intensifying. The prey was moving toward him.

Brett was hunting a narrow stretch of land between the Da River and the mountains that stretched most of the distance from Lao Cai to Hanoi. It was a good spot that offered unsuspecting farmers and preoccupied fishermen.

The prey came from the river. Brett opened his eyes and narrowed his gaze, scanning the green landscape for visual confirmation. He shifted on his feet, the callouses scraping against the wood and his knees clicking as he moved.

He gripped the thick tree branch with his clawed hands to steady himself. Nine of his ten fingers, or what resembled fingers, were adorned with long, hooked claws. One of the fingers was missing a claw. Brett lost the weapon fighting a woman in the river. It didn't diminish his abilities to pounce, slash, and feed. It had been more than ten hours since he'd fed. Warm saliva pooled in his mouth and oozed from his lips, mixing with the omnipresent stain of blood that painted his face.

Then he saw it. The prey. Brett leaned forward. He was ready to pounce.

"Wait for it," growled the woman's voice that occupied his head. She was always in control. "It will come closer."

The hunger in Brett's gut screamed at him to jump, to use his speed and agility to overtake the prey and feed. The ache emanated from his stomach to his chest and into his throat. He longed for the warmth of raw meat and the delicious satisfaction of blood.

The prey moved closer, carrying a net of silver and coral basa fish over one shoulder. Even from a distance of fifty yards, Brett's bloodshot eyes could see the basa's tiny heads, their eel-like eyes, and the thick underbelly that distinguished them from others in the catfish family.

He wasn't interested in the fish, though, and his glare darted to the chunky man carrying the net. He was walking with the low energy of a man who'd spent his day fighting for his food. Brett inhaled the sweet odor of the man's sweat. His eyes narrowed on the beautifully full artery running along the man's strained neck.

Another flood of saliva poured into his mouth. His sinewy muscles tensed, twitching almost, as Brett awaited the command. He was so hungry. So. Hungry.

"Now," snarled the voice. "Get him now. Kill him and feed."

Brett pushed with his thighs and jumped from the branch to the muddy ground below. He landed solidly on both feet, his shoulders rolled forward, as he caught the fisherman's full attention.

The man froze. His eyes grew wide. He dropped the net.

Brett sniffed the distinctly acidic smell of urine. His lips pursed and popped. His joints clicked and snapped when he dropped to all fours.

In the time it took the man to open his mouth, but before he could force a scream, Brett was on top of him. Brett's razor teeth ripped at the man's throat. His lips found that juicy arterial flow and he fed. Oh, he fed.

Brett grunted and snarled and slurped as he worked the prey to a pulp. He scratched and clawed the meat free of the bone when his teeth and lips were otherwise occupied.

When he was finished, when he'd put the hunger at bay for the moment, he squatted on the jungle floor, admiring his work.

"He was delicious," said the voice. "Mmmmmm."

Brett snatched a thin bone from the ground next to him. It was a finger. Maybe a toe. Brett picked it up with his own clawed hand and slid the bone between his lips. He bit down and raked his teeth across it until the last remnants of flesh were stripped away.

Brett then tore what was left of the man's nose from his mangled face and held it tight in his hand. It would make a wonderful addition to the cord around his neck.

He stood and then crouched on his knuckles like an ape. He inhaled deeply through his nose, threw back his head, and howled. Even after a decade, it was a sound that chilled what little humanity remained in Lieutenant Trevor Brett. That speck of his former life couldn't reconcile the monster he'd become. That speck, that spot of reason and love and compassion, was buried so deeply within his core, it might as well not have existed at all.

ACKNOWLEDGMENTS

My love and thanks begin with Courtney, Sam, and Luke. You always have my back.

Big ups to my editor Felicia A. Sullivan, who is brutally honest and fiercely loyal. She's also brilliant at finding the words I overuse. Brilliant. Brilliant.

Thanks also to Pauline Nolet and Patricia Wilson for their critical eyes and outstanding proofreading of my schlock and to Stef McDaid for the wonderful formatting of both the digital and print versions of this story.

Cover artist Hristo Kovatliev is truly a rare find. He takes ideas and runs with them. My favorite part of the process is seeing the first drafts of each new design. Steve Kremer, master of all trades, is an outstanding reader and friend who thinks of things I hadn't.

And Kevin Pierce, who I wish could narrate everything I do. My life would be much cooler than it is. You rock.

Thanks also to my parents, Sanders and Jeanne, my siblings, Penny and Steven, and my mother-in-law, Linda Eaker, for their support and loud cheers.

Oh, and you. You. For picking up this book and reading it, for giving Marcus Battle life, and for demanding more of me. I am always grateful.

Made in the USA
Coppell, TX
29 January 2025

45149526R00152